Love at Last

The Bachelor Series, Book 4

CHERYL BARTON

Published by: CRBarton Productions

CRBarton Productions, LLC
P.O. Box 962
Reisterstown, Maryland 21136
www.crbarton.com

Ordering Information:
Quantity sales. Special discounts are available on quantity purchases by corporations, associations, and others. For details, contact the publisher at the address above.

Orders by U.S. trade bookstores and wholesalers.
Please contact prez@crbarton.com

ISBN 13: 978-0-9978779-4-6
ISBN10: 0997877944

Dear Reader,

Wow, here we are with book 4 in the 'Bachelor Series' and I'm so excited to finally bring you Brian's story.

We started off with Duron Knight's story in, Bachelor Not for Sale, where the sexy bachelor was auctioned off at a charity event when he spots a beautiful woman in red who stood out unlike any other woman. Could she be? Would she be? Can she be the one woman who can make him forget about being a bachelor?

Then we have, Michael Bailey's story in, A Designed Affair, where he could no longer fight his attraction to his best friend, Duron's sister, Loren. The passion was so hot that he would do anything to keep her in his life and his bed, including keeping their affair a secret. What happens when that secret is no longer a secret?

In the third installment, A Perfect Combination, we meet Tyrone Davis and what was supposed to be a one-night stand turned into his search for the perfect woman until he discovers she has a fiancé she forgot to tell him about. Tyrone didn't let that stop him from proving to her that they were perfect together.

Now, in book 4, "Love at Last", Duron's brother Brian wanted love, needed love and fell in love until love left him with no explanation....and then there were three...a baby someone said? Follow Brian on a journey across states in search of the woman who left him and didn't tell him about the baby she carried.

I hope you enjoy this series and trust me, it's not over yet! Thank you for reading. I am because you read!

Cheryl

CHAPTER 1

A Few Years Ago

A comfortable bed would do the trick right now, Brian thought as he sat down, pretty much exhausted, in the black, high-back leather chair in his cramped office on the campus of Morehouse College. If it weren't for the fact that he had a lot of work to do, he would be home, stretched out catching up on some much-needed rest. Lately, his life had become one class after another, passing by his eyes like a blurry mass, often aiming for him as if it were going to attack him. That, he knew, was the sign of a man doing too much without time to enjoy the fruits of his daily labor.

As a professor teaching Marketing and Finance to undergraduate and graduate students, there wasn't a lot of time spent out of the classroom because to him, education was the key to success and he held the careers of young African American men in his hands and helping them get to the next level in their lives was a priority. There was a time when there were professors who did the same thing for him.

After graduating from Morehouse College, Brian never had a doubt that he would return to give back to the school that helped shape him into the man he turned out to be. That's not to slight the great job his parents, Earl and Barbara Knight had done bringing him up right and how their support got him to this point. His parents instilled in him and his siblings the importance of education as the path to becoming whatever they choose.

Brian grew up in a loving household with parents who had high expectations for all of their children and one of his proudest days was the day he presented his college degree to his mother as a thank you for always being in his corner. Now, the real work began by pouring into students the same way he had been poured into for undergraduate and graduate school.

Turning to the stack of assignments in front of him, Brian exhaled and knew it was time to get caught up on reviewing assignments submitted by his students. Before he could get to the first one, his cell phone rang and he grabbed it, seeing his brother, Duron, was calling.

"What's up?" he said answering.

"Not much, bro. I'm checking to see if you are still hanging with Silas for the game tonight?" Duron asked.

Brian checked the time on the wall in his office, which was barely visible behind the stacks of books that climbed the wall and noted that time had gotten away from him and though he'd been in his office for a few hours, he hadn't gotten much done.

"I forgot all about the game. I'm behind in getting these assignments back to my students. Are you going to the game?" he asked.

Duron chuckled.

"Not on your life. With the firm really taking off and working on the final design for my new office park, I don't have time right now for football games."

"I know that's code for a woman is on your agenda. Some woman will have you hemmed up, I presume, and knowing you, that means everything else becomes secondary. I've learned that you being too busy for things doesn't include your proclivity for beautiful women," Brian said, chortling.

"Normally that would be the case since you know there is never a shortage of sexy women, but tonight, it's actually business that'll keep me tied up."

Brian smiled, proud of his brother who was embarking on a career path that he'd planned out since his first year of college. After making the decision following his graduation from Howard University to go into business with his two best friends, Michael Bailey and Tyrone Davis, together they started their own architectural firm, Pioneer Architecture & Design, and business immediately began booming, shooting their company to the top of the list of firms to seek out for new, modern structures. Requests for their services had begun pouring in almost immediately and he knew one day, Duron and his partners were going to make it big. They had started out with small jobs for quite a few years and now, they were at the top of their game after recently being featured on the cover of Black Enterprise Magazine as a company to watch. That article had surged Duron's company to the top almost immediately.

He also knew that his brother had become so focused on business that his personal life had begun to suffer which probably led to the thought that Duron was digging deep and hard into business to get over his failed relationship with a woman none of them really liked, even their mother, who liked everyone.

Duron had gone through a recent breakup that had sucked the life right out of him, just as he was on the crux of his rise to the top. Being older, he felt a protectiveness for his brother and he, for one, was glad the relationship ended when it did. If that woman, Allison, who had left Duron for a guy who already had money, had gotten a whiff of Duron's business about to really take off, she would have stayed around, taken advantage of his brother and Duron would be stuck with her. He was thankful for small blessings.

"I'm glad to hear you're no longer sulking over Allison. That chick was bad news from the start just like Jake and I both told you," Brian said.

Duron snorted on the other end and they both laughed. He was glad they could finally laugh about the demise of that relationship because he knew that there was someone better out there for Duron and until he found her, his brother was making a name for himself in Atlanta where the stigma, *'Ride the Knight'* followed him wherever he went. The women did love his baby brother.

"I know and trust me, Allison is a long-distance memory that I'm glad to say I'm over. In the beginning, it really got to me because I didn't have a clue that she had been stepping out on me. I was so in love with her that I never thought that she could betray me, but you live and learn. Anyway, you know me, I don't let much grass grow under my feet, especially when it comes to the ladies. Remember I am that forever bachelor and I plan to keep it that way. Come to think of it, I may make it an early night and put a

4

call in to this woman who could help take some of the stress out of my day. The last time she came through, she surprised me and showed up with nothing on under her coat and I do mean nothing. When she dropped that coat, there was flesh and more flesh and it was curved in all the right place. I'm sure her visit tonight would be just as adventurous. Yeah, that sounds like a plan and definitely beats going to a football game."

"Even though you can't see it, I'm shaking my head at you on this end. You've gone back to your old ways of tapping everything that bats an eye at you," Brian said.

Duron laughed out loud.

"Hey, I'm just giving the ladies what they want. Did you hear that women call me the panty dazzler? I've heard them walk by me and say 'Ride the Knight', but panty dazzler is a new one," he said humorously.

"Yeah, I've heard and I'm still trying to decide if that's a good thing or not."

"Yeah, whatever. It's a great thing and you know it. Don't hate the player! I can't help it if the women find me irresistible," Duron shouted.

"Man, what do you want besides stroking your own ego? I know you didn't call me to talk about your prowess. Remember we grew up in the same house and I've seen your expertise with the ladies up close and sometimes way too personal. What's up?" Brian asked, putting away the papers. He'd return to them later, after the game.

"Right, I almost forgot the reason I called in the first place. Listen, I have a new guy starting who'll be doing some marketing for the firm and I need you to come in and talk to him. You know that stuff better than I do and I want to be sure I'm hiring the best. I could be hiring the best if you'd join the company. You could make three, four or even five times what you're making as a college professor at Morehouse. I know it's your alma mater and you want to give back, but you could be doing a lot more. I can even make sure you still have time to teach some of your classes. You know I need you on board so come on," Duron begged.

Brian had thought about the offer to join his brother's firm and so far, he'd turned him down every time. Maybe one day, he thought, just not right now.

"I told you I need some time to think about that. You are taking off faster than a rocket and I'm proud of you, Mike and Tyrone. Right now, this works for me. I know you can't understand it because you've always wanted to be rich and famous, but not me. I'm more about longevity in love, though wealth is important, too. I'm good for now, but you know in a pinch, I got your back. Let me know when you need me to come talk to this new guy and I'll be there."

"Leave it to my brother, the epitome of the face of a romance novel with all that happily ever after crap."

"Just because I don't want to hop from bed to bed with no connection doesn't mean I don't get mine."

"Yeah, I know. Remember I grew up watching you and Jake and all I've learned, I got from the two of you so if I'm going for woman after woman, I got it from the best examples."

"Don't blame me for the closet full of boxes of condoms I've seen at your house," Brian laughed.

"Whatever and thanks for talking to this guy for me. I want to be sure he knows his stuff and I knew I could count on you."

"No problem. Say, tell me what's going on with Mike and Tyrone? Between the three of you, is there a pair of panties that any of you haven't hung from your bedpost? You know women talk and you aren't the only one making a name for yourself with the ladies. I guess being at Howard together with all the antics you guys pulled with scoring with the ladies wasn't enough."

"Well, at least it's good names because it could be worse. Women could refer to us with names that would make others run for the hills when they saw us coming. We aren't out here making them promises and tossing out words like relationship and commitment and not following through. We're doing what young, virile men do and the women can't seem to get enough of us. Unlike you who's looking to be all in love and stuff, we're building our kingdom first and will worry about relationships much further down the road. I'm thinking of living my entire life as a bachelor and I never have to deal with the drama," Duron said.

"I'm going to remember you said that when you're in love like a little puppy and we won't be able to stand you," Brian laughed.

"Never, dude; never."

"Famous last words, Duron. I need to get out of here if I'm going to get to the game on time. Silas took off to go to the game and he'll have a fit if I don't show up. It's the only time his wife allows him to get out for fresh air," Brian said.

"Yeah, well that's how you'll be one day, brother."

Silas was Brian's roommate from their college days and they'd remained friends since then. Silas had once had plans to play professional football, but a college injury curtailed that, but not his love for the game.

"Like I said, famous last words. Text me the day and time and I'll slide through the office."

"Thanks, man."

After Duron hung up, Brian leaned back in his chair and thought over the conversation. He loved his brother, but they were completely different when it came to their viewpoint on relationships. Where Duron was more of a playboy when it came to the ladies, Brian knew that he wanted something on a deeper level with a woman than having her keep his bed warm. Of his siblings, Duron was definitely the wildest and he couldn't knock his hustle in business or with the ladies. He handled it well.

There was also Jake, who was the oldest and married to the love of his life, Kim. They had two children, his nephew Milo and his niece Lyric. Jake was a doctor like their father and being the oldest, they had all looked up to him. He knew that Jake had lived his days with the ladies like Duron is doing now, until his wife brought to the table everything he wanted in a woman and Jake had settled down. To Brian, their life was perfect and he hoped to one day find an incredible woman just like her.

He was next in line, followed by Duron and their sister, Loren was the youngest and the only girl. To him, Duron was the smartest of the group of them and was more of a thinker. When it came to the ladies, he had them all beat, especially with those hazel colored eyes that drew women in like a moth to a flame, a facial feature Duron and his sister had inherited from their father.

Loren was the quietest one of the group and he and his brothers took great pride at being her protectors, especially Duron, whom she shared such a close resemblance to, people thought they were twins.

Family was everything to Brian and though he'd been involved with women a few times while in college, he hadn't found that one woman to share his life with. There were times when he admired Duron's love for all things women and though he'd had his own share of one-night stands, that wasn't going to lead him to the one woman who would make his life complete. He wanted the kind of love he'd watched his parents share and knew that such a woman existed for him and one day, he'd find her.

Brian shook off his melancholy mood and focused on getting ready for the football game. It wasn't often he got to indulge in a lot of outside activities, but football was a must. He considered himself one of the biggest fans of their Atlanta team and being a season ticket holder, he seldom missed a home game. Putting the papers in his backpack to finish reviewing them at home, he gathered his things and made haste in leaving campus to catch up to Silas.

CHAPTER 2

"Hey, Brian, grab me a beer while you're getting yourself something to eat," Silas said, never looking his way, but kept his eyes glued to the cheerleaders out on the field.

Brian took the money Silas handed to him as he left his seat before the actual game started. He loved being at the Georgia dome and the one thing he secured with his salary as a professor was season tickets to every professional Atlanta football game. After investing in his first home, his next investment was to make sure he never missed a game.

On his way to the concession stand, he ran into a few students from campus and after chatting, grabbing food and beer, he made his way back to his seat. He enjoyed his exchange with his students and liked that no matter where they were, they remained proud and confident in the men they were becoming because of how their school impacted their lives positively.

Back in the stands, he made his way down the row, excusing himself as he mistakenly stepped on a few toes. As he got closer to his seat, he noticed a bizarre smirk on Silas's face as if he'd just gotten away with committing a crime. He watched Silas cut his eyes and nod his head toward the seat next to him, which was his seat and then back at him with a leer on his face, looking like a jester. Brian looked to where Silas was signaling and sitting in his seat was the most beautiful woman he'd ever seen. The woman looked to be quite a bit younger than him and normally he would steer clear, but he would almost admit that he had just experienced love at first sight. She looked his way, but not at him, smiling at something beyond him, but all he saw was her.

As he got closer, he saw that she was drinking a beer, so he knew she had to be at least twenty-one, maybe even a few years older than that. He looked at Silas again, who now appeared to be interested in the pre-game activity on the field, though Brian knew he wasn't. The look said that in any other situation, Silas would be openly making fun of him. For now, Brian wasn't amused though he was enthralled by the woman.

"You gave away my seat?" he leaned down and said to Silas.

Silas laughed quietly and kept his eyes on the field.

"I didn't give it away, she sat in it and I didn't say anything and trust me, there is a difference. Besides, I knew the moment you saw her, you would turn into a bumbling idiot, taken in by her beauty and from the look on your face, I would say my thinking was on point," he laughed.

"Clown!" Brian joked and shook his head as he moved passed him.

"Thank me later," Silas whispered and laughed harder.

Brian stopped when the woman appeared to move slightly to the side to let him pass. When he didn't move further, she looked up at him and he quietly died and went to heaven. This had to be the end of life, he thought, because he was looking into the face of an angel. When her smile turned to a look of confusion, he finally found his voice that so far, had escaped him.

"Excuse me, but I think you're in my seat. I don't know why my friend Silas here didn't tell you before you sat down," Brian said, pointing to Silas who faked not paying attention. The steady sneer on his face told him otherwise.

Her smile returned and Brian couldn't take his eyes off of how attractive she was. Her smile lit up her entire body and to him, the space around her, too. He was embarrassed standing in front of her lusting after her live a love-struck puppy, but he couldn't help it. Thankfully he could control his body and the flow of his hormones enough to not embarrass himself in front of her with a hard-on. That never happened to him, but he felt like it was about to and he needed to get into a seat. He'd never had an experience where a smile had turned him on that way hers was doing. He felt like a high school boy as his zipper appeared to get a little bit more snug. So, not only was she drop dead gorgeous, but nature had his entire body reacting to her and for him that was a first. She hadn't said a word and yet he was already into her unlike any other woman he had ever encountered before. She was about to speak and his eyes darted right to her perfectly shaped lips, which were hiding a perfectly white smile. Was he really thirty-three and acting like this, he thought and scolded himself.

"Am I?" she asked.

Brian cleared his throat in hopes it would help clear his mind enough to respond intelligently.

"I think so. I have season tickets for these two seats and

I sit in them at every game. Do you have your ticket? Perhaps I can help you find your seat if you like?" he said, hoping that her correct seat was the one right next to him that was still empty.

He wanted his seat back, but he didn't want her to be on the wrong row. If possible, he wanted to use this scenario to get to know a little more about her. As she reached for her ticket, he continued standing there looking out of place while behind him, Silas continued to quietly laugh. He would get back at Silas later for this. If it turned out bad for him, it would be worse for Silas, but if it turned out good, he would definitely thank him.

Brian looked down at the ticket that she pulled out of the front pocket of the black Baltimore Ravens hoodie she wore. Clearly, she didn't care that she was in Atlanta territory and her confidence gleamed like a bright beacon.

"Let me see what this says," she said looking it over.

Brian strained to look at it too.

"Yeah, it looks like you are one seat over," he said and inwardly thanked whatever force was with him at the moment. He would be sitting next to her for the entire game. Now, all he had to do was hope that she was at the game alone or with family, but not with a boyfriend or husband. He scanned her ring finger and though that didn't mean much since people didn't always wear wedding rings, it was a sign that he shouldn't just avoid talking to her.

"I'm sorry about that. I have never been to this stadium and I wasn't paying attention when I sat down. I knew it was on this row and thought I had the right seat. Let me get out of your way," she said standing to move over one seat.

"Don't worry about it. Silas, take this stuff," Brian said handing him the food and beers and then turning back around to sit after she'd taken her seat.

"At least the game hasn't started and I didn't make you miss any of it," she said, smiling and lighting his whole life up.

"No need to apologize. My buddy, Silas here, could have told you that you were in the wrong seat, but I guess he's engrossed in the on-field cheerleader show," he said simpering at his friend again, who was still smiling and giving him the thumbs-up.

Brian shook his head and turned back to the beauty in the seat next to him. He was about to say something else to her, anything else actually just to continue the engagement, when Silas leaned over and spoke to him in a hush tone so that only he could hear what he was about to say.

"Like I said, thank me later, dude," Silas said and then went back to focusing on the field.

"I apologize for the inconvenience."

Brian turned his attention away from Silas and back to the woman who had just spoken to him again.

"No inconvenience at all," Brian said.

"Thanks for being so nice about it. I know how football fans can be about their seats," she leaned over and said, smiling at him again.

"It's just a seat and luckily, there were two of them and all you had to do was slide over one.

"I'm glad about that because these are some good seats and the view is incredible," she said, looking directly at him before darting her attention back to the field.

"Yes, they are and yes, it is."

Brian was thinking more about who was sitting in the

seat more than the actual seat.

He turned toward the field and waited a few minutes before getting up the nerve to prolong their conversation.

"My name is..."

The rest of his statement was lost in the roar of the crowd as the announcer let them know that the players were about to take the field. Before he could get any more words out, the beauty next to him stood up along with everyone else to welcome the Atlanta team to the field. Without being too conspicuous, Brian looked between his new neighbor and the action on the field and found that looking at her was much better than any football player coming onto the field. He was a die-hard football fan and never missed a game, but today, he was already distracted and he could care less about what was happening on the field. The only thing he could focus on was how gorgeous his neighbor, who so far had no name, looked and so in the midst of all the noise as player after player came out from the tunnel, he took in everything about her.

The woman next to him was shorter than him, probably around five-foot-seven or eight. She wore her hair pulled up giving him a glance at her long, sleek neck. Brian's body reacted sharply to the thought of placing soft kisses along her neck, getting a feel and taste of her. He loved nuzzling a woman's neck, feeling and hearing her swoon in his arms, letting him know that she liked what he was doing to her.

Her face was actually beyond beautiful to him and she had a quiet zest about her that drew him in. He feigned being angry at Silas, but at the moment, Silas was his favorite person in the world because he was now next to a woman who seems to have dropped out of the sky into his life and he wanted and needed to know more.

After the pledge to the flag, everyone sat waiting for the game to begin and before the kickoff, he decided to take another chance at introducing himself. He leaned over a little closer to her after she finally took her seat again.

"My name is Brian Knight. Since we're neighbors for the game, I figured I'd introduce myself," he said offering her his hand for a shake and a kind gesture.

He watched her contemplate returning the handshake. He beamed when she smiled and took his hand in hers. His body rocked at the electric surge he felt the moment their hands touched. This was more than meant to be, he thought.

"Hello, I'm Sherry Braxton and it's a pleasure to meet you Brian."

"Likewise, Sherry. You mentioned you've never been to the stadium before. Is this your first time at a game?" he asked.

"Oh, no, not at all. I go to games all the time when I'm back home in Baltimore. I'm a Baltimore Ravens fan for life, as you can see from my shirt, but being here at school at Atlanta-Clark University, I miss the home games. My dad has season tickets and always takes me. Now that I'm here, he surprised me with tickets to a few of the games here since he knows how much I love football. My Ravens are still number one in my book though. Since you have season ticket seats, I assume you come to every home game?" she asked.

"When I can I do and I go to some of the away games if I get a chance to steal a few days away."

He started to add more, but then the game began and the crowd roared. For the next couple of hours everyone's focus became the game and intermittently, he and Sherry shared their opinions about the players and the game where Atlanta eventually came out on top. All too soon for him, the game was over and it was time to leave. Normally when a game was over, he'd be making his way to his car, but he was still enraptured by Sherry and he wasn't ready to leave.

"It was nice sitting next to you the whole game. I see there is no doubt about how much you love football. I thought any minute you'd get up and run onto the field to tell the teams how badly they were messing up," he said, hoping to hold her attention a little longer.

Sherry laughed.

"I do get passionate about the game. I do love me some football and I blame that on my father. I grew up with football on the television all the time and as his partner in crime since my mother hates sports, as I got older, he started taking me when he saw my interest matched his. It was a great opportunity for us to bond."

"Your passion shows and it's refreshing. I know women love football as much as guys do. Kudos to your dad for showing you the way to the light!" he joked.

"Yeah, he created a monster!" she replied.

It was now or never Brian thought.

"Hey, Brian, I'm heading out since you seem like you're not ready to leave anytime soon even though the game has been over ten minutes."

Brian gave him an annoying glance with a look that secretly signaled him to go away.

"Jokes, Silas?" he asked.

"I'm sorry, am I keeping you?" Sherry asked him.

"Not at all," Brian countered quickly.

Brian turned back to Silas and caught him trying to

suppress a laugh.

"Silas, I'll see you on campus tomorrow. One of my graduate students is leading my class tomorrow, so I'll be a little late. Are we still on for a pickup game tomorrow?" Brian asked.

He and some of his friends played a pickup game of football sometimes on campus against some of the students. A lot of them were away from home for the first time and Brian wasn't just a professor, but also a mentor.

"Definitely. It was nice to sort of meet," Silas said shaking her hand before turning to leave.

Brian then realized he had not introduced them.

"Well, on your way out, this is Sherry Braxton. She's from Baltimore and loves football."

"Again, nice to meet you," Silas said.

Brian turned back to Sherry who didn't appear to be in a rush to leave either. He looked around and saw a few other stragglers, but his attention was square on Sherry. He felt a connection to her and had a strange feeling that she was feeling the same thing since she didn't appear to be in a hurry.

"Nice to meet you, too," Sherry said to Silas.

Brian was becoming annoyed at his friend who couldn't see he was in the way.

"Maybe I'll see you around again sometime soon," Silas said looking from her to Brian, seeing that his assessment was correct from the beginning. Brian was definitely into her and from the look of things, the feeling was mutual.

Sherry looked from him to Brian and then responded without taking her eyes off of Brian.

"I hope you will," she said.

"Bye, Silas," Brian said with his eyes locked on her.

Silas laughed and walked away.

Now that it was the two of them only, he could get back to the woman who captured him from the moment she looked up at him from her seat.

"Sherry, I know the game is over and you probably have to get out of here, but do you think I could interest you in having dinner with me sometime?" he asked, going straight for what he wanted. Nothing ventured, nothing gained, as the saying goes.

Brian held his breath hoping this would not be the first and last time he'd get to see and spend time with her. His eyes went from her eyes to her lips which had yet to open to respond to his question. What was wrong with him, he thought? He was pretty much undressing her with his eyes right in the stadium and when his eyes landed on her lips, his body hardened at the thought of how soft he knew they had to be and wished he knew her well enough to get a sample. If given the opportunity, he hoped he'd one day get to show her how much he enjoyed kissing. He knew that a good kiss could lead to intoxicating intimacy.

"You sure can. I'd like that," Sherry finally said.

"What?"

Brian had lost his train of thought by being caught up in the possibility of more with her.

"You asked me out, I think," Sherry said with uncertainty in her voice.

Brian shook it off and rejoined the conversation.

"Oh, I'm sorry. I was distracted for one second. Let me just say this before I drive myself crazy. You are absolutely stunning," he said and waited to see if his comment would put her off. When she beamed with joy at his compliment, he exhaled.

"Thank you," she said shyly.

"Do you mind if I ask you a question? If it's out of line, I apologize up front because my mother taught my brothers and I that there are some questions you don't ask a woman, but I need to ask."

"Okay?" she said.

"How old are you?" he said hesitantly hoping that her next move wasn't to walk away from him.

Sherry smiled at him brightly. She thought he was going to ask something inappropriate. She got that question about her age a lot considering she looked young for her age even though she knew she was still probably quite a bit younger than him.

"I just turned twenty-four earlier this month. I'm sure you asked because I look young and trust me, I get that a lot. How old are you, if you don't mind me asking you the same question?"

"Absolutely. Turnabout is fair play. I'm thirty-three and I had a birthday last month. I'm a professor at Morehouse teaching Marketing and Finance."

"Wow, that's exciting," she exclaimed.

"Yeah, I enjoy it. Besides teaching, I'm also working on my doctorate degree in both fields of study. What are you studying?" he asked.

"I'm a biology major and a late starter. I took a few years off after high school and when I finally decided to go to college to study biology, I chose Clark-Atlanta not sure if it would be awkward being a twenty-year-one freshman, but it's been an incredible experience. I started out taking one of those gap years, which ended up lasting a few years, but I'm back on track now."

"It's never too late to figure your path out. I have a sister who recently finished college and she took a year off before starting and for her it was the best decision she'd ever made. She said it helped her grow and learn and also find out what she really wanted to do with her life."

"I can relate to how she feels. School has helped me find myself and even though I was older than the average freshman, I never felt older or different. So, now that you know how much older you are than me, are you still interested in having dinner with me sometime?" Sherry asked, bluntly.

Never had she felt as hopeful about the possibility of seeing a guy again as she was feeling about Brian and already she was acting out of character by reminding him that he'd asked her out. The moment she looked up into his handsome face, she was taken in by the handsome stranger. On first look, she could see that he was older than her, but that wasn't a deterrent. She'd wasted enough time on men her own age, who acted more like boys than men and finally discovered that she had a penchant for older guys. Knowing Brian was nine years older than her was intriguing and she hoped he was beyond the childish games men her age were into. She wanted someone who was interested in being with one woman, not several as if he was trying to conquer them all.

When she looked up at him, the sun was partially in her eyes, but once she'd gotten a better look when he turned to talked to her, she was a goner and since they were still sitting and talking to each other when thousands of others had already left the stadium, she wasn't the only one smitten.

"Yes, I am still interested in having dinner with you. If our age difference doesn't bother you, it doesn't bother me and I wasn't going to let it," he proclaimed.

Brian looked around at the near empty stadium as the workers began cleaning up the trash.

"I think they're going to throw us out of here in a minute. Did you drive? If so, I'll walk you to your car," he said.

"I did and thank you. Are you sure I'm not keeping you from anything?" Sherry asked and hoped not.

Brian stood and took her hand to help her walk through the row over the trash left on the ground.

"I'm positive."

"Okay," she said.

Brian stopped suddenly and turned to her, looking deeply into her eyes. He knew that they had just met, but he wanted her know that this wasn't a passing thing for him. He was seriously interested in her.

"There is no place I would rather be right now than right here with you."

He heard the words as they came out of his mouth and he couldn't think of anything he'd meant more in life about anything he'd ever said than what he'd just told her. As he walked with her hand in his, he realized he'd just become a believer of love at first sight.

As she walked behind Brian, holding tightly to his hand, Sherry smiled inwardly. Something in the back of her mind told her that her life was about to change and she knew it was for the better. She'd watched friends on campus and back at home get involved with man after man and she didn't want to be that kind of woman. It wasn't in her to test the waters with every man she came across hoping that the next one would be the right one and leaving a part of herself with each one of them. She wanted the right one to be the only one and something about Brian told her he was special.

There were times where she felt like an outcast from her friends when they talked about one man or the other and how good he was in and out of bed, a conversation she couldn't relate to. She dated plenty, but never had she gone to the point of giving her body to any. She was saving herself for the right man; the only man and something about Brian already made her feel like he was a man unlike any she'd ever met before. She had hope, as they left, that the first dinner date with him would be the first of many.

CHAPTER 3

Present Day

Hurt, anger, irritation and annoyance were a few of the feelings that were running through Brian as he made his way through traffic to the airport to board the private flight his brother Duron had secured for him. He was on a mission and nothing was going to divert him from his destination, not even the ringing of his cell phone. It was Duron. He wasn't in the mood to chat with anyone or to hear from anyone who wanted to tell him that taking the flight was a mistake. In the back of his mind, he knew that if he didn't answer, Duron would continue calling until he picked up and the constant ringing of the phone would only annoy him even more.

"What's up Duron?" he said after hitting the answer call button in the car for hands-free access.

"Hey, it's me and Jake on the line. I patched him in before calling you. We wanted to check on you before you got too far after you shot out of Tyrone and Victoria's wedding reception faster than a jaguar as if the place was on fire and we wanted to be sure you made it to the airport safely without killing yourself or someone else. I told Jake that the moment I saw you check your phone and hightail it for the door, you had gotten your answer from the private investigator. He also sent me a text with the confirmation you had been waiting for. I'm hoping your driving doesn't match how fast you escaped the reception," Duron said.

Brian had to admit that he was driving erratically once he pulled away from the reception, but he was focused and it wasn't on how fast he was moving or how fast the car was going. He had one thought and it was on Baltimore.

Stopping at home to change out of his tuxedo should have been his priority, but he didn't care. He would have Duron send him clothes from his house or he would buy clothes after he landed. Right now, he had one goal and that was to get to Baltimore before he calmed down and found his common sense. No sensible man would drop in on a woman he hadn't seen in a few years, but he was doing it and nothing was going to stop him. The only thing that mattered to him was the fact that he had a daughter and she had been kept from him by a woman he once thought he would one day marry. That woman had thrown a wrench in those plans and he hadn't been the same since the day she walked away from the love he thought they shared. Never had he loved a woman as much as he loved her, yet his love wasn't enough for her.

"Yeah, I'm good. I'm just anxious to get to Baltimore and find out why Sherry has kept my daughter from me. It doesn't matter what the hell happened to our relationship, I had a right to know about my daughter. If you're calling to tell me I'm doing the wrong thing, you're wasting your time," Brian shouted in anger.

He knew his brothers didn't mind the fury in his tone.

They had been each other's sounding board since they were kids.

"Brian, we're not calling to talk you out of it, but we want you to calm down. Are you headed home first? Jake and I are going to run by your house so that we can talk before you get on that plane. There's a lot you need to think through before you get to Baltimore and how this could possibly blow up in your face. You have no idea what you're walking into. I know the guy I hired to get to the bottom of everything confirmed what you already knew to be true, but I need to be sure you're thinking your next move through with a clear head. I've made the jet available to you any time, but I thought that once you got the information, you would take some time to process it before jumping quickly into a decision to just show up on Sherry's doorstep."

"D, I'm already on my way to the airport, not my house and I've thought about it plenty. I do need one of you to check on my house while I'm gone and overnight me some clothes. If I don't go now, I may think sensibly and I don't want to. I want answers and I want them now. I didn't want to believe that the woman I thought I loved would get pregnant with my child and not tell me, but to know that she did when I did everything to try and find out why she left me without so much as an explanation, is crushing."

Duron had hired a private detective for him after one of Brian's friends told him that he saw Sherry with a little girl that looked like she could be his sister's daughter. Loren, like Duron had a distinctive look because they were African American's with light hazel eyes and everywhere they went, people commented on how beautiful their eyes were. When Brian's friend made the connection of Sherry to Brian, he had a feeling he was looking at Brian's daughter. Though Brian didn't have the hazel eyes, it was still a family trait. Jake didn't have those eyes, but his kids did. The private detective had done the job he was hired to do and had located Sherry Braxton and brought back the information he needed about what could possibly be Brian's daughter.

Brian didn't want to be as angry as he was, but he couldn't see beyond the hurt. He had a child out in the world he didn't know and that child didn't know him.

It appeared that when Sherry left Atlanta, never wanting anything else to do with him, she was pregnant with their daughter and never told him. He wasn't just anxious, he was livid, something his brothers knew. The detective had sent back pictures of the little girl who could be Loren's daughter as Brian's friend claimed originally. There was no doubt the little girl was a Knight, which gave him no doubt that she was his. She had the same hazel eyes as Loren and Duron, but her facial features were all him.

Brian looked at the picture of the little girl who had his mouth, nose and he didn't care that he didn't have a confirmation that she was his, he knew deep down, he was looking into the face of his own daughter. His irritation reached the boiling over point every time he thought about it. Clearly the last time he'd tried to reach out to her she had been pregnant and didn't let him know, which meant that she deliberately kept him from his daughter. He would soon confront her and get some answers. Thankfully, he was on a break from teaching and if need be, he would take a leave of absence from work to make sure Sherry understood he wasn't going anywhere until she knew that he planned to be a part of his daughter's life whether she liked it or not. He had no intention of walking away from his flesh and blood. He wasn't that kind of man and would never be that kind of father. He was raised in a family where they loved each other and were a priority in each other's lives. He lived in a house with a loving mother and father and he didn't care if he had grown up and made a thousand children, they would all be special and would all get his love, affection and attention. How dare Sherry deny him that with his daughter? He thought.

"I hear you, Brian, but you don't know the whole story and I think it would be more beneficial if you waited until later today or even tomorrow," Duron said, still trying to convince Brian to pull his anger back a little.

"D, she kept my daughter from me. That's unforgivable in my book and I want to see her. I want to see my daughter. I need to see my daughter. She's my flesh and blood and she doesn't even know I exist. Neither of you know how that feels because you both have your children and have been with them from the beginning of their lives. That's not the case for me and I want to see my daughter. Eighteen-months-old puts her conception right at the time when she left Atlanta and ended things with me," he said through clinched teeth, trying to tamper down his anger.

"Brian, it's me, Jake. Listen, I know you're upset and believe me we hear the frustration, but you need to taper that off some before you get to Baltimore. I remember Sherry and the person you brought around doesn't seem like the deceitful type. You have no idea what the circumstances were then or are now, so don't get to Baltimore and throw accusations. Something happened that caused her to keep this from you and you need to listen with a closed mouth and opened ears. She's still the mother of your child, so respect that. Now, I'm agreeing with you that the little girl is probably yours, but it's not confirmed, so pull it back. No matter how much that little girl looks like our family, you have to handle this the right way. Don't go barging in on their lives making demands. You need to talk to Sherry with a level head and let her tell you that the little girl is yours and if she doesn't, I recommend you convince her to let you have a paternity test done. Again, you need to ask her for it and not demand it like I know you would do."

"It's clear we're not going to convince you to wait on this, so just remember to park in the private hangar at the airport and they'll be expecting you. When you land in Baltimore, get a breather before you go to her house. Check into a hotel and relax and think about going to visit her tomorrow and not today when you're this amped up," Duron said.

"I'm here at the airport now. I hear you both and I'm good for now. The flight will give me extra time to think about what I'm going to do and say. I don't plan to go off half-cocked at her, but I can't help how I feel right now. You know how much I love your kids and Loren's son, so you should know my feelings about what I've missed out on with my own daughter," he implored.

"We know and we're here for you. If you need to talk before you see her, call us. Remember what I said and watch your anger and again, if she denies anything, ask her for a paternity test so that you can be sure. It's not that you don't trust her, but you want to ease your mind and know for sure. We're here for you, Brian. The whole family is here for you," Jake said.

Brian pulled into his parking spot at the airport and jumped out of the car. He paced back and forth with determined steps after Jake told him what equaled to letting Sherry control what happens. He had no plans to do that since she'd been controlling things all along.

"I don't need a paternity test because I know she's mine. Both of you saw the pictures and there is no way anyone is going to tell me she isn't mine. Would either of you question paternity if it were you and you saw how much that little girl looked like you? The minute I saw her cute little face in those pictures I had no doubt she was mine. If Sherry tries to deny it, then yeah, I will ask her for a test. If she denies that, then I'll use legal means."

"Brian, are you sure you want to do this alone?" Duron asked. "Jake has offered to come along with you. You know I would if the twins were older," he added.

Brian thought about Duron's kids, Autumn and Brent, who were identical twins and though both of his brothers could sympathize, neither could possibly understand what he was going through. They were with their children day in and day out and he felt like he was about to be in the struggle of a lifetime for his.

"No, I'm good. By the time the plane lands, I promise to rethink my approach and handle this calmly, but right now I'm venting to the two of you, so that I could let off some steam, but I'm good. I appreciate the support and thank you for the love which you already know I appreciate. Thanks for the use of your company jet, Duron. I owe you a big one for this."

Duron smile. He knew that there was nothing like true brotherhood.

"You'll never owe me for anything. I look forward to meeting my niece soon. Call if you need anything and remember I have some attorneys in Baltimore that I can connect you to if you need them and remember your fraternity brother, Xavier McIntyre, is there, too. I don't want you to have to fight with Sherry, but we don't walk away from family and that little girl is our family."

"Thanks, D. I will call with an update when I land. I'm not sure how long I'll be in Baltimore. It depends on how things go. I should have stopped at home first, but I didn't want to wait or delay my trip to see my daughter any further. I've already waited what seems like a lifetime for the information to be confirmed," Brian said.

"I got you covered with whatever you need. I'll stop at your house later tonight after I get Taija and the kids settled in at home. By the way, what's our niece's name?" Duron asked before they got disconnected.

Brian smiled with the glow of a new father thinking about his daughter.

"The investigator only got me her first name. He was close enough to Sherry one day to hear her call her name. It's Sherice," he said before hanging up so that the plane could take off.

Brian took the time on the flight to remember back to a time when he was happier than he thought he could ever be. That was until the love of his life ended their relationship and turned his life upside down.

After that first day of meeting Sherry at a football game, they were inseparable. For months, she was his everything and he thought she'd felt the same way. He fell in love hard and fast. The holiday had come around and even though they had only been dating for about two months, he invited her to spend Thanksgiving with his family and he agreed to travel with her to Baltimore over the Christmas break to meet her family. Their relationship happened quickly and he had never been happier.

Neither of them had allowed their age difference to get in the way and found out that besides football, they had other things in common.

Sherry was a Baltimorean at heart and loved all things seafood, especially steamed crabs. Brian enjoyed them also even though he was from Atlanta where steamed crabs were not a favorite of the town. There were times that he'd visited Duron when he was in college at Howard University and a few times, they'd gone out for crabs and he became an instant fan.

He and Sherry both loved reading and though she enjoyed those sweet, sexy romances, he preferred crime, fiction and science-fiction novels. They equally loved action movies and had spent many evenings at his home in front of the big screen television enjoying the latest action flicks.

They loved to cook and when he shared with her that it was his mother who made sure he and his brothers could cook, so that they wouldn't starve if they took years to marry, they cooked many meals together. One night after making love, he'd watched her sleep until his stomach growled and figured by the time she woke, she would be famished as well. He remembered that night clearly because he'd gone to the kitchen initially to make sandwiches so he hadn't bothered with clothes. One thing he never had a problem doing was walking around his house naked.

Once he made it to the kitchen, he ended up cooking and had to jump out of the way several times as he boiled vegetables to avoid hot water splashing on him. He finally turned around to find Sherry standing in the doorway to his kitchen admiring his nakedness and when she dropped the robe she was wearing and showed him she was naked underneath, any thoughts of food went out the door as he turned the fire off on the stove and proceeded forward with them making their own fire on the marble countertops.

Making love all over his house was their vice of choice until the day it wasn't. Their last time together had plagued him for a long time because he couldn't believe the relationship had ended without him knowing they were over. He had even introduced her to his family and invited her to a few other family functions since his family was all about the time they spent together, especially over food and his mother enjoyed spoiling them all with her southern-style home-cooked meals.

Things were going great between them, or so he thought until one day she told him the relationship was over with no real explanation. The only information he got was that she never wanted to see him again. He had no clue what had happened and tried to get her to explain, but came up empty. He decided to let her cool off and when he went to visit her at her apartment in downtown Atlanta a week later, she had already moved out. It was the end of the semester, but he assumed the time apart would be good for them and allowed her to work through whatever was going on. He racked his mind trying to figure out what could have gone so wrong when to him, the life they were building together was perfect. He would never do anything to hurt her because in the months that they had been together, he'd fallen in love with her. Since they had become intimate months ago, he had never given attention to any other woman and he did his best to make sure she knew that there was no one else for him, but her. What had gone wrong?

Thinking more about their time together, Brian knew her parents lived in Baltimore and reached out to them assuming she'd gone back home. Whatever had caused their breakup had been shared with her family because it was her father who told him that he thought it was best that Brian leave their daughter alone because he had hurt her enough. He didn't understand, but he abided by her father's wishes. His parents had taught him to be respectful and he had his graduation for his doctoral degree to prepare for.

Brian had taken an online doctorate program and the graduation was in Ohio where he was planning to attend in person and had hoped that Sherry would be going with him. He was thankful his family had traveled with him, but the entire time, he still felt empty without Sherry by his side. When he returned to Atlanta, he tried reaching out to her again and feeling desperate, he took a weekend trip and flew to Baltimore to talk to her in person, only to be turned away by her father, this time in person. Knowing he was in Baltimore and she still didn't want to see him, he finally gave up, went back to Atlanta and tried to focus on life again. It was hard, but he'd made it through the loss of the love of his life. That was until information surfaced that Sherry may have had his daughter and he was thrown back into the turmoil his life went through when he lost her.

Back then she wanted nothing to do with him and as much as he cared about her, he moved on not wanting to beg for a woman who no longer wanted him. When he no longer heard from her he stopped trying to get answers to derail a path to something he thought would become more permanent. Others may have thought it was too soon, especially his brothers who he confided in, but nothing kept him from buying her an engagement ring that he was planning to present to her later that summer. He wanted to do the right thing and speak to her father first and his plan was all set to travel to Baltimore after his graduation once she returned home. While there, he was planning to speak to her father about asking for her hand in marriage, but he never got the chance. The relationship was over before he could.

Brian couldn't imagine then or now what could have gone wrong and after she'd walked away from him without cause, he no longer wanted to know. The only thing that mattered to him now was that they had a daughter together and Sherry had a lot of explaining to do about why she didn't tell him that Sherice existed. In a few hours, he planned to get answers and he wasn't leaving Baltimore until he did.

Looking out over the Atlanta skyline as the plane took off, he questioned his decision to drop in on Sherry, not knowing how she would receive his presence in her life again and if she would even allow him to see his daughter. He had hope that things won't turn into a blowout session, but he was determined to at least get some answers. What if in that time, she'd gotten married or was involved with someone else? He didn't want to be an intrusion on her life; all he wanted was to see his daughter. He was over her, so whatever or whoever was in her life didn't have to worry about him. His only concern was for Sherice.

As the plane soared, Brian began beating himself up that he didn't pursue her harder. If he had been persistent, he could have known about Sherice or they may have been able to work things out. He could kick himself for giving up so easily. He should have pushed to find out what made her leave him so suddenly. He could have been in on the early years of his daughter's life and not missed out on the love between a father and his daughter.

He watched Jake with his daughter, Lyric and Duron with his daughter Autumn and there were times that he wished he'd had the kind of life with Sherry that would produce children that he would coddle and spoil. That was his plan until it all went to hell for him. Now that he knew about Sherice, things were going to change and if he had to fight Sherry in court to be a part of his daughter's life, he would. There are some guys who would happily stay away and not have the responsibility that came with parenting, but he wasn't one of those guys. Family was everything to him and not having Sherice in his life, he knew a big part of him was missing.

Brian smiled when he thought of the beautiful little girl in the pictures he'd seen of her. She appeared to be a happy little girl and she was as beautiful as her mother. The detective didn't share much about Sherry's personal life, but he did say he believed she was involved with someone, but couldn't confirm it. He'd seen her with a guy a few times while checking things out, but wasn't sure if it was a boyfriend or not. He had asked Brian if he wanted more details on that and he'd said no. Hearing that she may be involved with someone brought out a bit of jealousy in him. He didn't know why since it had been several years since he'd last seen her. He was so in love with her back then that he didn't know anything, but love when it came to her.

Sherry had given him her virginity, trusting him with her body, something she had never entrusted another man with and that sealed a special connection between the two of them. Right now, he didn't want to think of her being with another man. She'd told him back when they were involved that the decision to sleep with him was an easy one because she had fallen in love with him and she couldn't see herself being as deeply in love with anyone else the way she was with him. Even though they had not discussed plans for a life together, it was unwritten that's where they were heading. Clearly, she was all talk because it didn't take much for her to walk away from him and probably into the arms of another man. To him, Sherry could be involved with anyone she chose to, but he had issues if the man was a father figure in his daughter's life and Sherice had a living and breathing father in him. That was something he would not settle for. He was here and he was here to stay and be a father to his daughter, not caring if Sherry liked it or not.

CHAPTER 4

Duron walked back into the wedding reception after he and Jake had finished talking to Brian. He couldn't shake how concerned he was for his brother, not knowing what Brian would be walking into. He remembered Brian telling him once that Sherry's father was the Police Commissioner for the Baltimore City Police department and if Brian didn't calm down before he got to Baltimore, there was a chance things could go extremely wrong for him. He had been turned away before with a warning to not come back again and Duron had a feeling it was about to happen again.

Of the four of them, including their sister Loren, Brian was the hot-head. He was the one most likely to act on impulse and the one more apt to react with emotions and not with thinking.

Duron had also discovered a big change in Brian the moment the relationship with Sherry had ended. He didn't know all of the details and whatever happened, Brian never shared it with any of them. He only told them that the relationship was over and that Sherry had left him.

The end of the relationship had hardened his demeanor

and made him question the love he had for her and whether he would be capable of trusting another woman with his heart again. Brian wasn't as happy as he had been even prior to meeting Sherry, but once he'd met and fallen in love with her, no one could stop the smile that was permanently plastered on his face.

Prior to dating Sherry, Brian had dated other women, but Duron had never seen him fall for a woman as quickly as he did for Sherry. The fact that he was quite a few years older than her didn't deter him for a second and for a time, it didn't seem to matter to Sherry either. They seemed to enjoy each other and he had to admit that he thought that Sherry was perfect for his brother. His first impression was, of course, that she may be too young for Brian, but she appeared to be just as into Brian as he was into her and neither of them cared about age.

Sherry had been at several functions at his parent's house and a few times, he'd taken his own date or two to Brian's house for one gathering or another and Sherry was always there. They seemed to be the perfect couple, both studying toward degrees and helping each other.

After two years of Sherry being gone from his life, Brian had finally gotten over her, though he couldn't recall his brother getting serious about any other woman. In fact, in order to try and erase Sherry from his mind, he recalled Brian becoming a serial dater, making a name for himself around Atlanta with the ladies. There were one-night stands and casual flings and whenever he asked Brian about a particular woman, he would always respond that there was nothing serious going on. He was simply getting an itch scratched and enjoying mutual satisfaction with willing participants. Brian had started sounding like him,

Duron thought and since he knew the kind of guy Brian was, Duron knew it wasn't in his character to not let feelings get involved. He assumed that had a lot to do with the hurt he was experiencing.

"Ready to dance with me yet?"

Duron put thoughts of Brian aside and hoped that things didn't go as bad for him in Baltimore as he knew they could. As soon as the reception was over, he was planning to call and check in on him to be sure he hadn't already gotten himself thrown in jail.

Putting all thoughts aside except for any involving his beautiful wife, who was now standing before him looking like a beauty queen, he took her in his arms.

"Baby, I would never turn down a chance to dance with the most beautiful woman in the room," he said leaning down to plant a sweet kiss on her lips, moaning quietly when he came in contact with them. He was blessed the day he'd met the love of his life. Who would have thought that he would find love after being auctioned off at a bachelor auction fundraising event? They had gone through trials in their own relationship including a rocky road that involved her ex-boyfriend, but due to Taija diligence, which he was thankful for, they had found their way back to each other and as a result of their love, they had two beautiful twins. He raced to give up being a bachelor just for her.

"I love how you love me," Taija whispered to keep their conversation between them.

"I love loving you any way you like, especially when we get home later. Seeing you in this dress, I have been trying to focus on the festivities, but all I can seem to focus on is you and how quickly I want divest you of this wedding gown. I'm hoping and praying *your* children will let us have a moment to get reacquainted," he swayed, walking with her in his arms to the dance floor. After spinning her around, he pulled her flush against his body, laughing out loud when Taija laughed.

"Oh, so now they're *my* children? How is it that they're my children when they're crying for us, our children when they are laughing and playing and your children when they're sleeping like little angels?" Taija asked.

Duron laughed out loud, the sound drowned out by the band playing music in the background.

"Well, when they are screaming their heads off, they sound a lot like you!" he quipped and feigned being in pain when Taija slapped him on the arm.

"You are lucky I love you," she said playfully.

Duron moved in as close as he could get to her.

"Yes, I am and I plan on getting quite lucky tonight," he said looking at her with roguish eyes, showing how deceitful his mind was being at the moment.

"Well, I'm ready to leave whenever you are. Now that Tyrone and Victoria have left, we don't have to stick around too much longer. Your parents have done a good job keeping the twins entertained, so they should both sleep like logs after I get them home, fed, bathed and in their beds and then it's you and me and whatever you want to do," Taija said saucily. Adding to her words a little wink of the eye, she knew Duron was tuned into what she had in mind.

Thoughts of the night he had planned for them hardened every part of his body, especially the part that was intimately pressed into her.

"Oh, yeah, you know I'm ready to leave right now. Can't

you tell," he said, moving his hips in a circling manner, hoping no one else noticed his display of a bedroom move he knew she loved.

Taija moaned lightly.

"I can tell and I can feel and I'm ready right now," she crooned in his ear."

"Before our night of me letting you have your way with me, I need to stop at Brian's house first and get a few things to send to him."

Taija knew some of what was going on and was just as concerned as the rest of the family, but she hadn't been able to get the full story from Duron yet.

Since marrying into the family, the Knight's had become as much a part of her life as her own mother and what hurt them, hurt her, too. She saw the pain in Brian when he was told he could possibly have a daughter he hadn't been told he had. She, like everyone else who was paying attention, had seen Brian jet out of the wedding. Something must have happened, but it couldn't have been too bad if after his phone call to Brian, Duron returned and didn't go on a chase after him.

"Is Brian okay?" she asked, quietly.

As they swayed to the music, Duron decided to share a little more of what had been going on.

"He's fine. Right now, he's on the jet and heading to Baltimore to confront Sherry about what could possibly be an intense situation regarding the little girl she has. I know I told you about the private investigator I hired for him and that there was a possibility that Sherry had a baby after being involved with him. He wanted to run to Baltimore when we first found out about the situation, but he didn't. Instead he waited for more information and that information came today. It appears his ex-girlfriend Sherry had his baby and never told him about it. There is more to this, but Brian had heard enough to know that he needed to get to Baltimore and so he's on his way. I always make the jet available to family whenever they need it and Brian took it to go see about his daughter."

That thought made Taija worry even more.

"You know how much I love Brian, who is more like a brother than a brother-in-law and I'm worried about what he may be walking into. You or Jake didn't think it wise to go with him?" she queried.

Duron leaned back and looked at her.

"I can't leave you and the babies to fly off half-cocked with my brother. He gets in trouble, then I get in trouble and just in case he gets in a lot of trouble, I need to out of jail in order to bail him out. I think he should have waited and so does Jake, who offered to go with him, but Brian said he needed to do this on his own. He looks at you and me and our kids and Jake and Kim and their kids and when he thinks of the fact that he has a daughter in Baltimore that he has never seen, he was hurting to the point that he needed this time to himself to deal with it. He left so fast that he didn't stop at home first to grab any clothes and is flying to Baltimore in the tuxedo from the wedding. I'm going to go by his house, pack a few things and ship them off to him in the morning. I don't even know where he's staying, but I do know that when Brian has his heart set on something, there is no turning him around, so we let him go alone. I'm going to check on him as soon as I know the plane has landed and before he has a chance to talk to Sherry. I don't want the next call I get to be of him calling me to bail him out of jail."

Taija shook her head in agreeance.

"Yeah, Brian can be pretty intense."

Duron laughed.

"Yeah, that's a good way to say he's a hot-head, something we all know. He's also very passionate when it comes to family and to him, that little girl is family and he's already missed out on so much."

"So, is it confirmed that the little girl is his?" Taija asked.

"Well, she looks just like me and Loren with our hazel eyes and from the picture I saw, yeah, she is definitely a Knight and has a lot of Brian's facial features. Our genes are strong as you well know from looking at our twins. You know I couldn't deny them even if I wanted to."

Taija leaned back in his arms and laughed.

"You are right about that. Those babies came out the womb with hazel eyes looking just like their Daddy. That will be a strong bond between the three of you."

"Baby, it's that kind of bond that Brian feels he has missed out on and according to him, he doesn't plan to miss any more time with her. Now, I will check on him and after that, I want the night to belong to us. I'm going to have a talk with our twin criers and beg them to give me a break tonight, so that I can make love to my wife slowly and not our quickie moments of late and then this night will belong to you and me. How does that sound?"

The moment Taija opened her mouth to respond, her words were lost on Duron's lips as he captured her lips for a searing kiss that gave her an early insight into how their night was going to be. She leaned into the kiss and when he sought out her tongue, while even in a room full of people, she gave into the love and into the feeling and knew that the fire in their marriage would never die because he had no problem letting the world see how much he loved his wife at all times. The kiss began to get hot and as she reached to clasp her hands behind his neck, pulling him even more into her, the need to get home, get their kids to bed and find their time alone was more important than ever.

When Duron pulled back, breathing hard as if he were out of breath and smiled, she knew his plan was to give her a taste of what was to come and she was more than ready.

"That sounds like more music to my ears than what I'm hearing right now. Let me get the twins together and you need to go talk to your parents. I know as soon as your mother is in close proximity, she's going to ask you about Brian and you need to be able to tell her that he's fine."

"I hear you, baby. I love you," he said as they walked off the dance floor.

Duron watched as the love of his life walked toward his parents who were playing with the twins at the front of the room. He walked toward the door and pulled out his cell phone to send Brian a text. He didn't want to call him since he knew the plan hadn't landed yet, but he wanted him to know that calling him as soon as the plane landed was a must or he and Jake would be on their way to Baltimore.

CHAPTER 5

Brian had drifted off briefly on the flight and as much as he tried to think of something else, he couldn't take his mind off of Sherry. Some of the happiest times in his life were spent with her and then one day it all abruptly ended. He was left with many remembrances of their time together and as much as he didn't want to think about it, his thoughts drifted to the first night they'd made love. He remembered it as if it had just happened since that night would forever be imprinted on his mind.

They had gone to a reception to celebrate a job promotion that his friend, Silas had gotten to department head of the Athletics department. He and Sherry had been dating for about two months and had fallen into a routine of spending a lot of their free time together. Things between them had been heating up and thankfully, he had enough will-power to pull back when things were getting too hot between them.

He had always enjoyed kissing and was of the mindset that it was the most erotic part of making love to a woman.

Others disagree, but done right, a kiss could stimulate the body in the right way, setting off all kinds of bells and whistles in the brain, the same kind that get lit during intercourse. Kissing Sherry was magic for him. Her lips were perfectly shaped for his mouth and it didn't matter how often they kissed, it was never enough. He heard himself moaning and every part of him hardened when their lips touched. Kissing led to letting their hands roam all over each other which led to him giving her pleasure she'd never experienced before. He loved being the first man to show her the kind of pleasure she should always expect and experience with the right man. It was his hope that she would never experience it with any other man. He wanted to be her first and only.

The night of the reception for Silas, they had left early wanting to have some down time after his long day at work and her day of classes. Instead of taking her back to the apartment she shared with two other friends, she'd met her first year of college, they went back to his house to relax. Prior to going to the party, Sherry had brought her things from her apartment to his house to get dressed and so the clothes she'd had on earlier were still at the house and they were both able to put on more comfortable clothing in order to really relax.

It was the week after the new year and with the coldness in the air, Brian had lit the fireplace in his four-bedroom house and they settled in to cuddle in his media room. He'd recently purchased the plush brown sectional and after finding a comfortable position, they settled in for a night of movies and snacks. Before too long, they were in each other's arms, letting passion control their actions. Kissing had turned into petting and petting eventually turned into

Sherry sitting across his lap with them pretty much devouring each other. The air was filled with the sounds of their moans of pleasure and before long, Brian was taking things to another level. He wasn't sure she was ready for them to make love, but he had been dreaming about pleasuring her so that he could experience the feeling she would get one day when they made love. Making her feel loved and desired was always top on his list and the way they had been going at each other told him it was time.

As they continued to kiss, he told her how much he wanted her, but didn't want to pressure her into anything. He shared his desire to pleasure her. He wasn't a virgin like her and so he knew when a woman was ready to experience more than just kissing, but he didn't want her to feel the pressure to go to the love making stage. Still, feeling her come apart in his arms would be as much for him as it was for her.

Brian remembered asking her if she trusted him to never do anything she didn't want. He looked into her heated gaze as she nodded her head yes. He told her how he wanted to please her and got her permission before standing her up and removing her jeans. He left her barely-there thong in place as he pulled her back onto his lap so that her legs crossed over his as she faced him. He thought about sitting her with her back to his chest, but he wanted to see the look on her face when she exploded from his touch.

Brian remembered starting with kisses that rose the temperature in the room several degrees. He kissed her lips softly while whispering to her how beautiful she was, how sexy she was and how much he wanted nothing more than to give her the pleasure that her body was crying out for.

The kiss deepened as both of his lips closed around her bottom lip and she shivered as he began a sucking motion that stimulated her desire even more.

As they kissed, he reached between them and lightly caressed her womanhood through the thin material of her tiny, black thong. Not much of a surprise to him, she was already dripping wet from their kisses. He commented on how wet she was for him and how he loved that he could do that for her and then told her how much more he wanted to for her. The moment he slipped his finger past the thin material and came in direct contact with her wetness, his world began to spin and nothing existed in the world, but the two of them. This was a woman he had fallen quickly in love with and who trusted him with bringing her pleasure as she freely gave control over to him. Brian didn't take her trust for granted and as much as his body wanted to find release inside of hers, he held on to the control of his own pleasure as he dispensed pleasure on her.

Kissing around her neck and down to her chest where he lapped at her chest with opened mouth kisses, Brian rubbed her essence around her intimate spot, taking note that her nub had swollen under his ministrations and the thought of tasting her overwhelmed him, but he held back. This was about her and not him and though he had no doubt she would enjoy him tasting her sweetness, he needed to go slow with her and there would be another time down the road for that.

As Sherry's body began feeling the deep, intense pleasure of his finger coming in contact with her nub, her body began moving on his lap and Brian thought that for the first time since he was a teenage boy, he was going to relieve himself in his sweatpants because that's how hot she was making him. Focusing on making sure she felt everything, he focused on her.

When he asked her could she feel him, she said yes. When he asked her if she liked what he was doing to her, she said yes. When he asked her if she wanted more, she screamed yes. That made him smile as he slowly slid one finger inside of her while still using his thumb to stroke her hardened nub. He rubbed it gently as he slid a finger inside and slid it back out. Her essence began to pool in his hand as he increased the tempo. Brian leaned into her chest and held her tight as she wiggled and bounced on his lap, moaning louder and louder for him to not stop and he didn't. He didn't stop even when an orgasm finally overtook her and she leaned back with her eyes closed tightly and her mouth formed into a wide "O". He told her this was what he wanted; he wanted to see her come apart and enjoy the pleasure of a man making her wants a priority. He continued stroking her even when she gripped his shoulders, digging her nails into him. This was about her, he thought and he continued on and on until Sherry finally collapsed forward onto his chest as he leaned back on the chair, holding her close to him, letting her body calm down.

After a few moments, Sherry leaned back and the look of a satisfied woman stared back at him. He wanted to talk about what she was feeling, so that she wasn't ashamed of what they had done. He was happy that there was no shame because she loved him and she knew he loved her and that was all that mattered.

As she shifted on his lap, the rock-hard, massive erection he sported was not a secret to either of them. Sherry looked down into his lap and looked back up at him questionably, asking what about him? Brian loved her innocence and told her not to worry about him and that his erection would eventually go down and before the end of the night, a cold shower was on his agenda. What they had just experienced was all about her and not him. They kissed and Sherry got up to use the restroom.

Brian sat alone for a few minutes taking in what they'd just shared and knew that though he had been with other women, what he and Sherry had just experienced was more erotic than being with any other woman. He was lost in thought until he heard her walking back and he reached to find a movie that they could enjoy, something without love scenes so that his body could calm down. Right now, it was still raging. When a few seconds went by and Sherry wasn't on the couch next to him, he looked up to find her standing in the doorway in a black lace, short nightie and his mouth went completely dry. His eyes took in the vision of her standing there with curves for days. He wanted to shake his head back and forth like a cartoon character to make sure seeing her wasn't a dream, but he couldn't move a muscle. He was afraid that if he did, the image would dissipate. He looked at her from head to toe and then back up again.

Her hair that had been pinned up was now down and flowing loosely around her shoulders. Gone were the jeans she had picked up from the chair that he removed from her body and along with them somewhere, was the top that she'd had on as well. His eyes went straight to her chest where her large breasts were free from the confinement of a bra and her large dark globes were a beacon in the thin black material. Brian still couldn't move and he certainly couldn't find words to speak. Standing before him was a goddess and he was never more thankful than that very moment that she was his. The conversation was short.

"Well?" she asked.

"Well, is right," he replied, barely getting the words out. Clearing his throat, he didn't want to sound like a bumbling idiot though he had no doubt all of the blood in his body had now traveled to one part of his body, leaving him brainless.

"Do you like it," she said nervously.

"I love it," he groaned out in a deep husky voice.

"Are you sure because I'm standing here and you're still sitting," Sherry said.

"Do you have any idea how beautiful you are?"

"I'm glad you think so, now make love to me," she whispered.

He could see that she was nervous and this took every bit of strength she had, he had no doubt. He didn't want an uncomfortable moment between them, so he stood slowly, and walked over to her. Before he said another word, he leaned in and kissed her sweetly and then deeply, pouring every bit of love he had for her into it.

"Baby, you know how much I want you, but you also know that tonight was about you and it wasn't to get us any further. I wanted to please you and I could see that your body craved it."

Sherry put her arms up and stood on the tip of her toes to get as close to him as she could.

"Well, now you've awakened the beast and my body wants you. Don't you want me?" she asked sheepishly.

"I know that was a rhetorical question because we both know the answer to that," he uttered.

Brian followed her eyes as they traveled down his body and landed on his hardness which was now harder than he'd ever remembered being in his life.

"I can see the answer and now I want to feel it," she said.

Brian pulled her all the way into his embrace.

"Are you sure?"

"Yes."

"I love you," he said.

"I love you, too," he heard her say right before he lifted her into his arms to took her to his bedroom.

That night was the first of many nights of making incredible love to Sherry and with the passion they shared, he couldn't imagine how she could walk away from him without looking back. They didn't just have sex or just make love; they had a connection that is only found once in a lifetime and he thought that's what he had found.

The captain interrupted his trip down memory lane when he announced that they were pulling into BWI airport. Brian settled in for the landing and hoped that he could control his anger when he saw her. He could take that she didn't want to be with him, but he wasn't sure he could ever forgive her for keeping him from his daughter. Whatever the outcome, he was ready.

CHAPTER 6

Brian exhaled when the plane finally landed after what felt like the longest flight in history. After exiting the plane, he made his way through the airport to pick up his rental as his level of uncertainty increased at the thought of seeing Sherry again and finally laying eyes on his little girl. Would Sherry ask him to go away and would the little girl who shared a likeness to his family be afraid of him? He decided to not waste time checking into his hotel, which was not far from the airport. He'd called and made a reservation on the plane, but he was too wired up to do anything, except confront Sherry. It had been over two years since he'd last seen her and he was anticipating the feeling of finally setting eyes on her and his little girl.

Using the GPS in the car, he quickly made his way through traffic and thirty minutes later, he found himself sitting across the street from her parent's house in Laurel, Maryland, just outside of Baltimore city contemplating how to approach them without being thrown out before he even said a word. The last time he had walked up to the door and rang the bell, her father came out and told him Sherry didn't want to see him and that he should turn around, head back to Atlanta and never come back again. It was now or never, he thought. The private eye was able to confirm that Sherry still lived at home with her parents and he was bracing for whatever was about to come his way.

The house was large with a wraparound porch that circled the left side of the house around to the back and on the right side of it, he saw a two-car garage. The house had three levels and was about the same size as his house in Atlanta.

He was about to exit the car to walk across to the house when the front door opened and Sherry came out with the cutest little girl with long, thick braids held together by big pink and white ribbons, live and in living color. The pictures did not do her justice.

Looking from the little girl to Sherry, Brian felt like his heart had suddenly stopped beating and temporarily, he was transformed back to a time when they were in love and he would look into her beautiful face as they made love and declared their love for one another. Now, here he was, not really sure of what to say to her.

They must have been on their way to something fun because even at her little size, she was pulling her mother along as if she was in a hurry and Sherry wasn't walking fast enough. According to the investigator, he estimated Sherice was around eighteen-months-old, which would have made Sherry about a month along in her pregnancy when she left Atlanta without a word to him. He was amazed at how much Sherice not only looked like his sister Loren, but she also favored his niece Lyric. He wasn't close enough to hear what Sherice was saying, but he could see her little lips moving a mile a minute. She was dressed in a denim jumper that covered a pink and white blouse and little pink and white tennis. She was beautiful and no doubt, his. Yeah, he thought, test or no test, she was his daughter and his heart swelled with love for the little girl he had yet to meet.

He was so overwhelmed with emotion upon seeing Sherice that he didn't care if Sherry wanted to see him or not and he wasn't leaving until they talked. He didn't want to cause a scene, but now that he was here, he couldn't back away.

Taking a few breaths to calm his nerves, he exited his car and followed them to the playground down the block from the house. He felt a little uncomfortable in a formal tuxedo in the June heat, remembering he still had it on from the wedding, but he straightened his appearance and walked over to them where Sherry now had her back to him. He approached and cleared his throat, so that he didn't startle them as he walked up after Sherry placed Sherice in a swing and began pushing her. He was angry at her, but Sherry was just as beautiful as she had been the last time they'd been together. This was no time for a trip down memory lane again, he thought. He needed to deal with the here and now.

"Hello, Sherry," he said softly from behind her.

Sherry's body went numb. She had to be dreaming because there was no way the person attached to that voice was actually speaking from behind her. She went from being numb to her whole body feeling stiff as if she couldn't move even if she were to put one foot in front of the other. That was a voice from her past, a past she thought she'd left behind in Atlanta. Her heart raced, not out of fear, but out of nervousness. Moments of times in the past of hearing that voice call her name flashed through her mind. Their two worlds that had been apart for a few years was now thrusts together here in Baltimore. She didn't have to turn around to know that Brian Knight stood behind her. She would recognize that sexy, deep, husky voice anywhere as she wondered why she was hearing it behind her right now.

Brian saw the instant Sherry recognized his voice, though she didn't turn around. Her body language said it all. He saw her back stiffen and she ceased pushing their daughter on the swing. He didn't say anything else, giving her time to adjust to the fact that her blast from the past had shown up on her front steps, figuratively and literally.

Though Sherry didn't turn around, Sherice peaked around her at the mysterious man who spoke. She looked down and saw a questionable look on her daughter's face and knew that her chickens had come home to roost. Those Knight hazel eyes glistened with curiosity.

Brian looked at the little girl who was eyeing him and his heart melted when her hazel colored eyes stared back at him. She was even more beautiful than her picture and just like what he saw in her picture, he now saw in person, which was that Sherice was all Knight and there was no denying it. He cleared his throat again as his mind dared Sherry to even try it.

Now that Sherice had noticed him, there was no way Sherry was going to be able to ignore his presence. He watched her turn, as if in slow motion until she was standing face to face with him.

He tried to hold his composure as she plastered what looked like a fake smile on her face and he assumed it was for the sake of Sherice, so that she wasn't startled by his sudden appearance. He knew he looked out of place, especially with how fancy he was dressed.

He watched Sherry look from him to Sherice and then back to him. He knew she was trying to decide if she would say anything or pick Sherice up and go back to her house, avoiding him all together. Whatever her game plan was, he wasn't leaving. When she smiled at Sherice and then turned back to him again, he knew she chose to stand her ground. That worked for him.

"Brian, what are you doing here," she said, looking around suspiciously as if she was looking for someone else to show up. He looked around as she did wondering who or what she was looking for. Seeing nothing, he focused his full attention on her.

"I came to Baltimore to talk to you," he said.

"You shouldn't be here. What did you want to talk about after all this time?" she replied.

Brian felt his temper rising since he knew she already had the answer to her question, but he kept calm remembering what his brothers warned him about.

"Are we going to play a game now?" he said.

"Play, Mommy, push," Sherice said, drawing Brian's attention. She must have heard him say the word, 'play'.

Sherry hesitated, not sure if she should address Sherice or Brian. She was a little torn and a whole lot confused. She turned to Sherice.

"Okay, baby, Mommy's pushing."

"That's a beautiful little girl you have," he said with a serious tone, but also knew he was be facetious at the same time. He tried his best to not sound snide, but he could hear in his own voice that his best was an epic fail. He was angry and had a hard time suppressing it and now he masked it in humor. He was going for whatever worked to get his point across.

Sherry looked at him, realizing he had figured it out, but she didn't respond. In the back of her mind, the moment she'd heard his voice, she knew why he was in Baltimore, but what she didn't know was how had he found out about Sherice.

When she was pregnant and after she'd first had Sherice, she had rehearsed what she would say if he had found out and shown up, but now after so much time, the idea had gotten lost with the passing of time.

"Shall we play twenty questions about why you're here in Baltimore?" she asked.

"Were you going to tell me about her?" he asked.

"Tell you what, Brian?"

The last thing he needed was for her to start playing games as if what he was asking wasn't obvious to her. He'd flown straight to Baltimore from Atlanta, still in his wedding tuxedo and the last thing he wanted to do was go around in circles with her about the obviousness of his presence. He was going straight to the point with no gray area.

"Sherry, I don't even have to ask you for a blood test; look at her. I know you know my sister Loren and she looks exactly like Loren did as a little girl and could pass as her daughter right now. Are you going to tell me she's not mine?" he asked quietly not sure how much his daughter would pick up on.

"Mommy, push!" Sherice shouted impatiently at the her because of the non-moving swing.

Sherry didn't realize that she'd stopped pushing the swing. She was trying to contain her surprise at seeing Brian and knowing that he also knew about Sherice. To say she was caught off-guard is an understatement. If she didn't have Sherice with her, she would probably handle this differently, but thankful for her daughter's presence, a calmer response prevailed.

She started pushing the swing again.

"I can't do this with you right now," she said looking around to see if anyone was watching them.

"Oh, really? When is the time to deal with this, when she's graduating high school or were you planning on never telling me about her?" he said, standing with his hands in his pockets. That was one way of controlling his anger.

"There is nothing to tell right now. It's not a good time to have this discussion," she said trying her best to brush him off. She needed time to prepared for seeing him again. Why was he dressed so impeccably in formal attire? The one thing he could always do was look good in a suit. His tall, muscular body was designed for tailor-made suits. Add to that his handsome features that included dark piercing eyes, strong, perfectly squared jaw and a smile that could light a city and you had the strikingly handsome, Brian Knight. Had he been attending some event in Maryland and decided to look her up and then saw Sherice with her? Could it have been that simple?

"I came a long way to see you and her and I'm not going away, so we can talk now or we can do this later, but know that I'm not leaving Baltimore until we talk and I don't care how long it takes," he stated matter-of-factly.

She now had her answer. He had come to Baltimore specifically to see them after somehow finding out that she'd had a baby. This conversation could get intense and she didn't want to frighten Sherice who was already looking at her strange while she talked to the man who was unfamiliar to her.

"Smile when you talk to me. Sherice is a very bright little girl and she will sense the tension. I don't want her frightened."

Without giving it a second thought, Brian plastered a smile on his face and the smile turned genuine when Sherice smiled back at him.

"Thank you," Sherry said, happy that he was thinking about Sherice and that he didn't want to upset her.

"I'm not here to make waves in your life, Sherry. I would have left you alone as you asked me to if it hadn't been for the fact that you have my daughter and I knew nothing about her," he whispered, hoping to avoid Sherice focusing on their talk.

"You want to do this now?" she asked.

"Do you have a better time? I'm going to keep smiling while I ask you again. Are you going to tell me that she's not mine?"

Sherry hesitated knowing that there was no way she'd be able to honestly deny Sherice was his. Everyday her daughter looked more and more like a Knight and any denial would be useless. She gave Sherice a push and when she laughed out loud joyfully, she quickly turned back around to Brian.

"No, I'm not going to tell you that."

"Tell me something, please?" he said, adding a plea to his voice. He had come to Baltimore ready for a fight and now that he'd seen his daughter, all he wanted to do was get to know her and deal with the fact that he had a precious little girl. What he hadn't expected was the rush of emotions he felt standing close to Sherry again. He was furious at her, but he also remembered a time when he loved her more than anything.

Sherry's heart broke when he said please. The weight of what she'd done came crashing down on her. She had deliberately kept him from his daughter and for that she had no excuse, but now that he was here, there was no need to continue hiding. She looked him in the eyes, those dark luxurious pools of delight, as her features softened.

"This is your daughter," she whispered.

Brian was choked up even though he knew all along, but hearing it come from her mouth made it more real.

He looked beyond her to Sherice who now smiled brightly at him, showing the few teeth she had in her mouth. He waved at her and when she waved back, he sighed with relief. He was a goner for her already.

"Hello," he said to her.

"Brian, I'd like you to meet Sherice Briana Knight."

At first her words didn't register because he was focused on Sherice and her beaming smile and then the words sank in. He looked from Sherry to Sherice, who was oblivious to what was going on around her because she was enjoying the swing. She paid no attention to them as any fight he had come prepared to have dissipated. Sherry confirmed what he already knew which was that he was the father of this beautiful little girl.

"Hi, Sherice," he said and his heart melted a little more when she quietly said hi back.

Before he could say anything, Sherry stopped whatever he was about to say. She spoke softly since they were still making sure that Sherice didn't sense anything weird going on.

"Before you go all into father mode and start making demands, this is my life and my daughter and I don't want or need anything from you, so you can turn around and go back home," she said pointedly.

He didn't want to upset Sherice either, so he smiled brightly as she continued to wave at him. He had already had enough of Sherry controlling his presence in his daughter's life and like it or not, she had better get comfortable with him being around because he wasn't going to be a father in name only. Sherice was his daughter and he planned on making sure she knew it. He had time to make up for and he wasn't going to let Sherry be what stands between him and loving his daughter.

"This is not about you and like I already told you, I'm not leaving here without my daughter knowing who I am or without you and I talking about visitation and joint custody. You've selfishly kept me from my daughter long enough and that ends today. I'll let you decide whether we do this the hard way or the easy way, but now that I know she exists, I'm about to become a permanent fixture in your lives, so you're not getting rid of me now or ever. I let you walk out of my life before without any kind of explanation of what I did that sent you away, but I won't let you keep my daughter from me. I've already missed so much of her life and I'm not missing anymore. The only question I have for you is do we tell her together that I'm her father or shall I do that on my own? She may not understand what it means, but I still want her to know. I want you to know that I will use any means at my disposal to make sure you don't keep her away from me anymore. Now, I'm going to give you my card with my number on it and when you're ready to talk privately, let me know."

Brian was about to lose his temper and he knew it was time for him to leave and gather his faculties. As much as he would like to spend time with Sherice, now was not the time. He and Sherry need to air a few things out and they needed to be able to do it comfortably out of Sherice's eye and ear sight. He reached into his pocket, pulled out his wallet and handed one of his business cards to her. He watched as she, at first, hesitated to take it from his hands and when she finally reached for it, he handed it to her. Their fingers touched lightly and a feeling came over him that took him back to the day when they had first met and their first touch was electrifying. All these years later and with the slightest touch of her skin, he felt it again. Knowing how to read Sherry and her reactions to him, he knew that he wasn't the only one who felt it as he watched her jerk her hand back away from his. They still had that spark and that angered him more than the fact that she had kept his daughter from him. He was now pissed that in his heart, there was still something there connected to her and it wasn't just because of his daughter. For that, he knew it was time to leave. He leaned down to Sherice's height to address her.

"It was really nice meeting you, Sherice. You are a very pretty little girl and I hope to see you again, okay?"

Sherice didn't say anything, but she bobbed her head up and down as her long braids moved wildly about. She smiled at him again and took her mother's hand, pulling Sherry close to her so that she could lean on her while strapped into the swing.

Brian stood back up to his full height and addressed Sherry.

"I'll be staying at a hotel at the airport and I hope to hear from you either later today or tomorrow. If not, I'll come by again and I'm assuming your father still has an issue with me, so that reunion may not be pleasant. I meant what I said, we can do this any way you like, but I think that with level heads, we should be able to work this out as two adults."

He didn't wait for a response as he turned on his heels and quickly walked away.

Sherry didn't realize she stood standing, watching Brian's retreat with her mouth wide open. She didn't know what she was preparing to say, but what she did know was Brian meant business and deep down, she knew he had every right to. She had messed up in a major way and even if she didn't want to, she needed to fix it. The man she knew was never going to turn and walk away from his child that he now knew about. His dedication to family is strong and now that extended out to Sherice.

"Mommy, push!" Sherice screamed.

Sherry watched as Brian sped off down the street, not even glancing her way and then she plastered a happy smile on her face and turned her attention back to Sherice. Her chickens had officially come home to roost.

CHAPTER 7

"You're going to wear a hole in the floor if you don't sit down."

Brian smiled into the phone at his mother's words. It didn't matter if her children were in her presence or on the phone, Barbara Knight knew what they were going through on the other end. He had been pacing in his hotel room ever since he left Sherry and Sherice at the playground.

He had driven only a few miles away before his cell phone beeped. Pulling over to the side of the road, he saw that he had received a text message from a number that wasn't stored with a name. Clicking it, he saw that it was from Sherry. She had agreed to meet with him the next day to talk about Sherice. The message said she would get back to him later in the day about a time and place. As much as he wanted to iron things out today, he was exhausted and needed to get some sleep, so that he could deal with her with a clear and focused mind. This was about Sherice and not him and Sherry and he needed to remember that. Ever since he saw the text, he'd been pacing and hadn't been able to stop.

"How do you know I'm pacing?" he said, smiling.

"Son, I know my children better than they know themselves, now calm down and tell me about her."

Barbara had waited what seemed an eternity for Brian to call her. After Duron informed her of why Brian had suddenly rushed out from the wedding, she felt better knowing that he was okay and it looks like it wasn't as bad as she was thinking his interaction with Sherry would be.

She knew that Brian was the most intense of her brood and he wore his heart openly on his sleeve. The minute he set eyes on that little girl, she knew he would be a goner, but her concern was about his conversation with Sherry.

She remembered the woman her son had fallen in love with and thought back to the first time she'd met her. Her first thought was that she was too young for Brian, but after talking with her, she found that Sherry was mature way beyond her years, though she now questioned that after finding out that she kept Brian's child away from him. Thankfully, she was a Christian woman, a forgiving woman and she was able to think of that little girl and not Sherry's actions. For now, that kept her sane.

"Mom, she is so beautiful and she looks exactly like Loren did at this age. The only difference is she has my darker complexion instead of Loren's lighter one."

Brian couldn't see his mother's face, but he knew that she probably had unshed tears pooling in her eyes and probably pacing herself. His mother loved her children with everything that was in her, but she had a special kind of love for her grandchildren and to know that there is another one out here that she hasn't met, hugged and kissed yet, was overwhelming. He could relate because even though Sherice was not planned or expected, the moment he saw her, he felt a love like no other.

"How old is my granddaughter?" she asked.

"She's about eighteen-months-old, but I'll know for sure when I have a chance to talk to Sherry more. You should see her, Mom. I'm pissed at Sherry, but you can tell Sherice is a very happy little girl who loves the swing at the playground. That's where I saw them."

"Was she frightened to meet you for the first time?"

"No, she doesn't know who I am. She saw me, but she doesn't know I'm her father. I plan to talk to Sherry again either later today or tomorrow and I think after some much needed sleep, I'll be able to talk with a level head without getting angry. I wanted to be furious, but the moment I saw Sherice, that went out the window."

"That's because she became the focus and not the fact that Sherry didn't tell you about her."

"You're right, Mom."

"Keep that in mind whenever you talk to Sherry and make sure you talk and not scream, Brian. You know how short your fuse is and Duron told me how angry you were when you left. I still wish that you had waited a few more days to let your anger calm before you went to Baltimore, but I understand your desire to see your daughter and to get some answers from Sherry. Of my four children, you are the most emotional and when you have reached your limit with someone, you don't think reasonably before you let off steam. Don't make the situation worse by making demands or issuing ultimatums. You don't know what caused her to walk out of your life and keep that beautiful little girl from you. Try your best to listen, not judge and find a way to make sure you're in her life for good."

"I hear you, Mom."

Barbara breathed a sigh of relief and now it was time for

her to be the mother and grandmother her children and grandchildren expected her to be.

"Good, now I know I'm telling you to tread lightly, but I also want to make it very clear that we do *not* leave Knight's behind for any reason and you and Sherry had better work something out before I have to get on a plane and make my way to Baltimore. I want to see my granddaughter soon and I want her to know who we are and that we love her."

Brian smiled and shook his head. That's the mother he was raised by and no one had better cross her or her children or grandchildren because she was definitely a momma bear! Family was first to her and that's what she instilled in all of her children, which is why they were all so close. He could never forget one time as a child, a family member on his father's side had cursed and talked down to him. When he arrived at home, he was upset and his mother could see it. After telling her what happened, she didn't wait for his father to drive her to his uncle's house to find out what went down. He watched Barbara Knight slip on her tennis while his father was trying to convince her to let him deal with it and she walked over a mile to his uncle's house and made sure even family knew never come for her children for any reason without expecting her wrath. Brian never had an issue like that again with anyone in his family after word spread. When she promised she would get on a plane and fly to Baltimore to handle this, he knew she meant it.

"I promise I'm not here to make waves and I don't want to disrupt the life Sherry has carved out for herself and Sherice, but you can trust and know that now that I know about her, I'm never letting her out of my life again."

"Tell me everything you know about her and don't forget to email me some pictures. I'm still figuring this cell phone thing out when it comes to texting, but I'm a master at email."

Brian did smile and laugh, knowing that the anxiety he was feeling could only be calmed by the sound of his mother's voice.

"Well, one big shocker is that Sherry gave her my last name and I wasn't expecting that at all. Oh, and her middle name is Briana and I won't assume she gave her that name for Brian, but I will ask her. She's a tiny little thing with long, thick black hair and she smiled and waved at me when I said hello to her."

"Milo and Lyric have a touch of those hazel eyes and we already know Loren's baby Chase has those eyes, too and there is no doubt the twins have them since we all saw them the first time they opened their eyes at the hospital. Your father has some extremely strong genes, since those hazel eyes run in his family."

Brian couldn't help, but gleam at hearing his nephew Chase's name. Before getting the news that he had been waiting for from the private investigator, he was planning on spending some time in California with Loren, Michael and his nephew, knowing he needed a break before classes resumed for the fall semester. He wasn't sure what was next for him on the life agenda, but something was telling him that he would need to take a semester off from teaching since his daughter lived in Baltimore and until he and Sherry figured out what the next step was, he wasn't going back to Atlanta. He didn't know what he would do, but for now, it looked like he wouldn't be teaching summer classes unless they were on-line classes.

"He does and I'm glad Sherry didn't try to say that Sherice wasn't mine. Anyone looking at her who knew the Knight family would know that she was me all over except for the hazel eyes. She has my nose and her facial features show that Sherry only carried her, but she is all mine."

He could hear his mother's silent cheer on the other end of the phone and he couldn't wait for her to meet Sherice.

"Oh, I can't wait to hold her, hug her and kiss her. What do you know about what Sherry has been doing all this time?" she asked.

"Not much at all. The private detective was able to find out that she had actually finished out her last year of college here in Baltimore after having Sherice and she now works for a forensics lab. She graduated with a degree in Biology and she's in the middle of getting her master's degree. Personally, he wasn't able to find out much, but I didn't really ask. I was mainly concerned with finding her and finding out if she actually had a baby. I do know that she still lives with her parents and I'm sure it's so that they can help her with Sherice. She really is beautiful, Mom, and you're going to love her."

"I already do, son. Whenever they're ready, please let Sherry and her family know that we don't want to impose on their lives, but we do want to be a part of Sherice's life. I'll let your father know that you arrived there safely. Have you talked to Duron or Jake since you landed? He was heading to your house after we left the reception earlier and then he was going home. Those twins can be a handful, so he doesn't like to leave Taija alone with them without his help, especially at bedtime. I think it has more to do with the fact that he doesn't want to miss any time with them and not because Taija can't handle them."

71

CHERYL BARTON

Brian knew the feeling. He'd only seen his daughter briefly and even as tired as he was, if he could see her tonight, he would, but it was late. He need to run to a store and buy some clothes and toiletries until Duron sent the items he picked up from his house.

"Yeah, I talked to Duron right after I landed and I called Jake on my way here to the hotel. Duron is going to overnight my things to the hotel and I should get them in the morning. Tonight, I just need a hot shower and a bed."

"Good, I know you need the rest. Where are you staying and after you meet with Sherry, what's the next step?"

"In a hotel at the airport. I have a fraternity brother, Xavier McIntyre, who lives here in Baltimore in a condo downtown, so I'm going to connect with him while I'm here. He's an attorney and I'll try and talk things out with him to see if I can get some help from him about how to handle this in a legal manner, so that everything regarding Sherice is done by the book. I'm not leaving here without knowing my rights when it comes to my daughter."

"I remember Xavier. He and a group of your fraternity brothers came home with you one year for dinner after a step show while they were visiting your chapter at Morehouse."

"Yes, that's him. He's a partner in his father's law firm, so I know he'll be able to help. I'll give him a call to let him know I'm here and to see if we can talk this week. I promise you, I'm going to try my best to not make waves, but I want full access to my daughter and I get the feeling that Sherry will probably try and push back. Her father is Police Commissioner for Baltimore City and I'm sure he's got some powerful people behind him. I have no idea what they'll try and pull and the last time I encountered him, it didn't go over well. He pretty much threw me off of his property and told me to stay away from his daughter or he'd have me arrested for harassment even though I only asked to speak with her. Two sentences in and he was threatening me."

Brian heard his mother gasp on the other end. It was at that moment that he realized he had never told anyone other than his brothers about that incident.

"He did what? Why is this the first time I'm hearing about this? Nobody messes with or threatens my children and I don't care what position he holds, he still has to abide by the law, too. I guess it's a good thing you didn't tell me about this when it happened. I would have given him a piece of my mind. Did your father know about that?"

Brian laughed. His mother could be quite gangster when it comes to protecting her children. She knew she raised good kids and there was no reason for anyone to threaten any of them.

"No, he didn't know. Only Duron and Jake knew and I told them not to tell you and Pop. I know you would have walked to Baltimore to confront him if you had to. I didn't rock the boat and I turned around and walked away. I never would have if I had known that she was pregnant. He didn't let me see her and though I tried reaching her by phone a few times, she never responded to me," he said somberly.

"I remember that she was a sweet girl. Are you sure you don't know what happened between you that made her leave and never come back, other than the fact that she obviously was pregnant with your child? I know there was an age difference. Do you think she just wasn't ready for a serious relationship at her age?"

"I don't know, but I thought we were on the same page. Age never played a role in our relationship. We knew about the age difference going in and though in the back of my mind, I was a little hesitant, I fell in love with her hard and fast. For a junior in college, she was a few years older than most juniors because she started college a few years later than most do, but she was mature for her age and that's what made us click so fast. It was fate that I met her and I had no idea I would connect with her the way that I did, but it happened. I thought we'd fallen in love and you saw her when I brought her home to meet you and Pop. She was happy and as far as I knew we weren't having any problems. Months after that, when the semester was just about over, I went to talk to her to see if I could see her over the summer break in Baltimore and she had already left. There was some tension about something that I don't know about and I tried to give her a few days to cool down. I tried calling her cell and checked with her friends and I got nothing. It was around exam time and we were both busy, so there was about a week or so that we didn't have any contact. The only thing a friend of hers would tell me is that she told them if I came around, to tell me she never wanted to see me again. That was the time I flew to Baltimore that summer after we all returned from Ohio when I got my doctorate. I think I said I was coming here to visit my fraternity brothers, but it was to try and talk to her, which as you know didn't happen. I spent a few days hanging with Xavier and finally got to meet his family and then I came back home. I figured, if I have to beg someone to be with me and they still don't, it wasn't meant to be."

Brian heard the words, but didn't really believe them. He desperately sought her out because if he had done anything to hurt her or upset her, he wanted to make it right, but he was left clueless. He would have been able to deal with her telling him directly that she wanted to move on, but instead, she left him hanging and kept his daughter away. He could forgive one day, but he'll never forget. He would remember her deception every time he looked at his daughter and wondered what she was like as an infant coming into the world brand new. He missed that and that was on Sherry.

"Son, that's all in the past and whatever happened, get the closure you need and find a way to co-exist with Sherry as a co-parent to that little girl. Every little girl needs her father. I'm assuming Sherry's not married or do you think she may be? I know you said she still stays with her parents, but that doesn't mean there isn't a man or husband in the picture."

"I don't know anything about her private life and at this point, I don't care as long as whatever her status is, it doesn't impact my ability to get to know my daughter and become a part of her life."

Brian hadn't thought much about another man being in Sherry's life and if that's the case, he would like to sit down with them together and talk through his role in Sherice's life. He was willing to compromise in any way possible as long as his role in Sherice's life is solidified.

"How long do you think you'll be in Baltimore?" Barbara asked.

"Until I figure out what I'm going to do and how this is going to work, I'm not going anywhere. I may have to put in a leave of absence at work depending on how long this takes because I'm scheduled to teach during the summer semester. We may have to go to court and talk things out like visitation and child support and whatever it takes is what I'll do. Right now, all I can think about is getting to know Sherice and making sure she knows who I am. I also don't want to love my daughter from a distance, but I don't have a plan for how to deal with that right now either. For now, I'm going to meet with Sherry and talk."

"Son, you can't stay at a hotel indefinitely. That could get costly and cramped."

"It's extended stay and it's pretty roomy, Mom. As far as cost, you have taught us well when it comes to balancing out our finances and I'm good. I'll be fine and I'll keep you and Pop updated on what's going on here. I don't want you to worry too much because I didn't come all this way to get arrested or cause any trouble. I came for my daughter and I'm entitled to that and believe me, the least Sherry can do is not fight me on this. She's taken enough from me already. It's getting late and I want to try and connect with Xavier tonight since I'm meeting with Sherry tomorrow. I probably need to get some advice from him before speaking to her. Promise me you're not going to worry," Brian said.

He knew there would be no stopping his mother from worrying about him, but he would feel better about all he needed to do if she could hear in his voice that he was okay, causing her to worry a lot less. He laughed when he heard her huff and puff on the other end of the phone. That was a joke amongst he and his siblings. When their mother was about to lay down the law, they would joke that she was about to huff and puff and shut everything down.

"Now, Brian, that's asking a lot. I will promise that I won't worry as much as I was going to worry before I talked to you. How is that?" she asked.

That would due for now. Only his mother, the gangster, he thought.

"I'll take that. I love you, Mom."

"I love you too, son."

Brian disconnected the line and immediately called Xavier's cell number, not sure if he was at the office or home. He knew there was a possibility that he was going to need some legal advice.

CHAPTER 8

Xavier McIntyre smiled as he walked around his condo, not being able to forget the incredibly beautiful woman he'd met while grabbing dinner at his favorite seafood restaurant in downtown Baltimore. After a long day at the office where he worked as a senior attorney at his father's firm, he needed that kind of distraction after a day that left him dog-tired. If he played his cards right, he'd be seeing her again real soon.

He was about to settle in for the evening, one of the rare days he got where he had a work-free evening to himself, when his phone rang, signaling one of his fraternity brothers was calling. He had a special ring for them who all were as close as blood brothers. He grabbed it and was glad to see Brian Knight was calling. They had plans later in the summer to spend a weekend fishing with a few of his brothers and Brian was one of the first to acknowledge that he was going.

"Brian! What's up frat? It's good hearing from you. Don't tell me you're calling to cancel out on our fishing trip later this summer," Xavier said.

"No, not at all. I'm still looking forward to that, but I

may have to make a change of plans depending on how my present circumstance turns out," Brian admitted.

There was a pause before Xavier chimed in.

"Circumstances? What's going on and is it something I can help with? You know whatever you need, I got you."

"Well, for starters, I'm here in Maryland," Brian admitted.

"Seriously? Why didn't you tell me you were coming? How long are you here for and where are you staying? I hope not at some hotel," Xavier said.

"My trip was a last minute unplanned one. I'm not sure how long I'll be here yet and yeah, I'm at a hotel, but it's an extended stay spot at the airport, so I'm good here."

"Nonsense. If you're going to be here for an extended period of time, you can stay at the corporate condo. No one is using it right now and it's in my building right on the water. I fell in love with the corporate condo we use for visiting attorneys from our Los Angeles office, so I purchased one of the condos for myself. No one is using the guest suite and while you're here, it's yours and I won't take no for an answer. I spend most of my time at my house in Montgomery county, but I'm actually here tonight, taking in the Baltimore scene. What kind of a fraternity brother would I be if I let you come to town and didn't put you up?" Xavier asked.

Brian appreciated the life-long friendship he'd developed with his fraternity brothers, especially Xavier. He was happy to hear that Xavier's younger brother, Spence had continued with their family legacy by pledging the same fraternity and he was proud to call them both brother.

"How could I turn down an invitation like that. How

about we connect tomorrow and I'll stay here for this one night? That flight was exhausting and I'm still in a tuxedo, which is another story for another time."

"Are you good? What brings you to here unexpectedly?"

Brian didn't hesitate to fill him in, but relented.

"Like I mentioned, I have a bit of a circumstance and I was hoping I could get some insight from you on how to proceed forward. I'll keep it brief in the hope that you have some time tomorrow for me to give you more details."

"Take all the time you need. I'm all ears and if I can help in any way, you know I'm there for you."

"I know it and I appreciate it. I may need your help with a legal matter, since I'm not sure how this circumstance will play out. Do you remember Sherry that I went out with for a while? I introduced the two of you once during one of your visits to Atlanta and I think you met her when I visited with her family over the Christmas holiday season a few years back."

"Of course, I remember her. She was a beautiful woman and had a love for all things science and the way you fell in love with her hard, there is no way to forget her. I also remember what you went through when she disappeared on you a few years ago, breaking things off without telling you why."

Xavier remembered things well.

"Yeah, that's her and she's the circumstance that I had to come here to deal with," he added.

"I remember you telling me she was from Baltimore which is why I remember her because it's my home town. So, what's going on?" Xavier asked.

"I'm here to actually see her sometime tomorrow. To give you the short version of what's going on, I found out that after breaking up with me and disappearing, she gave birth to my daughter; a daughter I recently became aware of. She never told me about her and I came to Baltimore to get some answers and to find out why she kept her from me. I may need your help, legally, to find out what my rights are when it comes to the baby, who is about eighteen-months-old."

"What!" Xavier exclaimed.

"You heard it right. I have a daughter I didn't know about and I have no intention of being kept from her ever again," Brian exclaimed.

"Wow. Did Sherry confirm the baby is yours?"

"She did and she named her Sherice Briana Knight, so yeah, she's pretty much mine."

"Did she say anything about you not being able to see Sherice or be a part of her life? You do have rights once paternity is established, which I think you should do through legal channels even though you have no doubt about her parentage. I still recommend doing it right in order to protect yourself now and in the future," Xavier explained.

"That's another reason why I'm reaching out to you besides hanging out some while I'm here. When I talk with Sherry, I don't want to push her, but I'm not letting her keep me from my daughter anymore and I want to be sure whatever is done, is done on the up and up, legally. Once paternity is established, I want to be sure Sherice is taken care of with whatever she needs and I need to know how visitation is worked out. I live in Atlanta and Sherry lives here with Sherice. That doesn't make for maintaining the best father/daughter relationship, but for now, I want to get to know my daughter and knowing that Sherry never told me about her, I'm guessing she won't be happy with what I want."

"Frat, whatever you need, I got you. Be careful what you say and don't make any demands. Let's connect after you've talked to her and I'll get some more information from you to begin the process to get your rights established."

"I'm hoping this doesn't get nasty. Can you believe she would do that? This is a woman I thought I was in love with a few years back. If you recall, this is the woman I was planning to marry. I never would have imagined she would do something like this."

Xavier was one of the few people outside of his brothers and sister that he told about asking Sherry to marry him. They thought it was a whirlwind relationship, but he knew from the moment that they had met, that she was the one for him.

"You never know what someone will do until they do it. Do you have any idea why she left you and never told you about the baby?" Xavier asked.

Still, he had no clue, but he hoped meeting with Sherry about Sherice would also shed some light on why she left him in the first place.

"I'm hoping to find out, but at this point, I don't even know if I want to know why she left, though I want to know why she didn't tell me about Sherice. I am a forgiving guy, you know that, but I don't know if any excuse she provides will be totally forgivable. This is my kid we're talking about and the part of her life that I've already missed, I can never, ever get back."

"I know how much your nieces and nephews mean to you. I remember getting those pictures of your brother

Duron's kids when they were born and you were smiling holding them. I also remember you telling me about Jake's kids Milo and Lyric and how much they love their uncle Brian. Try not to talk to Sherry in anger even though I know you're angry with her over the situation, but play it cautiously. I would really prefer if you not meet with her yet and wait for the legal process to kick in, but that can also make the situation worse if you show up talking about lawyers, visitation and rights. Do what you need to do, but tread lightly until you and I can talk. I'll do some looking into this. You know I do entertainment and finance law, but I'll bring in one of our junior attorney's who's more familiar with family law. That will save me some time with research and all the paperwork that we'll need to get filed. Long term, what are your plans, especially with Sherry and Sherice living here in Baltimore? I know you mentioned it, but a judge is going to ask you how you see this playing out and you'll need to provide an answer. We'll be making demands and how you're going to deal with the distance will be a key factor in any decision," Xavier warned.

"I haven't thought about that other than until things are resolved temporarily, I'm not leaving here even if I have to put in for a leave of absence from work for the next semester."

"What are you going to do for months here in Baltimore? You're going to drive yourself crazy."

He hadn't thought about that. The only thing on his mind was Sherice and he totally forgot that he had a life, which included bills to be paid, back home. He had plenty of money saved up, so that wasn't a real big issue, but he would eventually have to go back to work. He could do some work for Duron's company to keep the money flowing in. For a few years, Duron had been trying to get him to officially come on board to lead one of his marketing teams and to do some financial reconciliation work, another specialty of his which was his focus for his doctorate. He would check with Duron about any work he could do part-time remotely while he's in Baltimore. He needed to keep busy and like he mentioned to Xavier, his brothers and his mother, he wasn't leaving Baltimore without a deeper connection with Sherice.

"Yeah, I'm going to reach out to Duron about doing some side work for him while I'm here. I don't have to be in the office to do that. I'll have to have him overnight me my computer and some other items, but I think it'll work out for now. If nothing else, it'll keep me occupied while I'm waiting for this to work out."

"Your brother is still trying to bring you on, huh? I have a meeting with him next month about putting my firm on retainer."

"Yeah, when he called me for your number, he mentioned he was hoping to do that. He has a few friends who are attorneys here in Baltimore, but he said he wanted to use your firm because if I trusted you, he knew he had nothing to worry about."

"I appreciate the referral. I was looking over the financials he sent me and Duron's company is booming and expanding by leaps and bounds. He could use your financial wisdom and you're not too shabby on the marketing front either," Xavier joked. Brian had assisted Xavier's brother, Spence, with some marketing for his car dealerships.

"I was planning to do that this summer anyway since they've really expanded. He asked me to join the firm on a part-time basis since I didn't want to give up teaching and I was going to have a full load three days a week this summer. I think I'll do one or two online classes and give up the others and then focus on getting myself acclimated to his company. I still love preparing these kids for the world of finance and marketing."

"Well, that's something. What time is good for you tomorrow to get you moved to the condo?"

"Anytime is good for me after I get the clothes Duron is overnighting me. Sherry didn't say an exact time for us to talk or meet, but I told her it needed to be later today or tomorrow or she would find me on her doorstep. As soon as she reaches out, I'll let you know."

"Good and be prepared to check out of that place. I'm going to have a service check done on the condo to be sure it's fully stocked and cleaned and ready for you and remember what I said, you can stay there as long as you need to and don't you dare insult me about money. I know that was the next thing out of your mouth. It's a condo that's paid for and maintained free by the law firm. A cleaning service can come in when you want them too and I'll give you the rundown of other building amenities you can take advantage of. I'll have everything ready for you tomorrow including the key and garage passcode for you to park. It's good hearing from you and I'm already claiming that this is going to work out for you. I can't wait to meet your little girl. Congratulations, Daddy!" Xavier shouted before hanging up.

Brian closed his cell phone and sat down at the table near the window, looking out over the dark sky. Xavier had just made his day by calling him Daddy, words he couldn't wait to hear Sherice say. All in due time, he thought. For now, he needed to run to the store to get some clean clothes and other needed items and then prepare himself mentally for the talk that has been a long time coming.

CHAPTER 9

Sherry had finally gotten Sherice to bed after a bath and then being forced to read three bedtime stories to her. She stood at her bedroom door and watched her as she slept peacefully. For over two years, it had been her and Sherice and of course her parents, but she only had to share her with them. Now that Brian was in Baltimore and demanding his rights as a father, she had to deal with the repercussions of her decision to not tell him about the baby.

When her father had gotten home from work, she was close to telling him about Brian's sudden appearance, but didn't want to cause trouble. She needed some time to think over what to do next. She wanted to tell her mother, but that would only lead to a conversation she wasn't ready to have. Right now, she needed her girls.

Her two best friends, Rayven and Candace, would be the ear she needed and she needed to talk to them tonight. She was planning to meet with Brian while Sherice spent some time with her parents tomorrow, but tonight, she knew she would be far from sleepy. Her mind kept drifting back to the many nights she'd fallen asleep in Brian's arms and when she turned around and saw him standing in front of her looking as sexy as he ever had, she felt like that woman who had given the love of her life her virginity and never regretted doing so, not even now.

He had always been handsome and sexy, but in that tuxedo with those bowlegs, he looked scrumptious and the mere thought of him had her sex throbbing.

She remembered a time when they were together when her body hummed at the thought of him and how he made love to her. He taught her about sex and how to derive the pleasure she needed from their coupling. Even as she turned and walked toward her bedroom, she had to rub her thighs together to relieve some of the pressure between them. How could she still have such a hot, deep carnal reaction to him when she hadn't seen or talked to him in years? She may have tried to forget about him, but her body had a mind of its own and it remembered. Since her parents had gone out for a late movie, she had some time to talk to her friends open and free without having to whisper or go outside to talk to not be overheard. She searched in her purse for her cellphone and placed a call to Rayven first.

"I need a three-way call," Sherry said the minute she answered the phone. After Brian left her and Sherice at the playground, she stayed about thirty more minutes before heading back to her house. She held her composure and kept a smile on her face for Sherice's sake, not wanting her to sense that anything was wrong or out of the ordinary. Brian's sudden appearance was beyond what she would call a shock.

"Uh oh, this sounds serious," Rayven responded.

"Oh, it is. Can you patch Candace in? My fingers are

shaking."

Now that she heard Rayven's voice, she couldn't stop shaking or pacing. Her life was officially turned upside down and she couldn't see a way out and tomorrow, she would have to deal with coming face to face with Brian and there was no doubt in her mind that he would ask her about the past before they talked about the present and future when it came to Sherice.

How could she have been so stupid and immature to keep him away from Sherice? Karma had come back to haunt her for the way she'd left him. She held her head up, though, knowing that she'd had no choice. After what she'd heard, she was crushed and had to get away from him and Atlanta. Lucky for her, the semester was over and it was time for her to return to Baltimore anyway. Now, just when her life was getting on track and she was planning to move out from her parent's house into a home that she was looking to buy for her and Sherice, Brian shows up looking all yummy and her body was all ready to jump him. She groaned in frustration at herself.

"Are you okay?" Rayven asked.

"No, I'm not which is why I need you and Candace on the line at the same time."

"Getting her right now," Rayven added.

Sherry didn't mean to make her worry without giving her an explanation for the three-alarm fire that was her life right now.

"Hey ladies!" Candace said after getting on the line.

"Something's wrong," Rayven said solemnly.

There was a moment of silence before anyone spoke and Sherry paced, still trying to gather her thoughts.

"Sherry? What's up? Do you need us to come over?"

Rayven questioned.

"Sherry, what's going on?" Candace added.

Sherry exhaled loudly and tried to calm her nerves. Soon her mother and father would be home and she knew she'd have to tell them what was going on, but right now, she needed her best friends to help calm her down.

"Okay, so I took Sherice to the playground like I do every Saturday afternoon because you know it's one of her favorite things to do. I'm planning on buying a house with a yard big enough for Sherice to have her own swing set," she said babbling on.

"You're dragging this out. Stop rambling and get to it. What's going on?" Rayven said impatiently.

"Oh, right, sorry about that. Well, I'm swinging her on the swing, again her favorite thing to ride on and up walks Brian."

Sherry waited for a reaction and didn't get one. She didn't know if they were shocked or had no clue what she was talking about and had not yet made the connection to the name.

"Okay, so someone named Brian walks up and then what happened? What's the emergency?" Candace asked.

Sherry blew air into the phone. She guessed neither one of them caught on and it had been a few years since she last spoke his name to them.

Even though she had gone off to school in Atlanta after a few years of struggling after high school to figure out her life, her two best friends from high school had remained her two best friends for life. She had told them everything, but time had made them forget.

"No, you didn't hear me, it wasn't some guy named Brian, it was *Brian!*" she said loudly.

And then there was silence.

"Wait, are you serious? *That* Brian?" Rayven asked.

"Whoa, are you talking about Brian Knight?" Candace added.

Now, Sherry exhaled now that they were on the same page.

"Yes, I am. He walked right up to us on the playground and I swear if a hole could have opened up on the ground where I stood and swallowed me whole, I would be in a better place right now," she razzed while exhaling.

"What is he doing in Maryland? Doesn't he live in Georgia?" Rayven asked.

"Well, from what I could gather, he came to see Sherice."

"Wait, he knew about Sherice? For how long and where the hell has he been then?" Candace asked.

"I don't know all of that. We didn't get the chance to talk that through because Sherice was there and I didn't want to have a heated discussion in front of her. I had a feeling if she wasn't there, we would still be hollering at each other. Somehow, he knew about Sherice before I had a chance to say anything and he came to Maryland specifically for her. I don't know what else was going on, but he was in a tuxedo as if he'd come right from some black-tie event and you remember me telling you how that man could wear a suit. He still can and apparently better than ever," she said without hesitation.

"Okay, focus Sherry and turn the heat down. I know you need some, but focus," Rayven laughed.

"Girl, all kinds of things started running through my mind when I saw him and they were all about hot, steamy nights."

"You still go it bad, I see," Candace chimed.

"Whatever," Sherry added.

"I wonder how he found out and also, what did you do and say?" Rayven asked.

Sherry had to finally sit down in order to calm her nerves. Sitting and then stretching out across her bed, she told them the whole story.

"I didn't say much because his sudden appearance caught me off guard and like I said, Sherice was there. I could tell he was pissed off and I've never seen him angry before. He told me he knew about Sherice and how much she looked like his sister. I told you guys that. Sherice looks exactly like Brian's sister Loren. I've seen pictures of her as a little girl and those photos could be Sherice. He came right out and asked if I was going to deny that she was his daughter and I couldn't lie to him. I may have kept the fact that I was pregnant from him, but I would never lie about something like that. If I was planning to do that I wouldn't have named her after him with her middle name and making sure she had his last name. That didn't ease the conversation any because then he started demanding that we talk about his rights as a father and that he wasn't leaving until he could spend time getting to know Sherice and not without making sure his rights to her were secure. Brian has always been a take charge kind of guy, but this time, he was more serious than I had ever seen him before. One other thing I saw was hurt at knowing that he had a daughter who was already walking and talking some and he was just setting eyes on her."

"Oh, I'm sorry you had to go through that. I know how much you loved Brian and how it crushed you to overhear that conversation. I said it then and I'll say it for the record now, you should have talked to him about what you heard and not made an assumption. Suppose you were dead wrong and you wasted years being apart from him and it's time he can't get back with Sherice."

Sherry wasn't expecting to hear that from Rayven, but the reason why they were friends is because they always told each other the truth, straight with no chasers. It's why she loved them like sisters. The look in Brian's eyes when he saw Sherice had burned right through her. She remembered the close-knit family that he'd come from and knew what having Sherice meant to him and she had a hand in destroying the early relationship he should have been able to have with her. For that, she suddenly felt overwhelmed and before she knew it, she started crying out loud and had to cover her mouth with her hand to not wake up Sherice. She quickly ran into her adjoining bathroom after grabbing the baby monitor to listen out for Sherice, and she shut the door and took her hand down to let her cries and tears flow.

"Aww, Sherry, don't cry. We're here for you. Rayven didn't mean to be so harsh, but you had to know that there was a possibility that this day would come," Candace said.

Through her tears, she responded.

"I know, but I wasn't ready for it yet and I wasn't ready to look in his face and see the look that was similar to hate when he looked at me. How could I have been so bitter to do something like keep her from him? I'm not sorry I broke up with him, but I'm sorry for not telling him about his daughter."

"Girl, that is now water under the bridge and you can't do anything about it, but you can work through what you're going to do now. Get some tissues, wipe your eyes and let's talk this through," Rayven said.

"How did you leave things with him?" Candace asked.

After wiping her face and gathering herself, she focused on the question.

"Well, he asked to talk to me about getting to know Sherice. He handed me a card with his number on it and said he would wait until tomorrow to hear from me and if he didn't he would come back. I'm afraid of what my father would say or do if Brian showed up. I told them what I'd overheard and they knew how crushed I was and then to find out I was pregnant, that pretty much sealed his fate with my father. My mother is a different story. She's the one who wanted me to reach out and talk to Brian and I refused. You both know how stubborn I can be," she acknowledged.

"Yeah," Rayven and Candace said together and that made them all laugh.

"Well, I sent him a text not long after he drove off and I told him I would meet with him tomorrow, though I have no idea what I'll say."

"Just tell him the truth and don't hold anything back. You know you've been waiting a long time and the time is now to let it all out and let the chips fall where they'll lay. Brian can forgive and forget and focus on bonding with his daughter, if that's what you want, or he can continue being pissed off at you. The best thing would be for the two of you to cordially discuss this and figure out how to make this work. You know how much you love your father and you know I've never known mine and I wished my entire life that he would walk back into it, but now that he's dead, he can't and I will forever long for the father/daughter relationship I can never have. Don't do that to Sherice,"

Rayven explained.

Sherry perked right up.

"Oh, I would never do that. Now that he knows about her, I have no plans of keeping her away from him. I'm just hoping I can deal with his wrath. I have no doubt he is furious with me and even if I don't like it, he has every right to be."

"Well, the past is just that, it's the past. Leave it there and figure out co-parenting together," Candace said.

"I know, you're right. It was just the initial shock of seeing him that has me turned all around. By tomorrow, I'll figure out a way to deal with this."

"Good. Now that we've talked that through, tell us again about how he looked?"

Sherry smiled and giggled like a school girl into the phone.

"Whew!" was all she could find to start with.

"That good, huh?" Rayven said.

"Goodness, that man is fine and he's gotten better looking over time. Tall, sexy and those legs had me remembering all those sexy nights with him. He had hair on his head back then, but now he's bald and so damn fine!" she cooed.

"He still has it, huh?" Candace said.

"Yes, he does."

Sherry meant every word of that. That man was runway male-model fine.

"Do you know if he's involved with anyone? Married?" Rayven asked.

Sherry stood still as her mind went there. It never dawned on her that he could be involved with a woman or perhaps even married. It wouldn't surprise her because even though she broke up with him, until the day she overheard a conversation he was having about her, he had treated her like a queen. She never thought she'd ever meet another man who treated her as good as he had.

"I don't know and I didn't think about it. I was so shocked to see him that I didn't check for a wedding ring. He looked better than ever, still with that same Brian Knight sexiness and swagger that he's always had. So many emotions flooded through me and I didn't know whether to be upset or leap into his arms. It wasn't until I saw him that I began to miss him like I did when I first returned home."

Then there was silence again and she knew why.

"What about Lance? How does he fit into this equation and are you going to tell him about Brian anytime soon?" Candace inquired.

Another piece of the puzzle she hadn't thought about. She was so busy focused on Brian that she forgot to think about the implications of his reappearance on her current relationship with Lance Solomon.

She had met Lance a few months back and things had been going pretty good between them, though she was still keeping him at arms-length. Lance wanted to take their relationship to a more serious level, but with school, working and Sherice, she didn't have time to invest in a serious relationship. To her they were dating and building something, but at a slow pace. Now, she had to tell him about Brian's presence in Maryland. She had never told Lance much about her time with Brian, though she'd told him Brian's name and that she'd had a whirlwind relationship with him that ended and she found out she was pregnant after she broke up with him.

Lance worked as one of the directors at the daycare where Sherice spent her days, a center that was owned by his sister. They'd hit it off quickly and after a few months of dancing around her, he finally asked her out and she said yes. They had done the couple thing of dinner, movies and just pretty much hanging out, but that was it. To her, things were still pretty new, though she could tell that Lance was pretty much smitten with her. She didn't feel the same way yet. She was taking things slow with him.

"I haven't spoken to him today. I was planning to have a late lunch with him tomorrow, but I'll need to cancel that now since I'm planning to meet with Brian. I'll let my parents take her to church with them and go see Brian then. I guess I'll go to wherever he's staying, so that we can talk in private, just in case he needs to release some steam. I'll talk to Lance on Monday and tell him about Brian and assure him that Brian's only interest is in Sherice and not in me, which will be obvious since there is nothing between Brian and me anymore."

She waited for either of her friends to respond, but all she got was total silence.

"Call us after you meet with Brian and let us know how the conversation goes. Just remember to lay it all out on the table. I think you've been stuck a little bit in the past because there was no real closure. Get that tomorrow and then settle in to discuss the specifics of arrangements regarding Sherice. Do you think you'll need to get a lawyer? Is he talking about doing this through the courts or are you going to work something out between the two of you?" Rayven asked.

Sherry didn't know, but she would find out tomorrow.

"I don't know, but considering the circumstance, I'm

thinking he's going to want to do this through the court system to be sure he's never kept from her again. I'm never going to do that, but even if I said it a million times, he wouldn't believe me. I'm sure he didn't expect me to keep her from him all this time," she said.

Hearing herself say it brought the weight of her decision back on her. She knew the moment she didn't make the call to tell him that she was pregnant would come back to haunt her one day and that day had arrived. She quickly thought into the future about the conversation she would probably have one day with a much older Sherice who will want to know why she did what she did. It hurt her heart to think of the consequences of the hasty decision she made and nothing could turn back the hands of time. She had to deal and tomorrow was that day.

She was startled when she heard her mother call her name, signaling that they were back from their movie.

"I have to go. My parents just walked in and I need to talk to them about this before they go to bed. One fight at a time, is my motto for the next several days when it comes to them, Brian and Lance, just in case he has an issue with Brian showing up. I wish there was a book somewhere on how to deal with all this. This will be a tough conversation with Brian and I know I'm going to need answers to a lot of questions. I'll call you both tomorrow and let you know how things go. Thanks for always being here for me. I feel much better already and I'm hoping I'll get some rest tonight though I doubt it. I haven't been able to think about anything else other than Brian."

"Yeah, she still has it bad for him," Candace said.

"Both of you are certifiable," Sherry quipped.

"Really? Just us?" Rayven added and laughed.

"Alright, well, you know we're here for you if you need us. Good luck tomorrow," Candace added before hanging up.

"Thanks!" she said and hung up.

After checking herself in the mirror, she went in search of her parents to start the conversation.

CHAPTER 10

Brian woke early not sure what time he and Sherry were going to meet. He was expecting to hear from her so that they could set a time and place.

He was glad he was up early and refreshed because the concierge service had called to tell him he had a package, which he was sure was the items Duron had overnighted him. After a hot shower and a few minutes of watching some movie, he was out like a light the night before and had missed the text from Duron telling him to expect his things in the morning.

When he woke, the first thing on his mind was his daughter and how fast he and Sherry could work something out, so that they could ease Sherice into his life and explain to her that he was her father. There wasn't much an eighteen-month-old child would understand, but early impressions were lasting impressions. Sherice was his one and only concern, though he still couldn't dismiss how good Sherry looked. Having a baby had thickened her up in the sexiest way and she was even more beautiful than he remembered.

Nothing could have prepared him for the shock of

seeing her in person again after so long. Throughout the night, he remembered tossing and turning, thinking of better times with her and rekindling the days when he missed her the most. He'd never been in love before and never again since her, though he'd been involved with more women than he wanted to count. None were serious or memorable like his relationship with Sherry. He would come face to face with her again today and even now, he still wasn't sure of exactly what he'd say. All he knew was he wanted to see Sherice, talk to her and hopefully develop a bond with her that he should have had since birth.

He had also heard from Xavier earlier and they were planning to get together late that night over dinner and drinks so that they could talk about what he was recommending after conferring with one of the other attorneys at his firm. He was looking forward to that talk and hopefully Xavier would come with good news about how to proceed.

Brian was just about to check the time on his cell phone when it vibrated with a call. It was Sherry, so he hurried to answer it.

"Hello," he said.

"Hi, Brian. Did I catch you at a bad time?"

"No, not at all. I was about to grab something to eat."

"Okay, great. I know it's Sunday, but I was wondering if you were free this afternoon around one?"

"Sure, if that works for you. Where do you want to meet?" he asked.

Silenced greeted him as he waited for her to think about his question.

"I'm trying to think of a place where we could talk privately without people overhearing our conversation."

"Well, if you want to come here, that'll be fine. I'm supposed to check out at noon, but I can get a later checkout time, so that we could have some privacy to talk."

Checkout? He was leaving? She thought he was going to stick around until things were resolved. He couldn't possibly think that they would solve everything in a few hours of chatting.

"You're leaving today?" she asked curiously.

"Trying to get rid of me already?" he asked.

"No, not at all. You mentioned checking out," she said.

"Yeah, I'm checking out of the hotel to move into a condo temporarily that belongs to one of my fraternity brothers who lives here in Baltimore. His law firm owns it and since it's currently not being used, he's loaning it to me for the rest of my stay here in Baltimore."

"And how long do you plan on staying?" she asked cautiously.

"I'm not sure yet. It depends on how our conversation goes today and how much time I get to spend with Sherice. We haven't worked out any details yet and until we do, I'm staying right here."

"I understand. Coming where you are will work. What's the hotel?"

Brian gave her the information and before he hung up, he made one last comment.

"Sherry, Sherice is a beautiful little girl."

Sherry smiled even though she was pacing nervously around her bedroom. Her parents were entertaining Sherice in the kitchen while she spoke to Brian privately.

"Thank you, Brian. She is the light of my life. I'll see you about one o'clock."

"See you then."

After hanging up, Sherry released the breath she had been holding. Just talking to him again brought out all kinds of feelings, some she thought she'd put away long ago. Something was still there and that frightened her and she wasn't the only one concerned about his return in her life.

When she finally broke the news to her parents that Brian was in town and that he knew about Sherice, her mother was calmer than she thought she would be, but her father wasn't as gracious with his demeanor. He threw a million questions at her and in the end, he realized that he had to let her make her own decision when it came to Sherice and Brian and whatever she decided, she asked them to support her. After much coaxing from her mother, her father yielded and agreed to watch his boundaries when it came to her private life. Whether he liked it or not, Brian was Sherice's father and now that he knew about her, she had no intentions of fighting with him about anything when it came to his role in Sherice's life.

She wasn't sure how it would work out with him living in Atlanta, but they would have to figure it out. She shared with her parents about the weight that had come down on her when she saw him and now she felt that weight lifted from her life and her daughter was going to finally meet and get to know her father. As much as she loved her own father, she wanted Sherice to have the same kind of relationship with her father that she and her own father had shared her entire life. She was a daddy's girl and she had a feeling, Sherice would be, too.

Sherry looked at her bed which was covered in various clothing items. She had a hard time choosing what to wear when she went to meet Brian. Clearly, she was losing her mind because he didn't care what she had on or what she looked like. He was only interested in getting to know his daughter.

Deep in thought, she still wondered how he'd found out about Sherice. What or who could have tipped him off? She never told him she was pregnant when she left school and decided to finish her degree at home in Baltimore because she didn't know herself until two months after she'd returned home. She couldn't go back after what she'd overheard, tell him she was pregnant and then have to deal with him for years to come knowing the way he truly felt about her, unlike the love he wanted her to believe he had for her. She couldn't go back to Atlanta and back to a man who considered her a sexual fling, someone he bided his time with until the woman of his dreams came along.

Now, here he was, in Baltimore and still looking just as chocolaty and sexy as he did the first time she'd laid eyes on him. She was going to need help as she faced him again because she was dealing with something she didn't think she'd ever have to deal with again; buried feelings she still held for him that were brought to the surface the minute she laid eyes on him again.

Meeting Brian Knight was the best day of her life, or so she thought. She'd fallen in love with him right away and for months, she was happier than she had ever been. She had always been attracted to older men, but he was the first one that she had actually gotten involved with until Lance who was also older than her by seven years. She still had Lance to deal with and she needed a few days to address the Brian issue with him. For now, she needed to get through her meeting.

Sherry yawned, unable to control it, knowing she had

gotten little sleep the night before. She'd tossed all night as memories came back in waves of night after night of making love with Brian and the way he'd made her body feel time after time. His attentiveness to her needs had her remembering what it felt like to be held, touched and kissed by him, something she would only admit to herself that she missed. All night, her body yearned to be touched like that again, but only by Brian. She had to resort to self-pleasure to finally get some sleep, something else he'd taught her. Shaking off her lust-filled night, she went back to getting dressed.

She finally decided on a comfortable outfit in purple and white along with staple high heeled shoes. After checking her makeup for the millionth time, she turned out the light and left her room to join her family in the kitchen. She was thankful her parents agreed to watch Sherice while she met with Brian. Sunday was the one day a week that my father agreed he would focus more on family than work, especially when they were looking after Sherice who could be a handful. She knew Brian may have been hoping to see Sherice sometime today, but the last thing she wanted to do was have Sherice in the room while they worked out their issues.

"Mommy!" she heard the minute she walked into the kitchen where Sherice was seated in her high chair at the table. She leaned down and kissed her on the cheek, causing Sherice to giggle. She loved her baby and knew that she was conceived in love even though that love didn't last. Love or not, it was her responsibility to make things right for Brian and Sherice to have a relationship.

"Are you sure you're okay doing this alone? I could come with you or perhaps your mother could," her father said.

"Oh, no, don't volunteer me for that duty. I told you last night to let your daughter handle this on her own. She's not a little girl anymore. She's a woman with her own child and she needs to work this out with Brian, making sure that whatever decisions she makes, she is thinking of Sherice first," her mother said, looking up at her with a stern look on her face that said now was the time for her to do the right thing by her daughter.

"Sherice firth," Sherice tried to repeat, but couldn't quite say the word 'first', causing them all to smile with glee over her attempt.

"Yes, Sherice first," Sherry said.

"Dad, I got this covered. Brian has a right to as much time with Sherice as we have and unless he is being unreasonable with his demands, I'm going to make this work out for us all, so don't worry. I have a few things to do before I meet Brian, so are you good if I leave now?" she asked.

"Absolutely. We're about to leave for church in a few minutes and will probably get a late lunch afterwards. Take as long as you need to with Brian," her mother said.

When she looked over at her father, she could see that he wanted to say something else, but out of the side of her eye, she could see her mother give him a look that quieted him quickly.

"Okay, well, I'll see you later."

She kissed Sherice and headed for the door.

**

Lance checked the time and wondered why he hadn't heard from Sherry yet. They had a date to do a late lunch today and he had hoped she'd call by now to tell him what time and where she wanted to go. Due to her busy work and school schedule, their time alone was limited and of course there was Sherice, the sweetest little girl ever. He didn't have any children of his own, but he had begun considering Sherice as his since he'd started dating Sherry.

The day she walked through the doors of the daycare center that his sister owned was one of the best days of his life. Once he got up the nerve to ask her out, knowing he was somewhat older than her, he had fallen head over heels in love with her almost immediately. She was not only beautiful, but smart and kind and he could see himself married to her. He knew not to bring up the "M" word with her because it was too soon, but only for her; he was already there and ready.

Their relationship was going at a slow pace and the more he was around her, the more he was ready to get even closer, so that he could get them to the point where she would declare her love for him and he could be free to share that he had been in love with her since the first moment he saw her.

It was going on one o'clock in the afternoon and he hadn't heard anything from her, even though if she had gone to church, she would be out by now. Taking the lead, he decided to call her and she answered on the first ring.

"Hey, Beautiful!" he said.

"Hi, Lance."

The first thing he noticed was that he didn't feel the excitement in her response to hearing from him that he was accustomed to.

"Did you forget we were having a lunch date today? I thought you were going to call me early to plan what and where we were going to go. Are we still on?" he asked.

Sherry could have punched herself. In all that was on her mind, she forgot to call Lance to cancel for today and reschedule for another day later in the week.

"I'm sorry, Lance. I forgot to tell you that I had something come up at the last minute and I need to cancel for today."

Yeah, something was wrong, he thought. Even without looking at her, he could tell by the way she was responding to him that mind was someplace else.

"Is everything okay?" he asked.

Sherry wasn't ready to tell Lance what was going on yet, so she thought of something quickly. She was already running late for her meeting with Brian and she was nervous about their conversation. She couldn't handle dealing with Lance today, too.

"Ah, everything is fine," she stuttered out.

"Okay, well why don't you call me later when you're free and maybe I can stop by for a while or maybe we can just take a ride and go down to the inner harbor for a stroll and some ice cream. I know Sherice would love that."

Beyond seeing Brian, she couldn't think that far ahead right now.

"How about I call you later and we'll see."

"Sherry, are you sure nothing is wrong?" Lance asked now concerned.

"I promise nothing is wrong. I'm a little out of sorts about some things I need to do today, but I promise I'll call you tonight when I get back home. I have to go, so I'm not distracted while driving."

Lance started to respond, that was until he heard the sound of her phone clicking off, cutting off their conversation. Sherry was more than distracted, he thought.

Something else was going on.

Her emotionless response reminded him of the end of his last relationship and no way was his relationship with Sherry going to end up in the toilet like his relationship with Malina had ended. He was putting everything he had into Sherry to show her what he was all about and to prove that he cared about her. Sherry was his and if her distraction had anything to do with another man, he doubted she was ready for his comeback. Malina hadn't been, but lucky for him, he'd scared her enough that she would never tell anyone what he'd done to her when she cheated on him with another guy. He shook off thoughts of that awful woman and refocused back on Sherry, the woman he loved and who he hoped would soon declare her love for him. They were going to be in love, whether she knew it yet or not.

CHAPTER 11

Sherry walked on shaky legs to the elevator that led to the fifth floor of the hotel where Brian was staying. She'd tried preparing for the meeting with him, but without knowing where he stood with everything, she was going to have to wing it.

Getting into the elevator, she watched as one floor passed and then another until the numbers lit up with the number five. She walked toward the room number he'd given her and when she was standing in front of it, she knocked lightly. Waiting a few seconds and thinking he may not have heard her knock, she was prepared to knock again when the door opened and Brian stood on the other side.

"Hi," she said as he moved to let her in.

"Hello."

Sherry walked in and quickly looked around at the expansive suite.

"This is a nice hotel," she said, not sure what to say when she turned around and Brian was staring at her as if he could look right through her.

"Small talk is what we're going to do?" he asked.

"I don't know what to say and I just got here," she countered, with a little more tension in her voice than she'd planned on having.

"Okay, would you like a drink because for some reason, I feel like I'm going to need one. The air in here is already feeling a little thick," he declared.

Sherry knew it was in her voice and in how she carried herself that made him defensive. She was all ready to come in and talk about Sherice, visitation and what they were going to do going forward, but the minute he opened the door, the words from that conversation she'd overheard where he called her a casual fling to some of his friends came back to her in vivid color and sound and she couldn't shake the way it made her feel then and now. She felt exposed then, just as she did now. Even though years had passed, she couldn't get over the way he'd categorized her back then after she'd given herself to him completely.

"No, thank you. Can we just talk about this, so that I can get back to Sherice?"

Brian had a feeling this wasn't going to go as well as he hoped.

"Alright, have a seat," he said pointing to the sofa and chairs in the living room area. He watched as she took note of where he was going to sit and she sat as far away from him as she could.

"Thank you."

"Okay, so where do you want to start this?"

"This meeting is all you Brian, so start wherever you like and I'll chime in," she said, nonchalantly.

"Well, let me just say that I wished I was talking to the Sherry that was less aggressive and angry than the one I'm talking to right now. I thought this was going to be a civil discussion with a lot less tension."

Sherry didn't know why she was being awkward and it was unlike her to act this way. Being around Brian again and being alone with him brought back memories she wasn't ready to deal with, but here she was about to hash up their history with him.

"You wanted to talk about Sherice and I'm here, Brian, and that's all you get; a conversation about her."

Now, Brian was feeling on edge as if he needed to defend himself against an invisible enemy.

"Wait, so you think I want something from you? I don't want anything from you other a few explanations and then some kind of agreement about when I can spend time with Sherice because I want her to know I'm her father."

Yeah, the heat in the room was rising, she thought as she avoided eye contact and instead looked out the window and not at him.

"I already told you that you were her father and I'm not trying to hinder any relationship you'll have with her."

"Oh, right because you've done that for the past eighteen or so months," he countered glibly.

Sherry did turn to him then and her anger officially boiled over and it wasn't just about what he just said, but she felt the rage over all the things she wanted to say to him back then that she never did.

"Well, I had my reasons and trust me when I tell you that Sherice and I have been doing just fine these past few years."

Brian looked her in the eyes and then looked from her face, down her body and back up.

"I can see that."

"Don't," she said.

"Don't what?"

"Just don't," she said again.

"Over two years ago, you walked out on me, no word, no explanation, no goodbye, no screw you Brian, no sayonara or nothing. You just bounced, took the knowledge of my child with you and moved on with your life. Is that how women your age deal with things? You don't address them head-on? You get pregnant by someone and decide he wasn't worth being a part of his child's life? You make a man believe he's your everything after he treated you like a queen and the result is, forget about you Brian, I'm through? You call all the shots and make all of the decisions? Was that it?" he demanded to know.

"We're here to talk about Sherice, not our broken relationship."

"Is that what it was? A broken relationship? Because the last thing I remember was making love to you the night before at your apartment and then the next day, everything went to hell. I'm still trying to figure out what I did that warranted you treating me that way?"

Sherry started tapping her foot to keep calm and not let her full frustration out on him.

"Let it go, Brian."

She looked over and sneered at him before she could pull her anger back.

"Okay, then let's just talk about Sherice and get this over with because clearly, you still can't stand to be in my presence. How are we going to handle this? Should I retain an attorney and have something drawn up about visitation, joint custody and financial support?"

Sherry whipped her head around so fast, she felt a pain in her neck.

"Joint custody and financial support? This discussion is about visitation only. I don't plan on sharing custody of Sherice with you which would mean she would spend some length of time with you in Atlanta without me and that's not happening. She doesn't even know you and as far as financial support, we don't need anything from you. I take care of her just fine on my own, but if you want to set up some kind of college fund for her, that'll be fine. By then, she can discuss that with you directly and I won't need to be involved."

Surprising herself, she had no idea where all her attitude was coming from. This wasn't going anything like she had hoped and it was because she came in with an attitude she was having a hard time shaking.

If Sherry's intent was to piss him off, she was doing a damned good job of it, Brian thought as he wiped his hand down his face to calm his raging attitude. He didn't come to Baltimore for a fight, but it looks like Sherry brought the fight with her to the hotel.

"So, because you've controlled this situation all this time, you think you still get to have total control? Sherice is just as much mine as she is yours even though it seems that if it were left up to you, that wouldn't be the case."

Sherry stood as if she was getting ready to leave and they hadn't resolved anything.

"Look, you want to see Sherice and spend time with her, that's fine, but as far as any kind of custody, I'm not agreeing to that. That's my baby and you haven't been around her to be talking about any kind of custody, especially since you live in another state."

Brian stood with her.

"Whose fault is it that I haven't been around? Whose

fault is that?" he stated loudly.

Sherry turned to him with fire in her eyes.

"Yours. It's your fault because if you hadn't been such a jackass, we wouldn't be in this mess right now, but then again, I'm glad we are because at least I found out your true feelings about me. I see games men play with women don't end because the man gets older."

Brian paced as he tried to not let her engage him in a conversation about his treatment of her. He knew he was a damn good boyfriend, lover and friend to her and because of her, he hadn't been able to fully open up his heart to another woman the way he had with her.

"I'm not here for this Sherry. If you want to throw stones about something that clearly only you know about, then go ahead, but do that when you're by yourself. It's been three years and you're right, we're here to talk about my daughter. You must have wanted to keep some kind of connection to me since you gave her my last name. Some part of you still wanted to be connected to me or was that just a moment of weakness and you decided to give her a piece of the man you loved and threw away like yesterday's garbage. How were you going to explain her name to her as she got older?" he asked.

"I don't know because right now she's only a year and a half and I don't have to deal with that yet."

"One day you will and I can't wait to see how you handle that discussion because so far, you've done a fantastic job with our current state of affairs. You can fight me if you want and if that's the case, then this conversation is over. This isn't some game we're dealing with here. We're dealing with the life of our daughter and how we're going to add me to her life, so that she knows me and my family just like she knows yours."

"Your family is more than welcomed to come here to see Sherice any time as long as it's planned out first. If you have any thoughts of taking my baby out of this state for any period of time, you need to think about another approach," she responded crossly.

Brian snickered at her attempt to come at him, but he was ready for her. They were talking about his daughter and he wouldn't be limited on his reach. He turned his attention full on her and without any hint of a smile on his face, he spoke direct and to the point.

"Like I said, I believe this conversation is over and I suggest you get an attorney and we'll let the courts decide what we will and won't do."

Sherry huffed and moved away from him.

"Well, I see the real Brian has surfaced again. I'll see myself out and I'll have my attorney contact you."

Brian reached into his pocket and withdrew a card.

"Don't worry your pretty little head about that. Your attorney can call mine whenever he is ready to discuss this with papers drawn up. I'll make sure Sherice is taken care of financially, whether you want it or not. You can put it away until she's grown or whatever you want to do with it and as far as visitation, I expect a judge will look at your antics of keeping her away from me and see that without any fault on my part, I didn't get a chance to be a part of her life and now, that's what I want. If you weren't so angry about whatever you're still harboring, you would see that I'm not trying to take anything away from you. I'm fighting to get a little bit of what you already have with Sherice and have had her entire life. I may not get joint custody, but I intend to petition for some kind of custody with her where

I can take her to my home and share my life and my family with her without you dictating everything, every step of the way. The address to the condo where I'm moving is on the back if your lawyer decides he needs to have any papers delivered to me."

Sherry clicked her teeth in frustration.

"You know what Brian? You're right, this conversation is over. I can see this was a huge waste of my time and gas."

"Then let me show you out," he countered.

Sherry looked at the business card he handed to her.

"I guess you came ready to work things out with me with an attorney already in your pocket or did you just happen to have this handy?" she said solemnly.

"I was ready to work something out, but you came in the door with enough attitude to start world war three and all I want to do is see my daughter. Does this argument mean I have to wait until a judge says you have to let me see Sherice before I can see her?" he asked as she headed for the door.

He wasn't sure she was going to respond when she reached for the door handle and opened the door to leave. Before stepping out, she turned back to him.

"I'll let you know," she responded in a brusque manner.

With that, he watched her leave with more strain between them than ever. This didn't go well at all and now it looks like he had to really prepare for a fight as the door slammed as she left.

"Damn!" he shouted out loud. He picked up his cell phone and called Xavier.

"What's up, Frat," Xavier said.

"Man, I think I just survived a war and I'm not sure I came out of it unscathed."

"Uh, oh. What happened? Was it Sherry?"

"I should have taken your advice and not met with her. She agreed to meet with me and when she showed up, she was full of anger and attitude and that just drew out my anger over the situation and we blew up at each other. It didn't end well and it looks like I'm going to need an attorney to get her in front of a judge and find out what my rights are. I talked about supporting Sherice financially and she doesn't want it. I asked about some type of joint custody agreement and she went off about me never being able to take Sherice to Atlanta for a visit. I mean she went ballistic when I mentioned the word custody. I wasn't talking about right now, but she blew up and turned into a woman I didn't know. We were going to talk about visitation while I'm here and I think she just shut that down by telling me she would think about it and let me know. What do I need to do next?" he said, out of breath and full of frustration.

"First, calm down and deal with your anger over this. If you go in front of any judge with as much anger as I hear in your voice, you're going to have a hard time getting what you want. I have someone looking into everything and we'll get together tomorrow to figure this out. It's Sunday, so there isn't much we can do today, but tomorrow I'll have some answers for you and I'll have someone at the courthouse tomorrow if that's what you want. For now, I want you to refocus and relax, so that you can think clearly about Sherice and not Sherry. Can you hold tight that long?" Xavier pleaded.

"I guess I'll have to. I'm not trying to do anything that would work against me with a judge, so I'll lay low and focus on work."

"Good. Let's meet for steaks and drinks in an hour and I'll walk you through the condo afterwards. No matter what Sherry thinks, you have just as much rights to Sherice as she does as long as she doesn't try pulling any rabbits out of hats to discredit you."

"Trust me, she won't find any. Thanks for your help and I'll see you in an hour. Right now, I'm going to go down to the gym here at the hotel and work off the stress from my meeting with her."

Brian could feel even more tension rising up in his spine and working out was the only way he could think of to relieve the stress, though his body suddenly had another idea.

Being in the room with Sherry again knowing there was a bed close by had his body rising for an occasion he knew wouldn't happen, that was until she went from zero to sixty in less than sixty seconds. His obvious attraction to her even now was part of why he'd gotten so angry so fast. After all that had transpired over the past two years, he still desired her and he hated that about himself. He wanted to be angry while his manhood wanted to be buried deep inside of her.

"Hey, did she ever say why she left originally?" Xavier asked, breaking into his thoughts.

Brian thought quickly over the conversation and it was all still pretty sketchy.

"Not really. She said something about finding out my true feelings for her and somehow, I wasn't being truthful about the way I said I felt about her. It was pretty cryptic and at this point, I don't care. All I care about is my daughter," he said.

"We'll make it happen. We'll go over our strategy later,

but for now, do whatever you need to do to calm down and call me if you need me."

"Thanks, Xavier."

Brian hung up and went in search of his workout gear. His mind was reeling from that conversation with Sherry, yet still, he was bothered by what she said about finding out his true feelings for her. He wanted to know what she meant by that and hoped that one day, they'd be able to have a conversation without yelling at each other. They would need to find a way to coexist for Sherice's sake. He meant it when he said he wasn't going anywhere. It was time for him to make the call to his job for that leave of absence and to talk to Duron about some work with his company that would help occupy his time while he stayed in Baltimore. He had a feeling things were not going to be resolved any time soon.

**

Sherry had been driving around for a couple of hours still trying to calm down and quiet that rage that had boiled up in her. She was disappointed in her own reaction Brian, going off on him like she had done. Where had he anger come from because it poured fuel on a fire that burned within her. That wasn't her plan when she'd agreed to meet with him.

She had arrived for their meeting, ready to plan out his visits with Sherice and how they would start telling her that he was her Daddy and letting that sink in for them all. The moment she walked through the door and she felt her body heat up with a need and want for him that she hadn't experience in a long time, she became angry at herself which boiled over to her taking it out on him. If she had kept her thoughts on why she was there instead of how good he looked, she may have made it through without acting like some crazed lunatic. There was no reason for her behavior and once she'd reached her car, she sat in it for thirty minutes feeling sorry for herself and ashamed and how she'd let the conversation get completely out of control.

How could she react that way after telling her parents she was open to letting Brian have whatever kind of relationship with Sherice that he wanted? She knew how much the closeness she shared with her own father had meant to her and now, she'd ruined everything. Just as she'd done over two years ago, when she impulsively walked out on him, she let her emotions get the best of her again and now the situation was worse than it was before she arrived. It wasn't Brian that she was angry at, she was angry at herself. She was angry that she hadn't handled her business back when she first found out she was pregnant. She once loved him and he didn't deserve her temper.

Brian had every right to be furious with her and make demands for visitation and custody. If it were her, she would do the same thing. She was upset because she couldn't stop thinking about the way he used to kiss her, making her whole body sizzle. She could remember the touch of his hands across her body and the way he felt as he entered her and whispered things in her ear that had her shattering over and over in ecstasy from his torrential love making and the way he expertly drove into her again and again until she cried out from the overwhelming pleasure of it all. Her mind temporarily drifted to thoughts of other women she was sure he had been with since her who he had shared what she hoped he would only share with her after they became involved. She didn't want to want him now, but she did and that thought had her responding to him in alacrity with disdain.

Now as she made her way through traffic toward her house, she had to deal with the fact that she had now set them on a path where they would be in court fighting over Sherice and she didn't want that. She had thought about turning around and going back to apologize to him, but pride kept her away. She didn't deserve his forgiveness for her antics today or for what she did when she disappeared on him and never looked back.

As she drove down her street and parked her car, she sat for a few minutes contemplating how to tell her parents about the meeting. She knew that her father's first reaction would be to try and get in touch with a lawyer tonight. She looked down at the console in the car and looked at the business card for Brian's lawyer and recognized the name of one of his fraternity brothers that she'd met before. It looks as if Brian was ready for a legal fight with her if he had already reached out to an attorney. She had again, reacted out of anger and the last thing she wanted was some nasty court battle. It was time to face her parents as she turned off the car and prepared to get out. She was startled by the sudden appearance of someone outside her passenger side window and when she looked over, it was Lance. What was he doing here?

Getting out, she locked the car doors and came around to meet him on the sidewalk.

"What are you doing here, Lance?"

"Well, do you want to try saying hello first? What's wrong with you? I came by to check on you because of how out of character you sounded earlier. You had me really concerned. Now, I see you pull up and literally sit here in your car for quite a few minutes without getting out, so now I know something is wrong. Talk to me."

Sherry took in everything he said and didn't let it go by her that he knew how long she had been sitting in her car.

"How do you know how long I had been sitting here in my car?" she asked questionably.

Seeing a change in his stance, she knew she had caught him off guard with her question.

"Oh, I was just guessing about that, but that's not the point. Something is wrong and you're keeping it from me. You know you can talk to me about anything. You know how much I care about you and we're in this relationship together."

Relationship? She thought. As far as she was concerned, they were dating and enjoying each other's company, but they hadn't talked about anything more serious than that. Right now, she wasn't in the mood to discuss anything with him. She was still focused on her argument with Brian and how she was going to explain to her parents the fact that the situation was worse than it was before.

"I can't right now Lance. I'm tired and I have a headache," she lied.

"Let's go for a ride with the windows down and enjoy the warmth of the early evening. I bet that will help your headache clear right up."

"I appreciate the offer, but I haven't seen Sherice all day, I'm tired and I just want to get a hot bath, spend time with her and go to bed. Let's do that another day," she said and turned to walk away.

Lance didn't stop her, but noticed she hadn't offered him one of her hugs and kisses that he enjoyed getting from her after one of their dates. Something was pulling her away from him and whatever it was, it was recent because a few days ago, when she'd picked Sherice up from daycare, they were fine and now he could tell he was the last thing on her mind and he didn't like it.

He walked toward his car after she went inside her house and shut the door without looking back at him. He would give her until tomorrow when she came to pick up Sherice and he would try talking to her again. He had no plans of losing her to whatever was going on that she didn't want to talk about. He wasn't losing another woman he loved.

CHAPTER 12

Three days had gone by and Brian hadn't heard anything from Sherry and he had not been able to see his daughter. To say he was going crazy was an understatement. He and Xavier had talked a few times and he was working on moving things forward expeditiously, but in the meantime, he was losing more time with his daughter. Luckily, the work Duron wanted him to do had arrived in his email and he was looking over some financials on a new project the company was taking on.

Xavier had given him the keys to the condo and he was impressed with the place. It reminded him of the condo that Duron owned in his office building. It was spacious with three bedrooms, an office, expansive living room and dining room area and the kitchen was bigger than those in some houses. There was an activities room with three gigantic televisions on the wall. He wasn't a fan of that too much considering you could only watch one at a time, but he had to admit the picture was crystal clear and sharper than the one he owned. He'll have to upgrade when he got back to Atlanta.

Duron had sent more of his things from his house and

he was settling in nicely for what he now felt was going to be an extended stay.

Several times, he thought about calling Sherry to ask about seeing Sherice, but with the anger she displayed at the hotel, he doubted he'd have a civil conversation with her, so he waited. He told his brothers and his mother about the situation and everyone offered help in any way they could, but this was something he was going to have to deal with himself. The last thing he wanted to do was overwhelm Sherry with the presence of his family getting in their business. He would let the court system do what it was meant to do, so for now he waited.

Pulling out his laptop after settling in on the leather sofa, he pulled up his email and got to work. Duron was expecting his feedback by the end of the day. He hadn't started on the first one when his cell phone rang. He reached for it without checking the number and then decided to let it roll over to voicemail.

After an hour of reading, he was hungry and got up to cook. Remembering his phone had rung several times, he checked the voicemail and shocking him, two of the four calls he'd received were from Sherry. Not sure he was in the mood for more fighting with her, he put off listening to her messages until later.

**

Walking through the lobby of the condo where Brian now lived, Sherry pulled out her cell phone again and dialed his number. She wasn't sure the guard was going to allow her to get on the elevator without his permission, so she needed him to at least answer the phone long enough for her to let him know she was in the building. She'd called and left him a couple of voicemails, but he had not yet returned any of her calls. No such luck when this time the phone rang five times before getting his voicemail again.

"Brian, it's me again. I don't know if you checked your messages or if you're still ignoring my calls, but I'm in the lobby of your building and I was hoping we could talk so that I could apologize for what I said to you. I'm really, really sorry about the things I said. I would never, ever keep Sherice away from you again and I'm sorry I didn't tell you about her. Well, I don't know what else to say or what else to do other than to say I'm sorry and I hope you'll call me back. I'm sorry, Brian."

She hung up the phone and looked for a place to sit and unwind. It wasn't until she sat down that she realized she was crying and tears were rolling down her cheeks.

She felt worse than she had when they broke up. After explaining to her parents about what happened, both of them gave her a piece of their mind when they told her that her actions were not of a woman who was putting her child first. Even her father was disappointed in her and they reminded her that it was her who asked them to be supportive in her desire to make sure Sherice got to know Brian and now it had all gone to hell because of her.

After dropping Sherice off at daycare that next morning, she went to work where she couldn't focus. Days had gone by and she hadn't rectified the situation with him to the point where they could at least talk like adults. Every time she looked at Sherice throughout the week, she saw how much she was letting her little girl miss out on when her father was mere miles away, a father who she knew would give anything to be with her. She was being selfish and she needed to stop.

How could she say such hateful things to a man that she

had once loved with every part of her being and when she looked into the face of her child, she saw him.

More tears streamed down her face as the guard spotted her and came around from behind his desk to see to her.

"Miss, are you alright?" he asked.

Sherry looked up into his face and tried to gather herself and wipe her tears. She didn't want to cause a disturbance, but the life had drained out of her over the past few days and she didn't have the strength to leave after she'd left work early and came straight to his condo after getting the address from the back of the business card he'd given her.

"Oh, I'm fine. I'm sorry, I was just leaving and I didn't mean to disturb you," she said getting up.

"Were you here to see someone? Can I ring them for you?"

She hadn't thought about that. Brian may not answer his phone, but maybe he would answer if the guard rang him in the condo.

"Yes, please," she said standing with his help. She followed him back to the counter as he went around behind it.

"Who can I ring for you?" he asked.

"Brian Knight. He's staying in the corporate suite on the eighteenth floor."

She waited and wondered if Brian would tell him to escort her back out of the building. When he hung up the phone and looked over at her strangely, she figured she was on her way out.

"Mr. Knight said to send you up. You can take the bank of elevators to you left."

Her heart began racing and her palms began to sweat. He didn't have the guard toss her out, so that was one step ahead, she hoped. She was going to talk to him and wouldn't leave until they worked out their issues enough to at least figure out what they were going to do about Sherice and it would be something that would work for both of them. She wanted him to spend time with Sherice and the sooner the better. If he still wanted to go the legal path, she would do that, but for now, he'd come all this way leaving his life behind in Atlanta and the least she could do is let him spend time with his daughter.

When the elevator reached the floor, she stepped out and turned toward one of two doors on that floor. The condo must be massive if there were only two on the entire floor, she thought.

Her nervousness went up a level the closer she got to the door. She was about to knock when the door opened and Brian stood on the other side, shirtless in a pair of jeans that rode low on his toned hips. Her attention first went to his abs which were a sign that he still worked out vigorously, something she remembered he was particular about when they dated. As he greeted her, he threw a shirt over his head. It was obvious he wasn't expecting anyone and had most likely been lying down.

"What are you doing here Sherry?" he asked, drawing her back to the present.

She started to say something and then pulled the words back. She was still stunned by how gorgeous he was and she remembered why she was unable to resist him when they'd first met. She got her nerve and found the right words. She wouldn't let his anger deter her after driving all the way downtown to talk to him in person. When he didn't invite her in, she assumed they were going to have the discussion with her standing in the hallway. If so, it was her fault that they'd come to this, so in the hallway it was, she guessed.

"I called you a few times and left you a few messages and I assumed you weren't taking my calls. I thought I'd try talking to you in person," she said.

"Why would I take your calls? I figured you've said all you wanted to say the last time we spoke."

The last thing she wanted was another explosive situation like their last talk.

"Brian, I was trying to apologize. I didn't mean to say those things. I was striking out and I don't even know why."

"You don't?" he asked, looking at her quizzically.

"So, are you going to hate me now? Giving me a taste of my own medicine?" she asked.

"This isn't some game Sherry. I'm not going tit-for-tat with you when it comes to my daughter. I came here to see her and get to know her, not get in a fight with you about the past. At the end of the day, we're going to have to find a way to coexist. You and I have to find a way to exist in a way that nothing negative impacts our relationship with her as her parents."

Sherry exhaled.

"Can I come in to talk or should I leave since you haven't invited me in yet? I don't mean to intrude on you unannounced, but I couldn't let another day go by without trying to apologize for my behavior."

"As long as we're not going to argue again, yes you can come in," he said moving to the side.

She walked inside the condo and marveled at the beauty of seeing windows from left to right that stretched from the floor to the ceiling, overlooking the Chesapeake Bay.

As she walked over to the window and looked out, Brian followed behind her coming up close enough that he could smell her perfume.

The minute he opened the door and found her standing there, anger went out the door and was replaced by lust. Even frustrated at her, she still turned him on like no other woman ever had. Today, she was in a dress that showed off her long, toned legs and she was in her usual high-heeled shoes, something he remembered she loved wearing and he remembered times where he took her to bed and all she had on were her heels. He'd even bought her a pair or two when they dated.

Not realizing Brian was close behind her, Sherry turned around and almost walked into him.

"I don't want to keep you long. I came by to talk and to see if you wanted to come over to the house and spend some time with Sherice tonight. I have to pick her up from daycare by six, but I was planning to pick her up around three today since I'm off for the afternoon. I have an on-line class to take, but you and Sherice can spend some time getting to know each other while I take my class."

Brian was at a loss for words as he listened to her invite him to her house. After the other day, he never thought this would be their next conversation.

"Are you sure it's okay? What about your parents?" he asked calmly.

"They'll be fine. My Dad is working, of course, and my mother will be at church for a while. I told them I was going to invite you over and they both plan to be there before you leave. We all know that what we're doing is going to be what's best for Sherice and she is the only priority. Again, I'm sorry for what I said and until we work out some other arrangements, you can see her whenever you like while you're here. I usually pick her up right after work around five o'clock. She likes to play until dinner, I give her a bath and then she's down by eight-thirty. What do you say?" she asked.

"I'd like that. Tell me a few things about her. What are her favorite things?" Brian said as they sat and talked, much calmer this time.

"She loves swings as you could see on the day that you arrived. She also loves books. She loves for me to read her several stories a night and I let her pick out the books. She never has enough books. She also loves Elmo from Sesame Street. I know that there are a lot of new cartoon characters, but she has a thing for him and every time I go into a store and she sees Elmo, she has to have a new one. She loves to eat carrots, raw and cooked though I have to mash them up because she's still growing teeth. Bananas are her favorite and one thing she has in common with you is she loves oatmeal. You know I could never stand the stuff, but I make it for her. If I take her out to eat, she loves waffles for breakfast, lunch or dinner, so we go to IHOP a lot on Saturday mornings. I haven't introduced electronic devices to her yet and I'm putting that off for as long as I can, so no cell phones or IPad games for her. Now that she's in daycare, they have been going over numbers and alphabets and so I pick one to work on to get her familiar with during her playtime at night. When she's really sleepy, she crawls into my lap and within seconds, she's fast asleep. Oh, one last thing is, she loves apple juice a lot and I mean a whole lot. I water it down a bit, but she still loves it. I use it to bribe her often and since it works, the house is never without apple juice," she laughed and was happy when Brian laughed along with her.

"I guess I have a lot to learn about her," he said excited.

"You do and you will. I don't want to keep you long. I wanted to come by and apologize and invite you over. If you come around six-thirty, you can eat dinner with her and maybe read her a story if you want to."

"I'd like that. Should I bring anything?"

"You mean food? No. If you must bring something, make it a book and any book will do. If you text me a picture of what you're trying to buy, I'll let you know if it's one she already has."

"Okay, I think I will get a book. I guess I had better get a shower, get dressed and make my way to the bookstore. I hear there's a big one at the inner harbor, so I'll start there. Thanks for doing this and I appreciate the apology and I'm sorry, too. I blew up and I shouldn't have. I'm not a threat kind of guy and still, I'm willing to work something out. I know you don't need my financial help, but she is my daughter and just as much my responsibility as yours."

"I know and we will work that out. For now, spend time with Sherice and let her get to know you and we'll go from there. Deal?" she said smiling.

"It's a deal."

Brian stood with Sherry as she stood to leave. He walked her to the door this time.

"Thanks for letting me up here and this condo is incredible."

"It is and I'm enjoying staying in it. So, I'll see you around six or so?"

"That's a good time. She'll be in full play mode by then."

"I really appreciate you doing this, Sherry."

When she stuck her hand out for him to shake, he

looked at it like it was a bee about to sting him.

"What?" she said smiling up at him.

"A handshake? Really?" he said and then without thinking he pulled her close to him for a hug. He held her not sure she would return the hug, but he wanted her to know that he was grateful for her concession. When he would have pulled away, he felt her arms come up and encircle his waist and he smiled. They were making headway and now when he really should let go, he couldn't seem to do it. Instead he leaned down and whispered in her ear.

"I don't know what you meant by finding out my true feelings for you, but I loved you. I loved you with everything in me and whatever you thought, if it wasn't that, you're wrong."

Like slow motion, Sherry leaned back and looked up at him. She wanted him to know what she'd heard, but didn't want to spend a lot of time on it.

"Brian, the morning after you spent the night at my apartment, you left and had ran into some guys right outside of my apartment. My window was open and I heard your conversation when they asked you about who you had spent the night with. I heard you tell them it was just some casual fling and that there was nothing to it. You told them it was nothing to you, but an itch you were getting scratched. I was crushed and thought that we were more than that."

Brian waited to respond thinking back to that time and he suddenly remembered the conversation. He had run into some guys and being that he liked to keep his private life private, which was why they seldom spent the night at her apartment, he didn't want the guys all in his business.

Besides the fact that they were college students that he ran into often on campus, he wasn't about to share anything personal, like his love for her, with them. He looked into her eyes and explained.

"Is that what happened to us? You broke up with me over that? Sherry, I said that for their benefit and for yours. You know I like my privacy and I didn't want them all in our business. They were students I have to see on campus and what we were sharing was none of their business. It was hard enough being involved with you, since you were a student even though I wasn't your professor. I wanted to protect your image and not spread our business like the other gossip that floats around. It was important to me that you understood how much I loved you and how I would do any and everything to love and protect you. Those guys were fishing to find out who I spent the night with and I was never going to reveal that. Our personal business was between you and me and no one else. Is that was caused all of this? Oh, my goodness, I am so sorry you heard that, but I wished you would have talked to me. Do you know how easily that could have been cleared up?" he asked with a seriousness to his voice. Two years down the drain like that, he thought.

Sherry wanted to cry. What she heard was him trying to protect her image and not words spoken in truth. She had ruined everything and the brunt of that was almost too much for her to deal with. As tears pooled in her eyes, Brian reached up and wiped away one tear before it ran down her face.

"I did this to us over something that wasn't even true?" she asked.

"Don't cry. We can't go back, but we have Sherice now

and she is the result of the love we shared back then."

She leaned into his chest and held on to him tighter.

"I'm sorry, Brian. I am so sorry for all of this. You missed all this time with Sherice because of what I did."

Brian reached down and lifted her face up, so that he could look into it. She was still the most beautiful woman he'd ever laid eyes on.

"It's in the past and I do admit, I was harboring some serious anger toward you, but today, I'm going to spend time with my daughter; a daughter you gave me and for that, despite what happened, I will forever be grateful."

"I hope you can forgive me. I don't think I'll ever be able to apologize enough."

"It's okay and I forgive you. Let's focus on Sherice and put that past in the past where it belongs," he said.

They stood like that for several seconds before a desire, buried deep inside of him burst open and he found himself looking between her tear-filled eyes and her lips and when she stuck her tongue out and rubbed it across her lips, he quickly captured it between his lips and kissed her with the pent-up lust he'd been carrying around for her for years and most recently since he'd arrived in town. He knew he shouldn't, but he did and any regret he thought he might feel for stealing a kiss at this moment when they were both vulnerable, dissipated the moment she joined him in the kiss. Standing in the doorway of the condo, the sweet kiss turned hot and heavy quickly as he pulled her up against him as his manhood hardened sensing her closeness. He was transported back to his house in Atlanta where they had spent many nights kissing and making love and he was reliving that moment having her in his arms. His head filled up with visions of her naked and writhing about wildly under him asking, begging and pleading for more from him.

He and Sherry were sharing an intoxicating, forbidden kiss and before long, they were both getting carried away as his hands began roaming over her luscious curves, driven on by the fact that her hands were caressing his back drawing him closer to her.

Sherry felt lightheaded. Brian was kissing her like a starving man and she was kissing him back and loving it. Before they went too far, she pulled back and took a step back from him while still focused on him as they breathed like they'd just finished a race.

He spoke first.

"I'm sorry. I don't know what came over me and I shouldn't have done that."

"I'd better go," she said and turned around and walked to the elevator.

"Sherry?"

Sherry was too overwhelmed to deal with what just happened between them. Any minute she would have asked him to take her back inside and make love to her.

"I'll see you around six-thirty," she said and entered the elevator, not looking at him as the doors closed.

CHAPTER 13

"I'm on my way to spend some time with Sherice and I need to know if I should take anything else," Brian asked his mother the minute she answered the phone.

"Really!" she exclaimed and he had to take the phone away from his ear she was so loud.

"Yes, really and I need your help. I picked out two books and texted the titles to Sherry. She said Sherice didn't have these already, so I'm good. Now I want to get her something else from me, but I don't know what to get. Sherry said she loves Elmo and I'm now in a toy store and there are so many Elmo dolls. I don't know which one to get."

"Brian, get any one that's all soft. If it has hard parts and she decides to sleep with it, it could poke her during the night or possibly come off and she could put it in her mouth."

He picked up a couple of them and found one he thought was all soft with no hard fillings or body parts.

"I think I found one. I knew I could count on you with all of the toys you've bought Milo and Lyric over the years."

"You're going to be a great dad, Brian. Make sure you

give that little one a kiss from her grandma."

"I will."

Brian was about to head to the register when he saw the cutest stuffed gray elephant. Something drew him to it and even though Sherry didn't say that Sherice loved elephants, he knew that Atlanta had one of the best zoos in the country and a big hit at the zoo was the elephants. One day he hoped to take Sherice to it, but until then, he would add the stuffed elephant to the bag and maybe one day, she'd grow to love it because it was from him.

"What else did you buy her?" Barbara asked.

"The two books, I just picked up a cute stuffed elephant and while I was at the harbor, I saw a cute boutique that sold little girl clothes and I asked Sherry her size. I picked up four little outfits, two in pink which Sherry says is her favorite color and another one in yellow and one in a pretty light green. I hope she likes them."

"Son, Sherice will like anything you pull out of a bag that's colorful."

"No, not her. I'm hoping Sherry likes them enough to put them on Sherice."

When his mother remained silent, he knew what she was thinking and he had a feeling the next question from her was going to be a hard one.

"Is something going on between you and Sherry?"

Should he lie?

"No, well, not really. I mean, we kissed earlier, but it wasn't anything. It was an emotional moment and it got the best of us. It shouldn't have happened and it won't happen again."

"Never say never and you don't have to explain this to me. You and Sherry are two adults, but I want you to watch your heart. She tore your life apart before and I won't be able to stand it if it happened again."

"I'm good, Mom. Now, is there anything else I should get for her for now. Of course, you know I may have to get another job to afford that fact that I want to buy out a toy store for her, but I won't for now," he smiled.

"I know you're excited, but don't go overboard just yet. Leave some toys for your father and I to buy her when we see her."

Brian laughed.

"I hear you. Thanks for helping me out with this. I'll call you later and I'll send a few pictures of her when I get there."

"Oh, that would be lovely. I'll keep my phone in my hand. Make sure you send them to your brothers and sister, too. They are all worried about you. I know you've stayed in contact with Duron and he's kept us posted, but send us all as many pictures as you can take. I can't wait to see more photos of her besides the one the private detective gave you."

"I will. I'll call you tonight."

Brian hung up, checked the time and was anxious to get to Sherry's house. He paid for his items, put everything in the bright pink gift bag he'd bought and headed for his car. He was going to see his daughter.

**

Sherry opened the door thinking that the ringing of the doorbell was signaling Brian's arrival. To her surprise, when she opened the door, Lance stood on the other side.

"Lance, what a surprise. Didn't I just see you a few hours ago, at the daycare? Is everything alright?"

"Yes, it is. I didn't get a chance to talk to you and in fact, we really haven't talked at all this week other than a passing hello and goodbye. I thought I would stop by on my way home and see if you and Sherice wanted to join me for dinner at Friendly's."

Sherry was uncomfortable as she looked around to see if Brian was pulling up. She didn't want them running into each other when she had yet to tell Lance that Brian was in town. She doubted she was going to be able to talk herself out of dinner without being truthful and now that she and Brian had come to common ground when it came to Sherice, it was time she shed some light on the situation for Lance.

"Lance, I can't tonight."

"Do you know this is the second time this week you're too busy for me? What gives?" he asked.

"Okay, what's going on is Sherice's father is in town and he's on his way over here to see her."

That news caught Lance by surprise.

"What? Where did he come from?"

"He somehow found out about Sherice and showed up on Saturday out of the blue and he and I have been working out an arrangement where he can spend time and get to know her."

"So, this guy, who has not been around for any part of her life shows up and you welcome him with open arms? Is he here to see her or is he here to see you and her?" Lance asked, now annoyed.

Now he knew why she had been acting strange. The man she never really wanted to talk about was back in her life and he wasn't sure it was just to get to know Sherice. As gorgeous as Sherry was, he had no doubt the mysterious Brian was out for more than just his daughter. If it were him, he would be.

"It's not like that. There is a lot about my history with him that you don't know, but either way, the bottom line is he is in town and he wants time with Sherice and I invited him here tonight as a starter for them to get to know one another. I want her to know who her father is."

So, Brian Knight was in town from Atlanta where she'd met and fallen in love with him and out of that came Sherice. Sherry never went into too much detail about what happened between them, but he assumed it was bad if the man had never made an attempt to see his own daughter and what made him suddenly appear now. He didn't think he would get the answer, but what he would get is a look at Sherice's father because as he stood talking to Sherry, a man got out of a car carrying a huge pink gift bag and he assumed that must be Sherice's father.

"I guess I had better go since it looks like you have company. Will I hear from you this week besides you saying hello and goodbye tomorrow?" Lance asked.

Sherry heard Lance say something, but for the moment, her focus was on Brian and specifically the kiss they'd shared earlier. She had been unable to think of anything else.

"What?" she said with her mind now befuddled.

Lance was perturbed, but now wasn't the time for a conversation since he was about to be a third wheel.

"Nothing, I'll call you later."

Where he thought he could escape, his path was now blocked by Brian as he walked up to the door.

"Hello, Sherry."

There was no getting around introductions, she thought.

"Hi. Brian, this is Lance."

She started to say boyfriend, but the word wouldn't come. When she continued to hesitate, lance spoke up for her.

"I'm Lance, Sherry's boyfriend."

Brian didn't say anything as he kept his emotions in check. He had to remember he was here for Sherice.

"It's nice to meet you, Lance. I'm Brian, Sherice's father."

"Yes, Sherry was just telling me that you were in town. I didn't know that the two of you were in contact since she never mentions you," Lance said with a hint of annoyance.

Instantly tension entered the space around them and Sherry knew the situation could possibly get touchy and uncomfortable. She turned to look at Brian.

"The situation is a little touchy and I haven't had a chance to bring Lance up to date on this, but I will Lance, a little later, okay?" she said, hesitantly.

"Sure. I'm going to go so that Brian you can visit with Sherice. She's a beautiful little girl. Sherry, I'll talk to you tomorrow."

Lance tried to lean in to give her a quick kiss, but Sherry was quicker as she moved back to let Brian in the house and to also avoid any public display of affection, which Lance found obvious. For now, he would let it slide, but he and Sherry would have to talk very soon as he turned around and walked back to his car without even getting a goodbye from Sherry before she shut the door behind Brian. He had a feeling there was a fox in his hen house and he didn't like it.

Brian entered the house and looked around for Sherice.

"She's in her highchair in the kitchen ready for her dinner. The daycare said she didn't eat much today and now that it looks like she has an appetite, she's hungry. I gave her a few carrots to keep her busy while I finish dinner. Why don't you come on in the kitchen and I'll take her out of her chair until dinner is finished? A lot of times, I have to keep her either in her chair or in a play pen because once she learned how to first walk and now climb, she gets into everything fast.

As soon as he entered the kitchen, he smiled as Sherice munched on a carrot.

"Sherice, you have a visitor," Sherry said and Brian came around where she could see him.

"Hi, Sherice," he said, beaming with pride.

When Sherice didn't respond to him, he looked to Sherry for help.

"Don't worry about it. She's not a big fan of new people. It takes her a while to warm up to anyone and I'm sure after a few visits, she'll warm up to you."

Brian didn't mind. He was just happy to be able to see her. He leaned down to her height and spoke to her.

"I hear you love carrots. I love carrots, too."

"Give me a second to wash my hands and I'll take her out. She may cling to my leg with a death grip like she tends to do around new people, but we'll sit for a bit and talk to engage her."

Brian shook his head and went back to talking to Sherice. While Sherry washed her hands and he talked, he was shocked when she reached her little arms out to him to pick her up out of the chair. He didn't know what to do. He had never been as nervous as he was right now. He looked from Sherice to Sherry and then back to Sherice who looked like she was about to get frustrated with him for not picking her up since she was reaching for him.

"Sherry, I think she wants me to pick her up."

"Really? Let me get her out."

Sherry went to untie the strap and pick her up when Sherice looked from her to Brian and again reached out toward him.

"This is crazy. She never likes new people."

Brian was officially a goner. His daughter didn't know him and already, she was reaching for him.

"Apparently, I'm not new. Do you mind if I pick her up?" he asked.

"No, go right ahead. I've already unsnapped the strap."

"You ready to get down?" he said turning to Sherice and without hesitation, she opened and closed her fingers while reaching out to him.

"Yeah, that's her signal for pick me up, not just let me down out of the chair. Try to pick her up and if she starts screaming her head off, I'll take her from you. Don't take it personal."

"Okay, got it," he said.

He reached for Sherice and picked her up and waited to see if she was going to scream. Instead of screaming, as soon as he picked her up, she threw her arms around his neck, laid her head on his shoulder and held on tight.

"Well I'll be. Now, this is a first. I guess she knows you're her Daddy. Dada?" she said to Sherice who grinned and looked at Brian with no hint of being fearful. In fact, to him she looked extremely happy to be in his arms. Brian didn't care what the reason was and as long as Sherice wanted to be in his arms, he wasn't going to put her down.

"Why don't I show her what I have for her in the bag while you finish cooking?" he asked.

"Okay, do that. You can go in the family room if you

want instead of sitting here in the kitchen. Just holler if you need me."

Walking with Sherice still in his arms, she lifted her head up the moment he left the room and stared in his face. They were a mystery to each other, he guessed. He walked into the room that Sherry pointed out as the family room and sat down on the chair holding Sherice in one arm and the big pink bag in the other.

"I have a few things for you that I thought you'd like. Do you want to see?" he asked.

Sherice looked in the bag and when she saw all of the bright colored contents, she reached inside and pulled everything out. Of course, she didn't pay any attention to the clothes, but reached for Elmo and the books. For an instant, he saw her eyes light up and then she threw Elmo to the floor and picked the elephant out of the bag and hugged it before turning to lay her head back on his shoulder, holding tightly to him and her new elephant. Brian smiled as his daughter officially had him wrapped around her finger.

"Well, look at what we have here."

Brian turned his attention away from Sherice and looked up to see that Sherry's parents had come in.

Brian tried to stand, but her father stopped him.

"Don't worry about standing. I see my Sherice here has already taken to you. How long did it take before she pried herself off of Sherry's leg? She does that around new people."

"She never did that, Dad," Sherry said entering the room.

"What?" her mother gasped.

"I'm serious. He came in the door, talked to her for a

few seconds while she was in her chair and then the next thing we knew, she was reaching for him like she already knew him."

"That's really is something," her father said. "Well, nice to see you Brian and I'm glad the circumstances are better this time."

Brian reached out with his free hand to shake hands with him.

"It's good to see you Mr. and Mrs. Braxton," he said greeting them both.

"It's really good to see you, Brian," Sherry's mother said, looking from Sherry to him and smiling.

"Sherice, are you ready to eat?" her mother said.

Sherice shook her head yes and as soon as she tried to take Sherice from Brian's arms, Sherice whimpered like she was about to cry.

"Okay, what is this, the twilight zone?" Sherry said. "Brian, bring her back into the kitchen. It seems as though, she doesn't want anyone, but you. Sherice, can you say, Dada?"

She pointed at Brian to help her make the connection, but Sherice didn't say a word. She continued holding on to a gray elephant with a death grip on Brian's neck.

"I guess my granddaughter has a new favorite person."

"Well, that's mutual because, so do I," Brian said.

"Where did the elephant come from? I saw Elmo on the floor and normally she's dragging Elmo by his arm all over the place. The only time we get to wash him is when she's asleep and now he's sprawled out on the floor," Mrs. Braxton said.

"I saw it at a store and thought it was cute," Brian said.

"Well, I'm guessing Elmo has been replaced," Mr.

Braxton said. "Let's all go in and eat and we can talk some more."

"Yes, sir," Brian said and walked into the kitchen with Sherice in his arms.

All throughout dinner, Sherice kept her eye on Brian and if he looked like he was moving too far away from her, she would whine until he moved back closer to her. Several times she took food from her plate and pushed it toward him to eat it and like a doting father should be, he ate it and each time and it made her laugh profusely.

Sherry knew it was the craziest thing and if she didn't know her daughter well and hadn't seen her actions for herself, she never would have believed it. By the time dinner was over, Sherice had started talking a mile a minute in her own language and when Brian entertained her by laughing at everything she said, Sherice would break out in a fit of laughter. She and her parents were mesmerized by the instant connection between Brian and Sherice.

"Do you mind if I use the restroom?" Brian asked.

"No, not at all. There's one just beyond the door to the family room," Sherry said.

Brian stood up to leave and to all of their surprise, Sherice screamed for him.

"Dada!" she said.

Brian stopped in his tracks and turned back to her.

"Dada?" he said pointing to himself.

"Dada, up," Sherice said and reached for him.

He looked around the table for help. He couldn't take her to the bathroom with him.

"Let Mommy wipe your face and then Dada will pick you up okay?"

Sherice bobbed her head up and down and Brian rushed off.

"She called him Dada," Sherry's father said, amazed and shocked.

Sherry smiled.

"Yes, she did. We've been calling him that all night and she made the connection. Today, was a good day," Sherry said and picked Sherice up to wipe her face and hands.

**

Lance had been sitting in his car at the end of the block where he could still see Sherry's house. He saw when her parents had come home and he waited to see how late Brian would stay at the house. His plan was to follow Brian to see where he was staying. He had a bad feeling about the guy and most of the time, his feelings told the truth. The way he saw Brian look at Sherry, he knew that he was there for more than just Sherice.

His eyes became heavy as the hour got later and later and Brian was still in there. It was now nine o'clock, past Sherice's bed time which meant that by now, Brian was officially visiting with Sherry and that made his skin feel like it was on fire. How dare this guy pop out of the sky and all of a sudden, he stepped into the role of family man where Lance himself had expected to be? Once again, he was pushed to the side by Sherry and once again, he didn't like it. He also contributed Sherry's cancellation of their Sunday lunch to Brian being in town. It was no coincidence that the change in her took effect after he arrived. It was all connected to Brian Knight. He'd have to see what information he could gather on this guy. When exhaustion had finally set in, Lance knew he needed to get on the road home before he fell asleep behind the wheel.

He was about to turn the car on when he saw Sherry's front door open and she and Brian walked out. He slouched down in the seat and hoped that Sherry wouldn't spot his car. He would never be able to explain why he was still outside of her house.

**

Thanks for inviting me over to see Sherice. I will never forget this night and the first time I heard her call me Dada," he said, smiling from ear-to-ear.

"You know, this was a weird night. I wasn't joking when I said she never, ever takes to new people. It usually takes her days, but with you it was a manner of minutes."

"That's what you call an instant father/daughter connection and I will cherish this forever."

"I think I have officially been replaced as the number one person in her life. She wouldn't even let me read to her tonight because it had to be you. While I was giving her a bath, she kept pointing to the bathroom door saying Dada, which now appears to be her next favorite word. I had to tell her that you were still there and would be reading her book to her as soon as she finished getting a bath. Suffice it to say, the bath was over as far as she was concerned or she was going to continue to serenade me with the word Dada until I got her out. She wanted to get to you and I swear, I have never seen her act that way before. She fell asleep with that elephant you bought her and I can't tell you the last time she let me put her to bed without her Elmo. You have our daughter under some magical spell."

Brian laughed heartily, glad that they could laugh and not argue.

"No, it's a connection that only fathers and daughters share. I've seen it between my sister and my father my whole life."

"Well, you certainly have won her over. Like I said earlier today, come by to see her any time you want or I can bring her to you for a visit."

"I'd like that as long as you stay for the visit, too."

Sherry didn't know what to say, but like many times before, there was an electric charge between them and she knew they both felt it.

"That I can do."

"What do you say to you and Sherice coming over Saturday afternoon and I'll cook something for us to eat and if you don't mind, I'd like to cut my computer on and let my family see her via webchat."

"Saturday is fine with me and that would be great. I know they are all anxious to see and meet her."

"Thanks again for tonight. If I promise to not stay as long as I did tonight, do you mind if I stop by for a bit tomorrow?" he asked. Sherice pricked a piece of his heart that made him want to see her as often as he could.

"Anytime you want to see her, feel free to call me to be sure we're here and come by. I know a little someone who will be happy to see you tomorrow."

"I'll be happy to see her, too. Good night, Sherry," Brian said descending the steps.

He hadn't gotten all the way down the steps when he turned back around. He hoped he wasn't about to rock the boat, but he needed to know.

"Do you mind if I ask you something a little personal?" he asked.

"Sure."

"Lance? I know I'm just coming into Sherice's life, but what kind of role does he play in her life? I know you said he was your boyfriend, but I do want to know about his interaction with Sherice?"

Sherry exhaled because she had a feeling the subject of Lance would come up.

"Well, I didn't call him that, he called himself that. Right now, it's kind of complicated to define it that way, but as far as Sherice, he sees her a lot because he's one of the directors at her daycare which is where we met. We keep things pretty light and I'm careful about my interactions with him around Sherice. I'm sorry about you meeting him like that. He showed up tonight unexpectedly before I had a chance to tell him who you are or tell you about him."

"Don't apologize for having a life. You are incredibly beautiful and a wonderful person. I didn't expect that I would be the only man in the world to notice that. I am sorry about the kiss earlier. I shouldn't have done that and if I had known you were involved with someone, I never would have done that."

Sherry stopped him before he went any further.

"Don't apologize for a kiss where I was a willing participant. I know we both got caught up in the moment and I'll forget about it if you do," she said, smiling to let him know everything was okay.

Brian moved a little closer to her.

"What if I don't want to forget about it?" he said smoothly.

Sherry didn't know how to respond because ever since she left the condo, she hadn't been able to think about anything other than the kiss they shared. It was brief, but filled with so much passion that she forgot she should still be angry at him. With him moving in closer to her, she couldn't help, but yearn for a repeat of the earlier kiss even though his visit wasn't about her. There was no more her and Brian.

"We shouldn't, Brian," she said breathlessly knowing her mind and body didn't match the words that came out of her mouth.

"I know, but I'm not sorry I kissed you. You may have left me, but I didn't leave you and to me, the moment I saw you, I knew you were still very much a big part of me. I know there's tension right now, but that doesn't cast a shadow over the fact that you are still one incredibly beautiful woman. I will, however, keep my distance because you are involved with someone. Nothing will make me regret the kiss from earlier or the fact that I want another one, but I'll move on."

"No regret on my part either," she said.

"Good night, Sherry and thanks again for the invitation. Our daughter is beautiful, just like her mother," he said as he turned and walked to his car.

"Good night, Brian," she responded and smiled when he waved.

What a man, she thought, knowing he wasn't alone in his desire for another kiss. She wanted it, too.

Sherry turned and went back inside after she watched Brian pull off.

"You're still in love with him, aren't you?"

Sherry was startled to hear her mother's voice behind her. She started to lie, but she knew her mother would see right through that.

"Yes, I am and I can't help it, Mom. I know I shouldn't be and I don't know what's wrong with me. I had a feeling that one day I'd have to deal with Brian again, but I didn't know it would be this soon and now I realize I may have left him, but I never stopped loving him. Do you know that all of this is my fault and not just because I left him and didn't tell him about Sherice, but the situation that made me break up with him in the first place was a misunderstanding on my part? I left a man who treated me like I was a precious jewel, I kept him away from his daughter and then I treated him nasty when we talked the first time. What is wrong with me?" she almost cried out.

Her mother put her arm around her for comfort.

"Nothing is wrong with you. For starters, you can't fight who your heart wants you to love. Then, there was no way for you to decipher that misunderstanding back then because you didn't go to Brian and talk to him about it. You can't make up for that, but you can move forward. I won't say fall back in love with him because that's up to you, but I will say, I watched my granddaughter with her father tonight and until I saw them together, I didn't realize how much she was missing out by not having him. I'm glad you were able to begin working this all out. Now, as far as you being in love with him, be careful if Brian doesn't feel the same way. He may have forgiven you for keeping him away from Sherice, but I doubt it if he'll forget. I'm going upstairs to bed. Make sure everything is locked up before you go to bed. Tonight, was good," her mother said before going up to bed and Sherry couldn't agree more.

CHAPTER 14

Saturday never looked so good, as far as Brian was concerned. He had been on the move all day anticipating his visit from Sherry and Sherice. After his visit on Thursday with Sherice, who blew his mind with how loving she was toward him, he had called Sherry on Friday and stopped by after she had gotten home from work. He and Sherice played and when he asked her about her day, he wasn't sure she knew what it meant, but boy did she love to talk and she laid it all out for him in her baby talk where the only words he understood were Mommy, Dada, Elmo and eat.

Learning from Jake's interaction with his kids, he knew to just keep talking back to her and when she laughed about something she said, he knew to laugh along with her because whatever she said was funny to her. Luckily, due to the summer time, darkness didn't settle over the Maryland sky until late in the evening, giving him time to walk Sherice to the playground and push her on the swing. Their time together was everything to him and his world was made whole when Sherry allowed him to read a book to Sherice before she put her to bed. He had stayed longer than he was planning to, but he couldn't seem to tear himself away from his daughter.

There was no talk between him and Sherry about custody, visitation or financial matters when it came to Sherice, but he was hoping they could touch back on the subject soon. He and Xavier needed to talk through things depending on where his discussion with Sherry led. Since Sherry was going to be at his place for a few hours tonight, he thought it would be a good idea to broach the subject at that time. He wasn't worried that Sherice would be with them because he felt that they were in a better place and were communicating better.

Xavier had called the night before and Brian asked for a few days to talk to Sherry before they proceeded with anything legal. They were getting along and how they would co-parent Sherice was a touchy subject. Xavier told him to call when he was ready to sit down and begin the process.

He had also spoken to Jake the night before and he was still excited about the pictures of Sherice he had sent to the family. Loren had sent multiple texts saying how she couldn't get enough of all of the pictures of her niece that he sent and she agreed with everyone else's assessment that Sherice looked a lot like her.

He mentioned to Jake that Sherry and Sherice were coming to his condo to spend some time and Jake gave him some tips on making sure the place had no safety hazards. The minute he knew the local stores were open, Brian ran out and got everything he would need to do as much child proofing as he could. He wanted Sherice to feel comfortable to walk around even though he knew he wouldn't take his eyes off of her. He had also confided in Sherry about adding a few items to his condo for any future visits from Sherice like a crib, toys and especially books. Sherry was happy to hear that with each day, he was thinking of Sherice first.

Excited about making a space just for Sherice, Loren was helpful in connecting him with an interior designer in Baltimore who was on her way with everything Loren had told her to purchase and set up in one of the spare bedrooms at the condo. Things were moving fast and Brian was thankful for his family who never failed to pitch in when needed. A few minutes after he called Loren for help, she was on the phone ordering a crib with all the trimmings and plush animals because he'd told her that Sherice loved them and had a room full of them at Sherry's house. Books he took care of since he was close to a Barnes & Noble Bookstore. Things were coming together nicely and now all he had to do was finish picking up everything he would need to make dinner after the decorator left.

He was roaming around doing a last check on his attempts at child-proofing when his phone rang. Seeing it was Sherry, he quickly answered and hoped she wasn't calling to cancel.

"Hey!" he said, answering.

"Hey yourself. I'm just making sure we're still on for today around five?"

"We sure are. I've been child-proofing, food shopping, toy shopping and I'm waiting on a woman whom my sister is sending who's bringing a crib and some other stuff that children need. I don't want to be presumptuous, but I want to be sure that I have what Sherice would need when she's here."

Sherry laughed.

"You are really getting into this Daddy role."

"Hey, I'm new at this and if it seems a bit too much, let me know. My family is leading me by the hand here," he joked.

"I totally understand and what you're doing is good. Do you need me to bring anything? I know you said you were setting up a crib, too. I didn't know if I should bring Sherice's carrier or not in case she falls asleep. I never put her on a regular bed even with pillows all around."

"No, you don't need to bring anything and a crib is one of the things Loren is having brought in. I'm expecting the delivery within the hour. You and Sherice just need to bring yourselves and anything she can't live without that's at your house."

"Well, other than that stuffed elephant you brought that she drags everywhere, I think we're good. I'll see you in a few hours," Sherry said and hung up.

Brian looked at his phone and smiled.

"Yes, you will."

Things had turned around after their first talk which had gotten heated and some not-so-good words were exchanged. He chalked that first talk up to them coming to the reality that though they hadn't seen each other in a few years, there was still a spark and neither knew how to handle it and their immediate reaction was to strike out at each other.

Spending time with them the past two nights gave them insight into how their lives could have been if they had stayed together. He shared with his brothers what Sherry told him about why she left him and neither could believe it was something that small, but to him, he felt that no one can measure the impact any situation will have on how someone responds to it. He didn't want to look back at what could or should have been; he can only move forward from today and that's what he was doing. He had to admit that since seeing Sherry again, old feelings had surfaced and though he apologized for the kiss they shared, deep down, he wasn't sorry at all. He'd wanted that kiss from the first moment he saw her with Sherice on the playground, though the desire was shielded at that time by hurt and anger.

The kiss they shared had stayed on his mind for the rest of the day, with thoughts of it marred temporarily by thoughts of her with Lance. He had no idea she was seeing anyone, but what did he expect? Did he believe no other man would want her? Hell, he still wanted her even after all that has happened. A man would be crazy to not want her. To him she had been the perfect woman, definitely perfect for him and now seeing her with Sherice, he not only wanted her, but he was still in love with her, which wasn't good; not good at all.

Brian knew he needed to bury his feelings for Sherry and focus on Sherice. She was involved with another man and every time he thought of that fact, he felt like he was going to be ill. He had been her first and he was supposed to be her one and only, but now he had to deal with the fact that another man reaped the benefits of the passion that flowed from her. He remembered how sexy and sexual she was and how much they loved making love all the time. His appetite for her was salacious and she responded with her own brand of fieriness that made their coming together explosive every single time.

He had been trying his best to keep his focus on Sherice, but in the back of his mind, Sherry and Sherice were his family, not just Sherice and he could see them together, even now, though he knew it wasn't possible. They can't go back and reclaim a moment that was gone and now that he knew she had moved on, he had no choice, but to respect that. It won't be easy, but he would try.

**

Sherry pulled into the garage under Brian's condo and looked for the other parking space that was assigned to him that he told her to park in every time she came to visit him. Sherice smiled at her from the backseat where she was still repeating, Dada, over and over again for the entire ride. When she told Sherice she was going to see her Daddy, she hadn't stopped calling his name. They had even turned it into a little song which seemed to please Sherice even more. Along with Sherice dragging her elephant with her, she had packed a bag with a change of clothes just in case her current outfit got dirty. She had put Sherice in one of the pink outfits Brian had bought and she hoped he noticed and liked it.

Reaching into the back seat, she picked Sherice up and grabbed her bag before walking toward the elevator.

"Dada?" Sherice said.

"Yes, Dada. You'll see Dada in a few minutes."

Sherice loved Brian so much it was crazy to her. It wasn't that she couldn't understand why Sherice loved him because she loved him, too, though she struggled with that fact. Seeing Brian again and watching him with Sherice brought out feelings she thought she had gotten over and left in the past. A life with him would have been perfect and she knew back then that one day, he would be an incredible father. If she hadn't been immature and selfish and instead of running away, talked to him, she knew they would have worked it out, but back then she was young and hurt and did what her first instinct told her to do. Now she knew that it was all for nothing because the situation wasn't what she thought it was and for that, she spent the last few years without him. If it weren't for having Sherice, she would have never known that she had been wrong about him.

Using the cardkey Brian had given her the day before, she was able to take the elevator straight to his condo without stopping on the main lobby level to be allowed up. Reaching his door, she rang the bell and within seconds, Brian opened the door with a gigantic smile on his face and her heart raced. He looked good in a comfortable gray sweat suit and only socks on his feet.

"My Dada!" Sherice hollered and immediately wanted out of Sherry's arms. When he reached for her, she let go and watched the display before her of a father and daughter who loved each other unconditionally.

"Sherry, can you take off your shoes. I left a couple of pairs of new socks and footies you can choose from in the basket right there on the floor. I had the carpets vacuumed in case Sherice is crawling around and I don't want outside stuff tracked in that she would walk or crawl through. I got that from my mom," he said smiling and walking ahead of her laughing and playing with Sherice who was giggling with glee.

She did as he asked and took off her shoes and found a cute pair of socks in the basket. Brian had thought of everything.

"Wow, look at this place," Sherry said admiring the added touches she didn't notice when she visited him before.

"Nice, right? I figure since I'll be here at least for a few more weeks, I may as well add a few touches of my own or should I say a few of Loren's touches. Remember I told you back when we dated that she was launching her own interior design business? Well, she did and it's been flourishing. She even opened a west coast branch besides the one in Atlanta. She had me walk around the place with my video chat open in order for her to see everything and when the designer showed up today with the stuff for Sherice, she brought a few new pieces of art."

"It's amazing. Xavier was okay with you adding your own touch and all of the stuff for Sherice?"

"Yeah, I checked with him and he said for me to do whatever I needed to do especially when it came to making it a comfortable space for Sherice. Go ahead and take a look at the room I set up for her. I hope you like it."

Sherry put her purse and Sherice's bag down and she went to check out the room. When she opened the door, she felt like she had walked into a castle made for a princess. Everything was pink and white and stuffed toys were everywhere. There was a large pink rug in the middle of the floor with a new shelf with several books on them, most duplicates of the books she had at her house of the ones Sherice loved the most. After getting a look and feel of everything, she went back out to join them as they sat on the floor playing.

"That room is incredible. I want a room just like it for me," she quipped.

"Well, feel free to spend the night in it anytime you want."

Brian didn't bat an eye and meant every word, though he wished he hadn't said it. He had to watch what he said and remember that they were not involved, so no subtle innuendos.

Not taking her eyes off of him, she was moved by the intensity of the way he was looking at her and if she didn't know any better, she could believe that there was more to his statement than the actual words. She didn't respond, but turned her attention to Sherice as she joined them on the floor.

"So, what are we having for dinner? I know you love to cook and it's going to be something good."

"Well, why don't we head into the kitchen and you and my favorite girl here can help me cook."

"For you and me, I was going to make a salad and some twice baked potatoes with crabmeat and sautéed shrimp along with salmon fillets. I have chicken nuggets, sautéed carrots and one of these potatoes for Sherice. You up for all that?"

"That's a lot of food."

"It is, which is why we're all going to cook together."

"Goodness, you're making my stomach growl with the thought of all that. You always did know how to cook. I bet if we had stayed together, today I would be three hundred pounds heavier," she joked and then thought about what she'd just said and wished she could take it back. She started to look away when the impact of her words showed on Brian's face. She waited for some type of comeback knowing she deserved it.

"Well, if we had stayed together and you were three hundred pounds heavier, I would still love you as deeply as I did back then. I know that you work out just as much as I do, so I don't think that would have been an issue, but if so, it wouldn't matter."

Brian didn't look away. He wanted her to see the sincerity in his words and he didn't care how much they

wanted to act like the air wasn't electrified every time they
came in contact.

"Tell me about all this new family you have," Sherry
said, lightening the moment.

"Well, my brother Duron met a woman at a bachelor
auction named Taija and after some ups and downs, they
got married and have twins Autumn and Brent. They are so
adorable and Duron is in daddy, husband heaven."

"I cannot believe some woman got Duron to commit. I
thought he'd never give up the single, bachelor life. I know
about him and his friends and their reputation with the
ladies."

"Yeah, well one of those friends married my sister,
Loren."

"What? Who?"

Brian chuckled. He had a lot to fill her in on.

"Loren married Michael."

"You're kidding me? They're married?"

"Yes, and they have a baby boy named Chase. Duron
was pissed at first, especially after months of them secretly
seeing each other. He was the one who caught them
literally in the act on one of his visits to California. Loren
was supposed to be decorating a house Michael purchased
on the west coast after he was tagged to open and run the
west coast offices of their company, Pioneer Architecture
and Design. Duron decided to surprise him with a visit to
the job site and he walked in on them practically naked.
After a touchy time and the revelation that they had been
seeing each other in secret, everyone realized that they
were really in love and after a woman who was obsessed
with Mike ran Loren over with her car, we knew nothing
was going to keep them apart. They are stupid, happy in

love."

"Wow, someone purposely tried to run her over with a car?"

"Yes, and it showed us all how fragile people are when love isn't returned. The woman is getting the help she needs and Loren and Michael currently live in Los Angeles."

"What about that other guy? I know they're in business together. I saw an article in Black Enterprise magazine about their company. It's been touted as one of the fastest growing architectural firms in the country."

"Yeah, they are and that's why Duron has been trying to get me to join the company full time, to help with the expansion. He needs someone with my financial expertise and to oversee his mentoring program for marketing graduates. I think he threw that in because he knows I have a passion for making sure our young men get to college and then out into successful careers."

"You finished your doctorate program in corporate financing?" she asked.

When she'd left him, he was months from graduating from an on-line doctorate program.

"I finished that summer," he said and looked over at her.

"I'm glad. I'll be finished in my next degree in December, hopefully. I've already been offered a job as a forensic pathologist and I'm also looking forward to buying a house for Sherice and I to have our own space. I'm sure my parents are ready to be empty nesters. I swear, it's frightening when you have to watch what room you're walking in with your parents who didn't get the memo that their activities were supposed to die down by now," she laughed. She had to watch her words around Sherice who repeats everything.

"Die down? Any woman married to me better be ready for it anywhere and everywhere until the grave," Brian joked, but really meant every word.

"I remember you saying that before and from what I remember, you're aren't joking."

Around them the room crackled with sparked.

"So, are you thinking about taking the job and working for Duron's company?"

"I've been doing some work already since I've been here in Baltimore. Thankfully technology allows me to work remotely. I don't want to stop teaching, but there may be a way to do both. I have to think about it some more. As for Tyrone, Duron's other friend, he's married to a great woman name Victoria. They got married the day I flew here, which is why I arrived in a tuxedo. I left from the wedding and got on a plane to Baltimore. As coincidences go, even though Taija and Victoria had been friends for a long time, she and Tyrone actually ran into each other while each were on a business trip someplace in Texas. That was a crazy situation because they had a one night stand and unbeknownst to Tyrone, she was engaged to some dude and didn't tell him, even though he was a fake fiancé. They have a perfect love though, so even a fake fiancé wasn't going to stand in the way of them finally realizing they loved each other."

"That's a lot going on. I should write a book or two about that," she chuckled.

They both kept an eye on Sherice who was entertaining herself at the kitchen table with a book.

"Do you still love to write?" he asked.

Brian remembered that she loved writing poetry and short stories and he once encouraged her to think about publishing them."

"I do still love to write, though I don't get to do it as much as I'd like. Sherice gets all of my free time and she's more important to me than anything. How is your other brother doing? The salad is finished. I'll cover it and put it in the fridge until the rest of the food is done."

Sherry moved around the kitchen as if being here with Brian was the most natural occurrence in the world.

"Jake is good. He and his wife Kim have two children, Milo and Lyric and you may remember them. They were babies when we dated."

"Yes, I do. Your parents? How are they doing?"

"They're doing great. Mom is anxious to see Sherice and calls me every day for pictures and updates and I promised them a video conference while she's here today. Are you still okay with that?" he asked.

"Of course, Sherice will love that."

Just when she thought she could get beyond feeling guilty, it crept back up again. Ms. Barbara had treated her like a daughter when she was in Atlanta. She would bake her nice treats and even invited her over for dinner, surprising Brian when he showed up and she was already at the house. He has a great family and none of them deserved being away from Sherice.

"I need to call and apologize to your mother. Actually, I need to apologize to your whole family. I honestly don't know what I was thinking at the time and all I can do is ask for their forgiveness."

"My family isn't like that and believe me, they have moved beyond that and are excited to meet her. We can't go back and my family understands that. I'm going to get the rest of the meal cracking because I'm starving," he said and after giving Sherice a quick kiss on the cheek which had her going into a flurry of calling his name, he went back to finishing their meal.

"A kiss on the cheek! What a lucky little girl," Sherry said with a grin.

Brian turn around and what she saw was undeniable as his heated gaze landed square on her.

"There's one for you too if you want it. All you have to do is ask."

**

With dinner out of the way and while Brian and Sherice played together in the living room, Sherry offered to clean up the kitchen. It was getting close to Sherice's bed time, but she didn't want to interrupt the time they were spending together. When she was finally done, and rejoined them in the living room, Sherice had fallen asleep and Brian was still holding her in his arms.

"I was wondering when she would tire out. It's eight o'clock, right at her bed time and I figured with the excitement of seeing you, she would crash eventually. Do you want me to take her?"

Brian stood up.

"No, I'll just lay her down in the crib unless you're ready to leave?" he said.

Sherry looked up at him and every honest bone in her body was telling her she never wanted to leave, but eventually she would have to, just not right now.

"No, not yet. Go ahead and lay her down."

"Good, I was hoping we could talk before you left. I'll put her down," he said walking into the other room.

Sherry was fidgety. She couldn't keep still, her palms were sweating and her heart raced. She was about to be alone with Brian again and the last time that happened, they shared a kiss that burned right through her. From the beginning, she was never able to resist his kisses because he was a master at kissing the same way he made love, with passion that had her mind and body screaming for more. Internally, she was screaming to be touched by him and the fact that she hadn't been since him had her body firing on all cylinders. She tried to act calm standing at one of the windows overlooking the harbor when he re-entered the room.

"She's out?"

"Like a light. I wasn't sure if she'd be comfortable in the unfamiliar crib, but snuggled up to that elephant and lightly snored," he laughed and joined her on at the window.

"You get to look at this view every night. I don't think I'd ever be able to sleep knowing this view was waiting for me."

"It is lovely," Brian said, looking at her and not out the window.

Sherry looked at him shyly and looked away.

"Do I make you uncomfortable?"

"I don't think I could ever be uncomfortable around you."

"Not even when we have to talk about uncomfortable situations? You know, I don't want to bring up the subject again because the last time we discussed Sherice and custody, visitation and child support, the conversation didn't turn out so well, but we need to talk about it. I can't stay here forever and we can't continue going on like the subject is going to go away."

She knew he was speaking fact, but she didn't want to get into it after a great time.

"After such a good day together with Sherice, why don't you and I table that discussion for a time when Sherice won't wake up at any moment. I promise you, whatever you want, I won't fight you on it. I can't say sorry enough to make up for keeping Sherice from you and I will never, ever do that again. I don't want there to be any tension tonight."

"When do you think you'll have some time to sit down and talk? I know you have work and school?"

"Well, I'm off Wednesday and if you'd like to get together then, that works for me. I can leave Sherice with my parents and we can iron everything out."

"Wednesday, it is. Now, what would you like to do until it's time to get Sherice home to her bed?"

Sherry shivered as soon as the word bed left his mouth. Speaking of mouths, she couldn't take her eyes off of his. His lips were a treasure she remembered delighting her body to heights she hadn't experienced since. How wrong would she be to tell him she craved another kiss? Knowing she was undeserving, she pushed the thought from her mind.

"Something interesting on the television?" she asked looking into his eyes as the feeling of her heart beating throughout her body seemed to be magnified.

"Not as interesting as watching you struggle through asking me for what you really want. This is me, Sherry. I know you and I see you. Come here," Brian said low and seductively.

"I can't," she said.

"Why? Because of Lance? We're not doing anything, but standing here talking."

"It's not the talking I'm worried about."

"Then what is it?"

Brian moved closer to her when she didn't move. If she moved away, then he'd back off, but if the signals were right, she wanted him closer.

They were now mere inches away from each other and he could see the rapid increase in her breathing. When she tried to look away, Brian reached out with his hand and lifted her head so that they were eye-to-eye.

"The kiss."

"What kiss?" he asked.

"The one from the other day. I keep thinking about it and I know I shouldn't."

"I told you I have no regrets about that kiss, Sherry and you shouldn't either. We stopped and you left. It didn't go further than that. I meant what I said when I told you any time you need another one, I have what you need, something you already know. I know how your mind works and you know I fully understand what your body wants, but in the atmosphere we're in, the ball is in your court. We can watch television if that's what you want, but if it isn't, say so."

Sherry could feel the warmth of his breath as he spoke in the sexy, raspy way that drove her wild. She knew she shouldn't, but a woman wants what she wants and right now she wanted to taste his lips.

"I don't want to watch television," she said with a soft, yet ragged voice.

"What do you want?" Brian said, coming even closer until their bodies were finally touching, even though it was only lightly.

"Your lips," she staggered out, whispering her desire.

"Where?" he said, coaxing her to open up to him.

Sherry looked away and then bravely looked back at him.

"Everywhere," she said unapologetically. The heat of the moment seemed to pass by slowly when what she wanted was for him to aggressively make a move before she did something like beg him. The silence in the room was deafening as the sound of a walk clock ticking along pierced the quietness. The sound of her breathing heightened as she watched him move closer and closer to her.

Caressing the side of her face, Brian brought her face closer to his.

"Mmmm," he murmured against the side of her mouth and then with a slow, tantalizing swipe of his tongue, he traced the crease where her lips met and went from one side of her mouth to the other, tasting her as he went along. He heard her moan as he slowly brought her even closer until their bodies were flush against each other.

"Yes," she breathed out on a sigh.

"More?" he uttered, dropping his voice to a hush against her mouth.

"Yes, more," Sherry said as she boldly reached to brace herself against his chest with the palm of her hand to keep from falling when she began to feel the effects of being this close to him again. The feel of his tongue gliding across her lips stoked embers in her that had not been lit in a long time; not since him. She closed her eyes in order to focus only on the feelings he pulled from her.

"Look at me, baby. I need you to see me and know it's

me."

Opening her eyes slowly, she felt intoxicated with a desire so fierce, she felt that any moment she would burst into flames.

Brian saw the fire in her eyes and knew that there would be no regrets from this kiss either as he finally leaned fully into her, using his tongue to coax her to open for him and when she did, he went on full assault. He made love to her mouth diving in slowly, but deeply, as their tongues dueled for more and more. The kiss went on and on and grew hotter the longer they stayed connected.

Reaching down, Brian drew her hands up into his, locking their fingers together and turned to press her firmly against the large window pane. Pressing himself into her, his head moved right, then turned left while going deeper and deeper. She wanted his kiss and he wanted to show her that he still knew how to give her exactly what she needed and the way she was practically climbing up his body and into his mouth, he knew she hadn't been this thoroughly kissed in a long time. This time together with her, like this was way overdue.

CHAPTER 15

Brian opened the door to the condo and on the other side stood a sight that made his heart leap. He and Sherry were getting together to finally iron out how they were going to co-parent Sherice, especially knowing that he lives in Atlanta. He also knew that they needed to address the elephant in the room and he wasn't speaking of the gray one Sherice loved dragging everywhere.

The other night, while Sherice slept in her crib at his condo, he and Sherry had engaged some pretty hot kisses, but were able to slow things down before they went too far. He wasn't so sure having her visit him alone was a good idea. It was clear to him they were struggling with keeping their hands off of each other.

"Hello beautiful," he said, moving to the side to let her pass. As she walked by, he couldn't help, but take in her exquisite beauty and the one thing he always loved about her was the confidence in her stride, especially when she wore very high-heeled shoes like the one's she had on now. He kept his eyes on her as she removed her shoes and grabbed a pair of socks to put on. He watched her every move and to him, she moved like a seductress because all he could think of was knowing how she moved when they were in bed together and already a fire was brewing inside of him.

In front of him, looking as beautiful as ever in white denim jeans, a white shirt tied at the waist with a blue top underneath that barely contained her large breasts, breasts he remembered never getting enough enjoying. He was really a sucker for punishment because knowing she is currently involved with someone else and no longer in love with him cut him even deeper. Despite his best effort, he had fallen in love with her again just as quickly as he had the first time. Sherry was no longer his, but he couldn't let go of the feeling that she was meant to be his.

"I think every time I walk into this condo, I'll end up right at one of the windows looking out. This view is stunning," Sherry said.

"Yes, it is."

Brian knew he wasn't talking about the view and the way Sherry turned and looked at him when he responded, she knew it, too, but neither of them addressed it.

"Thanks for having me over," she said, trying to tamper down the nervous feeling of wanting him that was creeping up. The way he was looking at her reminded her of the looks he would get when he wanted to make love. There was a time when he didn't care what they were doing or where they were, when he wanted her, all he had to do was give her a look and she knew the meaning behind it. Right now, she was seeing that look and her body responded the way it would have back then. She felt a tingle that spread throughout her body, making sure it pinged in her most intimate places.

"Are you sure I'm not keeping you from anything? I

know it has probably been a long workday for you and you're probably exhausted. I didn't know if you had plans tonight or anything. I know you, Sherice and I have been spending a lot of time together and I hope I'm not taking you away from anything else you would normally be doing if I weren't in town," he said.

She knew what he meant. He was probably thinking she may have plans with Lance later, but she didn't. Seeing Lance was the furthest thing from her mind at the moment. Lance was having big problems with Brian's sudden reappearance in her life, knowing how in love with him she once was.

When she arrived to pick Sherice up from daycare the day before, he wanted to talk to her and when she told him she needed to get Sherice home because her father was stopping by, she could see he was angry about being put off yet again. When he asked her about the depth of her feelings for Brian, she changed the subject and told him nothing was going on and he shouldn't worry. Her response may have ended the conversation, but it didn't put his worrying to rest. She had to lie to him today in order for her to meet Brian at the condo for their talk.

"My evening is free and I agree that we really need to iron this out."

"Before we get started, would you like a drink? I was going to make myself something light for dinner and I didn't want to insinuate that you would want to stick around long enough to join me, but there is plenty if you have the time."

"I love a drink and yes, a light dinner is fine. My mom has Sherice, so I don't have to rush off."

"Good. She tired me out on the playground yesterday

when I stopped by. I am going to make sure that I have a swing set built in my backyard for her."

"I need to think back because I believe her first words were swing and push," Sherry laughed.

"Have a seat while I fix you a drink. A glass of wine?"

"That would be perfect. I don't get to do that often because I never drink when I have Sherice, but there are times when I need something besides apple juice. Every now and then I hang out with Rayven and Candace so that I can finally get a big girl drink."

"I remember them. They came to visit you once and you brought them by my house."

"Yes. We're still as tight as we have always been. They share in godmother duties and spoil Sherice rotten. Say, how is Silas doing? The man who gets the credit for setting us up," she said.

"Silas is good. He's over the Athletics department at Morehouse and he and his wife just had their fourth baby."

"Four? Wow."

"He's got me beat. So far I have one and bringing up the rear."

"You're a great father, Brian. Sherice is one lucky little girl."

"I'm the lucky one. Thank you for her."

"Thank you for her. You know, she was looking for you today. Not long before I left out, a delivery guy rang the bell and she went full on Dada mode, thinking it was you. She grabbed that elephant and ran straight for the door. I told my mom to try and get it from her and wash it tonight."

"Has she ever been to the actual zoo?"

"No, I've been meaning to take her, but life has been

crazy."

"Do you mind if I take her while I'm here. I think she'd love it, especially seeing a real elephant."

"Sure. When do you want to do that?"

Walking back in to join her on the sofa, Brian handed her a glass of wine while he opened his beer.

"What about Sunday after your family gets out of church? I can meet you there and take her with me, if that's okay."

"Sure, that would be fine."

"You can join us if you like. We could take her together," he added. Brian didn't want to assume too much and he also knew she had a life that she had been putting on the side because of him. As much as he wanted her, he wanted to operate on her terms. If what she wanted was Lance, he would have to be okay with it, but if there was a chance that he could spend more time with her, he wanted that."

"Together? Are you sure?"

Sherry knew they were growing close again and that both were obviously avoiding acknowledging it.

"Yes, all of us, together and yes, I'm sure," he said.

"I see you are really settling into the condo. How long do you plan to stay here?"

"Still trying to get rid of me? I guess I'm overstaying my welcome," he said and looked over at her.

Sherry was stunned at how he must have received her comment. She didn't mean that at all.

"No. I like having you around and I know Sherice is loving having you here. I also know you can't stay here forever and eventually you'll leave and go back to your life."

"I don't know, we'll see. Right now, I don't have any plans to go anywhere that doesn't involve my daughter."

Sherry saw a perfect lead into the discussion they needed to have.

"If you want to take Sherice to Atlanta this summer, I'm okay with it. I didn't mean to say you couldn't take her anywhere. I trust you with her and you are her father. She deserves to know who all of her family is. I meant it when I said I was sorry. I don't want to fight about child support or visitation or anything else. As she gets older, I don't want her to have to beg me to see you or not get to be around you, so we need to work this out with you being in Atlanta and me being here in Maryland. We can start with a couple of weeks this summer and you can let me know what holidays you want and of course you get Father's Day weekend."

"Thank you. I'm willing to take the brunt of the travel and I'll fly here as often as I can to visit. Teaching poses a problem during the semester, but I'm thinking of switching to teaching all on-line classes and taking Duron up on his offer to join his firm full-time. That will give me more flexibility to travel and make my own hours for time with Sherice here and in Atlanta. My priorities have changed and everything I do will be based around her from now on. Now, I know we've talked about child support and it got touchy. I know you're your own woman and you can take care of Sherice on your own, but you don't have to because I'm here. I'm more than willing to cover everything for her since you do the day in and day out with her. Financially, I want to be sure she doesn't have a want or need for anything and I will set up a college fund for her. I want to have papers drawn up that leaves everything I have to her in the event something happens to me with you as executor to oversee it. I know you want to buy a house for the two of you and I hope you'll let me help with that. I don't want to control everything; I just want to contribute whatever you want or need. How is that?"

"Wow, you really have thought about this. I don't see anything wrong with what you want to do and I welcome every bit of it. Sherice will be blessed being a Knight and I know that."

"Thank you, Sherry. I didn't come to here for a fight or to mess up your life. Well, actually, I did show up expecting a fight and you gave me one that first time we met, but my sole purpose was to see my daughter and to be a father to her. I know my showing up has been an imposition especially on your relationship with Lance, but I hope he knows I mean no harm."

"Lance understands, at least I think he does. All of this has been so sudden that none of us have had a chance to adjust to it. I'm sure whoever you're involved with would like to have you back in Atlanta and not here for weeks or months dealing with this. Also, I'd like to know who Sherice would be around, though I know you wouldn't be involved with anyone who wasn't of the best caliber. I only want to know who she'll be around besides family, if that's okay with you."

Brian placed his beer on the table and turned to her.

"Sherry, only one of us is in a relationship. There is no one at home waiting for me to return and you don't have to worry about any women being around Sherice. I'm not about that and my time with her in Atlanta will be about me and her and of course letting her get to know her grandparents, uncles, aunts and cousins. They are going to love her."

"I hope I wasn't prying."

"You were, but it's okay because I understand. It's the same question I asked you about Lance. We'll have to figure out a way to adjust."

"When do you think you'd like to take her back to Atlanta with you?"

Brian knew she may have been offering an olive branch as a compromise, but he could still hear worry in her words and he didn't want that. He needed her to trust that he would take good care of Sherice whether in Maryland or back in Atlanta with him and his family. At home, he would have more than enough help with her. He also knew that she still felt that his family had ill-will feelings toward her for keeping Sherice, not just from him, but from them, too. He needed to be more compromising."

He turned toward her.

"I know you have reservations even if you're not telling me, but I know you and I know what inflections in your voice mean, even when your face has a smile. I want to offer a compromise here and let me know what you think. What do you say to my family coming for a visit here in Maryland for a weekend and Sherice can get to meet and be around them all? You'll see that she'll be fine with my family in Atlanta. We can talk about when and how long she can come for a visit after that. If you like, you can fly to Atlanta with us and spend a few days before coming back here. I promise you, she will be okay and I know my family will be on the first thing smoking to Maryland the moment I ask them to come because that's just how my family rolls!" he said cheerfully.

"Do you think they'll be receptive to that?" she asked.

"They can't wait to meet her and to soften the impact of all that has happened, I think they would all love to come here and meet her, especially my mother. She calls me several times a day."

Without thinking, Sherry moved close and threw her arms around Brian's neck. Brian was being more cordial than he had to be considering what she'd done. Having his family in town was an excellent idea. Before she could pull back, she felt Brian's hands come up and circle her waist, holding her in place against him.

Brian knew he was in trouble the moment their bodies touched. She was soft, supple deliciously sexy in his arms. His instantaneous reaction was to embrace her. The moment they realized they were embracing settled over them as he felt her slowly draw back, not out of his arms, but far enough back that they were now eye to eye and a whisper away from each other's lips. He looked first from her eyes, then darted his gaze down to her lips before looking back up into her eyes again. For a quick instant, he saw it. He saw that look that said she loved being in his arms as much as he liked having her there. When she tried to look away, he followed her with his gaze.

"Don't," he whispered. "Don't look away."

Sherry gulped at the intensity of his stare. His eyes were filled with so much love for her that it was almost too overwhelming to look into them. Too much time had passed since she'd felt this kind of attraction to any man and so far, the only man who has ever had her feeling this way was holding her in his arms.

"Brian," was all she could get out.

"Brian, what? I'm sorry, but I can't help that you still have the same impact on me that you had years ago. I can't just turn it off, though I know I should."

"Do you want to?" she asked.

"No," he said without taking a breath to think about it. "Do you want me to?" he asked and quietly held his breath waiting for her to reject him once again as she had done on the few occasions when his traitorous body couldn't deny his want for her.

Sherry tried to look away and he pulled her gaze back to him with a slight movement of his fingers on her chin.

"I don't know what I want."

"Of course, you do, Sherry. What you don't want to do is admit what it is that you want. I'm not trying to push you or get you to say or do anything you don't want to, but if there is a moment for honesty, it's right now. Do you want me to turn off my feelings for you? I didn't come here for this, for you, but just like when we first met, I feel connected to you and I can't seem to shake it."

She wanted him and she no longer wanted to fight it.

"No, Brian, I don't. I've been fighting an attraction to you again since the moment you arrived in Maryland. I know I don't deserve to have you still looking at me the way I remember with so much passion and desire, but I can't help that I never lost my desire for you even after I walked away. That kiss we shared the other night wasn't something casual, but meaningful. It was nature's way of telling me that there is still something between us. I had too much pride to allow myself to admit I made a mistake even though deep down, I knew I did even then. Since you've been here, I can't seem to focus on anything other than the fact that you're here and now that I know that I was so very wrong about you, I'm able to admit that I still want you. I still want you, Brian."

Brian smiled knowing those words were music to his ears. Knowing that what they shared had never really died, his heart and his body leaped for joy. When they had found each other at that football game, he thought he had finally found what he needed and looked to a future with her. Now that she was standing in front of him again and admitting that she still felt something for him, he wanted to live in the moment.

"You and Sherice are mine. I'm not talking about property as if you don't have a right to do you. I'm talking about in my life, in my love and in my heart. You both are there and not just Sherice. I don't have to convince you that I still have feelings for you. I think you already know it and I know you feel it being this close to me."

Brian was right. She knew he still had love for her in his heart and no longer buried deep was the love she still carried for him like a hot, burning torch.

Brian felt her tremble and he smiled a seductive smile that let her know he knew what she wanted because he wanted the same thing. Could he really cross that line with her again, especially knowing she was involved with someone else? That reality settled in and he closed his eyes and exhaled, working to get his body and mind in check.

"I'm sorry. What am I doing? I know I've had a few times around you when I couldn't seem to control myself, but I don't want to mess up the equal ground we now stand on by confusing it with what my body wants.

'No, no!' Sherry shouted in her head. She didn't want him to pull away from her again. She didn't want any rejection from either of them. She wanted truth, honesty and most of all, she wanted him. This was the one and only man she'd ever loved and that love still ran deep. No more would she be a participant waiting for someone to lead. She knew what she wanted.

"Kiss me, Brian. Please?" she all but begged. "I know what I'm saying, I know what it means and I know what I want. Kiss me."

"Sherry, there is no turning back from this at this point if we cross that line. I'm not talking about this being some booty call or me scratching an itch. This isn't even about you being unfaithful to Lance, though I couldn't give two shakes about that. I wouldn't want another man making love to my woman when that's my job. I don't want to just kiss you. I want to make love to you and if we do that, you can't go between Lance and I. I won't be able to handle that. I can't and I won't share you. I don't know what could be in store for us, but it won't be a one-night stand," he offered.

Brian knew he was now in a fight for his happiness. He came for is daughter, but fell in love again and the time for denying that was over. He wanted her and he wanted all of her.

"Brian, I know it's been a long time, but I am that same Sherry you knew years ago, especially when it comes to what I share with a man. I told you back then that you were the only man that I had ever been with when I gave you my virginity. I'm no longer a virgin, of course, but I've also never been intimate with another man since you. Lance and I have never taken that step, nor have I with any other man, except you."

He did pull back then, surprised to hear that she still had only been intimate with him. No other man had entered her body, but him, knowing her on that level of intimacy? That thought played with his mind.

"Are you telling me, in over two years, you've never been with another man in any intimate fashion or just intercourse?"

"No fashion at all; nothing. I've dated, but nothing on that level. I've been focused on Sherice and struggling with a love for you that I've never been able to get over. Because of that, I haven't thought of making love with anyone else. All I can see when I think of making love is you."

Sherry was about to say more when Brian pulled her to him and captured her mouth in a deep penetrating kiss. He didn't want to focus on any pretense of gently nipping or stroking her lips, he went in deep, relishing in the feel and taste of her. His body was harder than he'd ever known it to be knowing that in his arms, he held the one and only woman he'd ever loved, who'd given him a child he loved deeply and who had never let another man touch her in an intimate way. While his mind tried to process all that, he followed his instinct of how much he wanted to make love to her. In his mind, she was his and always would be his. Tonight, he would make sure she knew it too.

Still kissing her madly and passionately, he stood, pulling her up with him, reached for her luscious behind and pulled her up until her legs circled around his waist. His hands caressed her ample behind and back and forth across her legs as he tried to deal with the fact that he had her in his arms and she kissed him wildly like she had been waiting on it her whole life. They needed and wanted each other equally and he had every plan to make sure that need and want was satisfied.

He leaned in close to her ear as he walked with her in his arms.

"Spend the night with me."

Sherry didn't have a doubt of what her answer would be.

"Grab my phone so that I can call my mother."

Brian walked over to her purse, handed it to her and after a brief conversation, they turned their attention back to each other and picked up where they had left off before the phone call.

Sherry was in heaven and never wanted to come down. The feel of Brian taking her lips and possessing them, owning them, letting her know how much he desired her. She'd practically begged for the kiss and was getting so much more. Their tongues fought for control as she tried to climb deeper into his mouth doing whatever she needed to do to make them one. She felt his hands caressing her and she remembered the many ways those hands had pleasured her in the past. She was ready for her past and present to cross paths.

CHAPTER 16

Brian walked with Sherry in his arms until they were standing in the center of the room in front one of the large glass windows that overlooked the now darkened sky. Thankfully they were up high enough that no one would be able to see in. He released her lips and nuzzled her neck, planting soft kisses all around it. She held her head back giving him the access he wanted.

"Don't you want to find a bed?" she asked, breathlessly.

"No. I want you right here, right now. We'll find a bed later. For now, I need you naked and I don't think I can make it to a bed on my weak legs, weakened by the anxiety of having you in my arms. I need to make love to you with nothing around us, but the sight of this beautiful skyline. I don't want to stop long enough to find a bed and then find out this is all a dream. I want you right now."

No longer needing to talk, Sherry aggressively took his lips this time and didn't hesitate to demand entrance into his mouth. When he opened for her, she went mad searching out his tongue, using her hands to hold on to his face making sure he didn't pull away. She was mad with a thirst for him that only he could cause in her. When she finally pulled back, they were both out of breath, gasping to gather air into their lungs.

"Does that feel like a dream?" she asked.

"No, and neither do you."

Before another word was spoken, Brian lowered her to the floor, making sure he slid her down over his rock-hard erection that was barely contained in his jeans. If he didn't soon get them off, he knew his flesh would burst through the zipper.

"I want you," she whispered.

"Are you sure? I told you there's no turning back from this. If you give yourself to me, you're done with Lance. I'm sorry for the guy, but there can't be a him and me; there can only be me. Do you understand what that means? I don't sneak around and I don't share. You're mine, sweetheart. Mine."

"Yes, I understand," she said looking up at him. She would deal with that later. For now, she wanted and needed him and he was taking too long joining their bodies. It had been too long for her, though she knew he hadn't waited that long and had been with other women. She remembered his appetite for sex and he wanted it often and every time he reached for her, she went into his arms willingly as she was about to do.

Without second guessing, she reached up and untied the knot in her shirt and slide it down her arms. Never taking her eyes from his, she reached down and pulled her tank top up over her head and off, tossing it to the chair.

Brian could see that Sherry knew without a doubt what she wanted and it wasn't anything less than what he wanted. He took his t-shirt off throwing it somewhere behind him. Earlier, he'd slipped his jeans on without anything else underneath of them, so when he carefully unzipped them and slid them down his legs, he crouched before her naked, painfully hard and ready.

She smiled when she saw how ready he was for her. She remembered that unlike some men, Brian was hard in an instant and stayed that way until he knew she couldn't take any more of his lovemaking. After giving her a rest, she would turn to him again and again to be loved like there was no one else in the world, but the two of them, just like now.

"I never forgot how gorgeous your body is naked. I have missed this body," she said reaching out to caress first his muscled chest, gliding her hands across his hot flesh before sliding them down and caressing his pronounced abs. When her hand slipped to slide over his massive hardness, she heard his breath catch as the first essence of his need for her slipped out, wet and silky just for her. Looking deeply in his eyes, she used her finger to smear the slippery essence across the head of his manhood and watched as the vein in his neck nearly popped as he tried to hold back his desire.

"Damn woman!" he uttered between clinched teeth.

"Yes, I remember this body very well and it appears it remembers me, too."

"Baby, my mind and my body have never forgotten you."

As much as she was enjoying the floor, she wanted to be on the long chair that rested against the window. She stood, pulling him up with her and when he stood to his full height, she gave him a little push and he fell back onto the soft chair. Knowing her intent, Brian reached over and grabbed the towel he'd left on the chair after his shower earlier and placed it under his hips. He didn't want to mess up the chair with what was coming next.

Gripping his manhood in his hand and stroking it lightly, he watched as Sherry did a little striptease for him removing first her pants and then sliding her lacy black, barely-there thong down her sexy, toned legs.

"You're killing me, Sherry. Come here baby," he stuttered out. Brian knew he was barely containing his desire to get inside of her. He'd never wanted anything more in his life. When she went to reach for the back clasp of her bra, he stopped her. That was something he wanted to do. He remembered how much he loved her breasts and every chance he got, he loved on them as much as he loved on every other part of her body.

Sherry walked over and slid down until she sat astride his lap with her legs straddling both of his, opening up her womanhood to that part of him she could barely wait to feel.

Brian pulled her to him by putting his hand behind her head and drawing her face to his until their lips once again touched. This time their mouths mated slowly as their heads tossed from side to side pulling everything they needed from each other. As they kissed, he reached behind her and unsnapped her bra, letting the cups fall away as her large mounds fell into the palm of his hands. Sherry sighed into his mouth as he caressed them and then lightly pinched the nipples the way he remembered she would beg him to do. He knew she was ready for him the moment her hips began to grind on him. His erection laid hard and ready between them, pulsing with the need to connect their bodies intimately.

Ending the kiss, he leaned his head down and captured

one nipple in his mouth, sliding it around in his mouth until it pebbled to a hard tip. He moved his head to the other nipple as Sherry softly caressed the sides of his head, holding him in place at her chest. Little did she know, he had no plans of ever moving. He reached between them to stroke her sensitive nub and the first contact of his finger to her slippery entrance caused her to sigh even louder as her head fell back in pure enjoyment.

"Yes," she moaned out as her hips gyrated with a life of their own. "I've missed this."

"I've missed you," he said right before he slid first one finger and then two into her. She was so wet for him, her essence ran down his fingers and coated his hand. She was more than ready for him.

"I need you inside me, Brian."

"I need you to come for me first baby. I need to feel you come apart in my arms. I want to see that look on your face as you fly high. Come on, give it to me," he said, increasing the pressure his finger placed on her nub as two other fingers slid in and out of her as the sound of his fingers coming in contact with her wetness edged them both on. He loved making love to her in the quietness of a room. Some people loved music, but the only music he wanted to hear was the sound of her screaming out her pleasure, which was coming soon.

This was exactly what she needed and exactly what she'd been missing. She was luxuriating in the feel of him when he added a quick bite on her nipple and the barrage of him touching all of her pressure points sent her careening over the edge as her orgasm ripped through her causing her to scream loudly and move her hips on him faster and faster.

Brian smiled as he watched the one and only woman he'd ever loved come apart for him the way he always loved to enjoy. This is what he needed; it's what he wanted. As her body began to settle, he slid her closer to join their bodies. Taking her lips in a kiss that was meant to prepare her for his entry into her body, he lifted her until the head of his penis was at the entrance to her body.

"Look at me, Sherry."

Sherry opened her eyes, though they were heavy from the aftermath of her climax and when she did, she kept her eyes on his as he lowered her slowly onto his flesh, inch by delicious inch. Remembering how long and thick he was, she let him ease into her body and pull out, so that he worked his way inside slowly. She was truthful when she said she hadn't been with another man since him and the tightness of her body was a clear sign that it was fact.

"You are so tight, baby," Brian said through gritted teeth. Even with her body's juices from her orgasm putting ease on his entrance into her, she still gripped him tightly so he had to go slow to not cause her any discomfort.

Going in and out of her body had him restraining himself to keep from slamming into her. He couldn't remember ever feeling this good about making love to a woman since her and if it were up to him, there would never be another woman after her. Finally pulling her up slightly, he slid her all the way down until he was deeply imbedded inside of her. He leaned his head on her chest loving the feel of her body holding tightly onto his.

"I need to move," she said when the feeling overwhelmed her of him hard and powerful vibrating inside of her.

Brian braced his feet on the floor, slid down a little

further on the chair and set a pace for their lovemaking. When the slowness at first didn't work for them, he increased the pace as their lips joined with tongues mimicking the lovemaking that was happening where their bodies were joined below. Breathing hard into her mouth he could feel Sherry as her body once again set out to claim her next orgasm. She increased her thrusts down as he increased his thrusts up into her. Their hearts raced and their breaths quickened. He gripped her hips and held on as she danced on him, taking and giving at the same time. He could feel each time he slid out of her body, not quite all the way, when she gripped him tight with her muscles and each time she pulled more and more from him.

Now they were at a pace that let him know she wasn't far from letting go. He loved watching her as she gave her entire being over to their passion and before long, her face tightened, her neck strained and she shot off another powerful orgasm. Hers triggered his and he held on to her hips tightly to keep her from falling to the floor as he groaned and growled through his own powerful release.

"Yes, baby, yes!" he screamed.

"Brian!" Sherry screamed, not being able to hold her cries of pleasure back. She felt tears as they pooled in her eyes and slid down her cheeks. No one has ever made her feel the way he has and she couldn't believe she would ever walk away from him. She would never do it again; never.

As their bodies cooled, Brian leaned back and pulled Sherry with him, letting their heart beats return to normal and the reality of the fact that they'd just made love settle over them. He held her close in his arms as he felt her lay her head on his shoulder.

"I never stopped loving you," she said quietly in his ear.

"Never."

"I love you," Brian admitted, knowing as much as he came to Baltimore not wanting to still love her, he couldn't deny that he did, he always had and he always would, even after all the hurt. That hurt no longer mattered. He had his daughter and hopefully, he had Sherry back where she belonged all the time; with him.

CHAPTER 17

Brian woke disoriented trying to focus on where he was. When he shifted, next to him Sherry moved and he smiled, glad that the night before hadn't been a dream. Lying next to him was the sweetest sight he'd ever seen. Sherry was just waking up, stretching and yawning like a cat. He snuggled up close to her back and embraced her body as she continued to bring herself awake.

"Good morning beautiful," he whispered in her ear before licking and then kissing her earlobe.

"Mmmm, it's morning already?" she asked.

"It's early, but yeah it's morning and unlike me, I do believe you need to get to work this morning, unless you're taking the day off to stay in bed with me."

Brian pulled her back toward him, flush against his already aroused body. He laughed when Sherry yawned and then groaned.

"What's wrong?" he asked.

"I am going to be toast at work today. I hope I can get things done that are on my to-do list. Right now, all I want to do is sleep."

"Well, you had a busy night," he chuckled.

"Yeah, I guess it had something to do with the many times we made love over and over, all night long."

"True, very true, but I couldn't seem to get enough of you. I tried to sleep and let you sleep, but my body wouldn't let me and having you lying next to me naked, dreams of getting in you teased me beyond my ability to stay asleep. How many times did we make love?"

Sherry turned around in his arms and moved even closer into the crook of his neck.

"Too many times to count."

There was one thing they needed to talk about, yet he wasn't sure how to approach the topic. It needed to be done.

"As much as I loved making love to you over and over and over and I'd love to do it again before we leave this bed, but we have a problem," he said with a guarded tone.

Sherry stiffened hearing him say the word problem and wondered if in the light of day, he realized he'd made a mistake. She didn't move and refused to look in his eyes afraid of what she would see.

"Sherry, did you hear me."

"It depends on what you mean by problem. Are you now regretting last night?" she asked, still speaking into his neck, not looking at him.

"Baby, I would never, ever regret making love to you. I meant it when I said I still loved you and that hasn't changed in the light of day. Is that what you think I meant?" he asked moving back so that he could see her face.

"I don't know what you meant."

"Well, that's not it at all, but yeah, we have a problem. Look at me please," he said.

When she looked up at him, his heart raced with how much he loved her. Even early in the morning after sleeping and making love, passionate and sometimes wild love, she still looked incredibly lovely.

"What's wrong?"

"We didn't use protection last night. Now, I admit I don't have any because I didn't come to Baltimore with a plan to make love to you or sleep with any other woman, so it wasn't on my agenda to have any on hand. Are you on birth control of any kind?" he asked.

A moment of horror overcame her. It wasn't a horrible thought that she could get pregnant by Brian, but for her to be careless knowing what they are already going through with Sherice and child support and visitation was beyond her. The last thing Brian needed was another child he would be living states away from. She sat straight up in bed.

"When I told you I haven't been intimate with any man since you, that was the truth and because I haven't been or even considering being intimate with anyone, I'm not on any kind of birth control. That wasn't really smart of either one of us was it considering what we're already dealing with."

"I don't want either of us to worry about this and if you turn out to be pregnant, we'll deal with it and this time, better than we did the first time," he said reassuring her.

Sherry exhaled knowing that even if she was pregnant, there was no reason to be worried about a situation neither of them could now control.

"I think we're fine."

Brian pulled her back into his embrace, seeing the terrified look on her face.

"Let's not worry about that, but if you are pregnant, promise me you'll let me know."

"I promise. No more repeats of the past."

"Okay, so that I don't have to find myself abstaining around you, I'll pick up some condoms to keep them on hand just in case we find ourselves in this situation again."

Sherry smiled and planted a soft kiss on his lips.

"I'd say let's do that because if you abstain, that means I would have to abstain and I don't know about you, but I don't want to do that. I feel a part of you that's already wide awake and ready and apparently in agreement with me when I say no abstaining."

"Baby, trust, you don't need to convince me. Let's not play Russian roulette and we need to get up and get some clothes on before I jump in you again," he laughed.

"Okay, okay."

Brian got up out of the bed that they eventually made their way to the night before. After making love the first time on the sofa, he picked her up and they then found their way to the bedroom where they made love again. After that second time, he got up to find a meal for them in the kitchen, coming back with the salad and salmon filets that he was able to quickly nuke in the microwave.

"You never did tell me what your mother said when you told her you were spending the night with me?"

"She said it was about time. She was the first person to tell me how wrong I was to leave you and then to not tell you about Sherice. A mother knows and she knew that I never stopped loving you. She told me to have a good time and that they'd take Sherice to school this morning. I'm happy about that because looking at the time, I'll have just enough time to get home, change and get to work by eight.

I'm sure I'll be a zombie walking around there. I need to go home after work and get some sleep, but I'm sure Sherice will want to take a trip to the playground. I forgot I need to finish an assignment for my class when I get off."

"How much longer before you graduate?"

"I'll be done next spring."

"Congratulations to you for continuing with your education. I know it can't be easy raising Sherice, working and going to school."

"Well, thankfully my parents have been a great help."

After slipping on pajama bottoms he pulled from the dresser, he came around to her side of the bed.

"Let me help you out today. Why don't I pick Sherice up today and keep her busy, so that you can finish your assignment and maybe get in an afternoon nap. Can you add me to the drop-off and pickup list at daycare?"

"Of course, I should have done that already. I'll call them when I get to work and give them your information like name, address and phone number. Do you still live in the same house?"

"Yes. You need me to write it down for you?" he asked.

"No, I still know it, even if I haven't used it in a long time."

Sherry wished she could take the words back the minute they left her mouth. She wasn't sure she'd ever get over the guilt she felt over what she'd done. Her life with him was so perfect back then and last night, they had once again come as close to perfection as they could. They always were in-sync and it as clear they still were and not just when it came to making love.

Brian saw the look of horror on Sherry's face.

"Listen, I think we need to agree to leave the past in the

past. I admit, I showed up here angrier than I have ever been in my life, but after seeing Sherice and you, I've let it go and decided that all we can do is move forward and not look back. I promise you, it's okay."

Sherry smiled and shook her head.

"Okay, so by the time you're ready to pick Sherice up, they'll have your information on file and from now on, you'll be able to stop in, spend the day if you like and pick her up. It's getting late and I need to get home to change and get to work. Do you mind if I take a quick shower?"

"Go ahead. There are fresh towels in the linen closet in the bathroom. Would you like some company in the shower"?

Sherry smiled wanting that very much even though she felt a soreness she hadn't expected. After a night of their amorous activities, she should have expected it. Brian loved and made love deeply and passionately and she remembered a time when she walked around for days feeling as if he were still deeply planted inside of her.

"I would, but remember, no condoms within reach and I have no doubt neither of us will be able to maintain any self-control. Can I get a raincheck?"

"Anytime baby, anytime."

Sherry got up and walked toward the bathroom, not shy about the fact that she was completely naked. She stopped at the bathroom entrance and turned back to Brian who was ogling her from across the room.

"I'm serious, Sherry, get your fine ass in the shower before I tackle you back down on that bed. A brother can hold on to his control only temporarily when he's looking at you and that sexy body."

"Well, I was wondering if you'd like to join me and

maybe engage in a few things that don't require a condom."

Before he had a chance to answer her, she winked, laughed and switched her ass that made him melt every time he saw it. Knowing what her compromise meant, he quickly removed the pajama pants he'd put on and followed her into the bathroom with plans to make it fulfilling yet quick so that she made it to work on time. Quick didn't mean he wasn't thorough. Thorough was his middle name.

**

"What's up Brian," Xavier said as soon as he answered the phone.

"Not much. I'm about to get some work done before picking Sherice up from daycare later on."

"So, things improved after your last conversation with her?"

Things had changed in a positive way and better than he could have imagined.

"We talked it out and she agreed that she spoke in anger and that I should have just as much access to Sherice as she does. She no longer wants to fight or argue. She's making no demands at all."

"Does that mean you don't want to proceed with the court proceeding?"

"No, I still do, but I want to make a change. I still want to make sure Sherry is given money to take care of Sherice and I also want to file papers to make Sherice and Sherry beneficiaries on my policies and to also add Sherice to my health insurance. I want to lighten Sherry's burden so that she's not doing everything by herself even though she lives with her parents. I also want to be sure Sherice's daycare costs are paid directly from my bank account each week."

"Wow, things really have changed. At first, she didn't want anything from you. What changed her mind?"

"It wasn't really a change of mind. This is what I'm offering her and I've already told her that I plan to take care of my daughter and that she shouldn't fight me and let me do this."

"That's good to hear."

"Yeah, we also spent the night together."

When Xavier didn't respond, he wasn't sure if his reaction was positive or negative.

"Does that mean that you're working things out?"

"I don't know what it means, but I do know that my priority is still Sherice and making sure she's taken care of and whatever happens with Sherry will just happen. I admit I still love her just as much as I always have, but we're going to have to tread lightly. When I got here she was dating someone and though it wasn't serious, he's still there. Things are happening fast and I know I want her, but the ball is in her court when it comes to what's next for us."

"What about Sherice visiting you in Atlanta? Have you worked that out?"

"Yeah, she told me she wouldn't fight me about taking Sherice to Atlanta later this summer. I'm actually hoping things will progress between us and we'll find a way to work out our co-parenting and relationship at the same time."

"Do you frat! I'm glad to hear that this won't have to get ugly in court. It's always best to keep the courts out of your personal business, if possible. I'll draw up the papers and throw in a few other things I think the two of you need to consider and get them to you in a few days. How are you enjoying the condo?"

"This place is great. Are you sure I'm good staying here a while longer? I don't want to overstay my welcome."

"I'm sure. We have several condos in that building, so if we needed one for a guest, that's covered. Stay as long as you need to. Saturday the local fraternity chapter is having a fundraiser bull roast. My brother who is now a frat as well is one of the even coordinators and I promised I would show up. If you're up to it, you should come hang and meet some of the brothers you don't know from this area."

"That works for me."

"Cool. I'll text you the address to meet me there. I've already paid for a full table, so I have your ticket."

"That works. I'll see you then."

"Good and I'll bring the papers you and Sherry need to read over and get back to me and I'll have them filed. Since you're both agreeing, there won't be a need to be in front of a judge. It's more of a formality."

"Cool frat. I appreciate all the help. I'll see you Saturday."

"Anytime and let me just say this, when you and Sherry get married, make sure I get an invitation."

"Whoa, I didn't say anything about marriage."

"Brian, I remember how in love with this woman you were years ago. I'm already claiming marriage and five or six more children in your future."

Brian choked and laughed at the same time at that visual.

"X, it's too early in the morning for you to be drinking. Lay off the sauce, buddy and see someone about that fantasy you're spitting out!"

"Remember, I claimed it first!" Xavier said before

hanging up.

CHAPTER 18

Lance checked the time and wondered what was keeping Sherry. Usually she picked Sherice up between four-thirty and five o'clock every day and he waited around specifically to talk to her. He'd gone by her house the night before to talk to her and noticed her car was gone. He waited until he'd actually fallen asleep in his car. When he snapped awake, he looked at the time and once he saw it was after midnight, he knew she wasn't coming home. He wondered where she could have been at that late hour, especially during the work week. Ever since Brian showed up, things between the two of them had not been the same.

Sherry appeared more preoccupied than usual and now that she allowed Brian to see and spend time with Sherice, she was more sidetracked. This morning, he arrived earlier than usual to try and catch her when she dropped Sherice off. To his surprise, her mother dropped Sherice off. He could feel her slipping away from him and if the night before was any example, he had a feeling she hadn't been home because she was somewhere with Brian. He didn't have a clue as to where Brian was staying or he would have driven by there looking for her car. He considered following him the night he met him at Sherry's house, but he lost him in the heavy traffic going into downtown Baltimore.

Today, he was hoping to catch her so that they could talk and find their vibe again. He wanted to take their relationship to the next level and wanted to see if she wanted to go away for a weekend with him on a romantic trip. They could use some time away.

Lance checked the time again just as he looked up and saw Brian coming through the door of the daycare.

"Brian, right?" he asked walking up to him at the door.

"Yes," Brian said shaking the hand Lance had extended to him.

"I don't know if you remember me. I'm Lance Solomon, Sherry's boyfriend."

"Yes, I remember you. How are you Lance?"

"I'm good. I was actually wondering what happened to Sherry. She usually picks Sherice up by now."

"Yeah, she asked me to pick her up today and said not to pick her up until four-forty-five. I've been sitting outside in my car waiting to sign Sherice out."

"Is Sherry okay? Is she ill?" Lance asked.

"No, I'm going to take Sherice and spend some time with her to give Sherry a little break and time to work on an overdue class assignment."

"Right, right," Lance said.

Brian still didn't like him. He was rubbing him the wrong way and sensed that Lance was insecure. Little did he know he had reason to be. After the night he and Sherry spent together, whatever the two of them had was pretty much over. He would let Sherry handle that conversation while he kept his distance.

Before Sherry left to go home and dress for work, they talked briefly about Lance and what should happen next. She told him she needed to find the right time to apologize to Lance and let him know that they wouldn't be seeing each other anymore. She told him that Lance had already professed his love for her, though she never returned the sentiment. She liked Lance, but she wasn't in love with him.

Brian knew it wasn't his place to get in between the two of them, so he agreed to let her handle it. He hoped he wouldn't have to step in and aid in a more permanent separation between the two of them. He meant what he said when he told her he wouldn't share her with Lance and if they were going to try and see if they would work as a couple again, she needed to be free and clear of Lance and she agreed.

"Do you know if Sherice is ready?" Brian asked.

"Oh, I'm sure she is. She's in the first classroom on the left. You'll have to stop at the desk and provide identification so that they can be sure you have permission to pick her up. Did Sherry add you to her contact card already?" Lance asked.

"She was going to do that when she got to work this morning. I'm sure they have my information by now."

The word morning got Lance's attention.

"You talked to Sherry this morning? I've been trying to reach her since last night after I stopped by her house and she wasn't home. It was pretty late and I was surprised to see that her car wasn't there and it really was a late hour."

Lance was digging and he wasn't falling for it. It wasn't his place to shed some light on what was happening.

Sherry needed to do it and he would keep his distance.

"Yeah, she called me this morning. I think she said something about meetings most of the day and told me she would call in my contact information and I just needed to present my license."

"Right, Sherice does have your last name, so that shouldn't be a problem."

"She is my daughter, so yeah, she has my last name."

"Well, don't let me keep you from picking up your daughter. I'll give Sherry a call to be sure she's doing okay. It was nice to see you again, Brian."

"Likewise," Brian said before walking in the direction of the receptionist. Lance rubbed him the wrong way and he had a feeling the conversation Sherry needed to have with him wasn't going to go well. He would let Sherry handle it until she said she needed his help.

As soon as he showed his identification to the receptionist, she allowed him to go in the room to pick up Sherice where he found her sitting at a table with two other children and when she saw him, she dropped everything, stood and ran to him with the speed of light, as fast as her little legs would carry her. He had to think quick when she leaped at him and threw her chubby arms around his neck, holding on to him tightly.

"Dada, dada, dada," she repeated over and over as if she were trying to make sure he was real.

"Hi, baby. Dada missed you."

"Love you, Dada," she said gleefully.

"Dada loves you, too and he's here to take you with him. Do you like that? Ready to go bye-bye?"

Her head bounced up and down so hard her long plats swung around in the air with yellow bows swinging left and right.

"Okay, well you have to stand on the floor so that Dada can pick up the rest of your things. Mommy told me not to leave without your bag. Let's walk over to your cubby and get it okay?"

Sherice didn't answer. She took him by the hand, gripping his fingers tight and walked him to her cubby where her jacket and bag were. Her teacher walked up to them.

"Well, Sherice, it looks like you have a visitor. Who is this?" she asked her.

Sherice looked up at him and then back at the teacher.

"Hello, I'm Brian Knight, Sherice's father."

"Hello, Mr. Knight. I'm Ms. Cross, one of the classroom aides for Sherice's age group. It's nice to meet you. Sherice has been telling the class about her Dada. It's nice to finally meet you. I got word that you would be here to pick her up today."

"Yes, her mother needs some time to finish an assignment, so I'm going to take Sherice with me for some fun daddy and daughter time."

"Well, it was nice to meet you."

She leaned down to speak directly to Sherice.

"I'll see you tomorrow and make sure you bring your daddy back to visit again, okay?"

"Dada," she replied and smiled.

Brian picked up her jacket and bag and then he picked up Sherice who couldn't wait to get up in his arms. She wrapped her arms around his neck again and laid her head on his shoulder. The love he had for his daughter was unmatched to anything in this world. She was his everything.

"Let's go to Dada's place and get some dinner. I bought a few new books for you that I can read to you. Would you like that?"

Brian kissed her cheek as they walked out the door. As he headed toward the door, he was able to catch another glimpse of Lance staring at him, acting as if he were reading a piece of paper that to him appeared to be upside down. The vibe he was getting wasn't a good one. Lance was going to be trouble.

**

"D, how is everything back in Atlanta?"

"Bro, I've been waiting to hear from you. Everything here is going great. What's happening in Baltimore?" Duron asked.

"Well, my daughter and I were about to watch Frozen and eat some chicken fingers and carrots."

He heard Duron laugh on the other end.

"Are you telling me you're eating chicken fingers and carrots? I need to meet my niece. She's working wonders on you, big brother."

"Don't laugh too hard. Remember, I've seen and heard you talk in gibberish to your kids, so don't act like you can't relate."

"Oh, I can relate. It's a great feeling, isn't it?"

"Man, it's the best feeling in the world especially when she walks around saying Dada all the time. I love it! Listen, I was calling to run something by you. I'm planning on bringing Sherice back to Atlanta to visit for a few weeks this summer, but before that, Sherry and I would like for you guys to come meet Sherice here in Maryland. I know it's asking a lot and everyone probably won't make it, but whoever can, I would appreciate it. I don't want to spring everyone on Sherice at once in Atlanta away from everyone she knows here. I'm hoping to let her get comfortable with the family beforehand. Sherry and I are trying to take things slow, but you and I both know that I'm going to have to return home soon and my plan is to bring Sherice before classes start back up at the end of the summer. What do you say?" Brian asked.

"Are you kidding? You think there's an option here? Of course, we'll be there. Taija will be excited about it and she's been asking me every day if I've heard from you and when will she get to meet Sherice. I'm looking forward to it and we'll be there with the kids whenever you say. Make sure you call Loren and Mike, too. I'm sure they'll want to come from California. Have you talked to mom and dad yet?" Duron asked.

"Sherry wants to call them herself. She feels the need to apologize for all that's happened, though I've told her mom won't expect that, but she insists. She wants to invite her and Pop here herself. I'm going to invite Tyrone and Victoria too since they're considered family."

"I think that's a great idea and hopefully they'll be back from their honeymoon. They stayed in town a few days after the reception and then they were heading off for a three-week excursion. I'll check to see when they're coming back. You know mom has been making herself crazy worrying about you and how things are going in Baltimore."

"I know and I'm hoping a visit here will ease her mind and let her know that everything is okay."

"Is everything okay and I'm not just talking about with Sherice. What about things between you and Sherry?"

Brian didn't know how much he wanted to share yet

until he knew for sure where things were going. For now, he'd wait it out and not be too presumptuous about where he thinks they are headed. They needed time to talk and see how anything between them would play out. They've been on this road before and he wanted he to be sure about what she wanted and didn't want her decision to be based on Sherice, but on the two of them.

"Things are fine. We're getting along and it looks like we'll be able to avoid court and a judge, though I am filing legal papers adding me to Sherice's birth certificate and making sure if anything happens to me, she'll be taken care of. I still love her and she still loves me, something we've both discovered in my time here."

"I knew you were and I'm glad that you were able to work some things out. I won't tell you to be cautious about how you proceed because I know how much you have always loved her. Just make sure whatever steps you're taking with Sherry are separate from those you're taking for Sherice."

"I hear you and believe me, I have never stopped loving her and having Sherice has added to that."

"I can understand that and you know now that we know about her, she will forever be taken care of by this family, especially if anything happens to you, though I'm planning on you living forever."

"From your mouth to God's ears," Brian added.

"It's good to hear the happiness in your voice."

"I couldn't be happier than I am right now. I better get off of here. Sherice took a nap after daycare and she's waking up. I'll talk to you tomorrow and I'll have party details for you soon."

"No problem. We'll take the company jet to Baltimore

since we'll be traveling with the twins. I'm glad things are working out good. I know you left here on edge."

"It was a rocky start, but things have calmed down lately and getting much better. Thanks for the support D."

"You know I got your back always. Make sure you tell Xavier I said hello. I hope to catch up with him while I'm there."

"I plan to invite him when the family comes, so I'm sure you'll get a chance to catch up."

"Good. Kiss my niece for me."

"You got that."

Brian hung up and went in search of Sherice. He could hear her calling for him in the monitor he'd placed on the kitchen counter after putting her down for a nap.

"Dada is here," he said walking in the bedroom and picking her up as she reached her arms up to him.

"Mommy?" she asked.

"Mommy is at your house doing some work while you visit with me here. She'll be here in a little while to get you. Let's get you changed and find some food. Ready to eat?"

"Eat," Sherice said and he smiled when she showed him her pearly whites.

"Well, I have some chicken fingers and carrots for you to eat and we can read a book after that. Let's call mommy on the phone so you can say hello before you eat."

Brian dialed Sherry and hoped he wouldn't wake her up if she was sleeping.

"Hello?"

"Sherry, it's Brian. Were you sleeping?"

"No, I just finished my assignment for my class. How is Sherice doing?"

"She took a little nap and woke up asking for you. Here

talk to her."

Brian listened to Sherice's side of the conversation and smiled at the number of times she said Dada. When she was done, she gave the phone back to him."

"Well, that was entertaining," he said.

"Yeah, it was on this end, too. I asked her if she was ready to come home with me and she said no. I guess that means she's having a good time."

"I think she is. What about you? How is your evening going?"

"Well, besides being a little sore, I'm doing pretty good."

"Sore? Don't tell me it's because of what I think."

"Oh yeah. You know how intense our lovemaking can be and last night and well into this morning, we both were extra excited."

"I hope the soreness wears off soon. I'm sorry about that, but I couldn't seem to get enough of you. I should have pulled back some knowing it had been a long time since you've been that active."

"It's okay, I don't mind at all. The soreness reminds me of the incredible night we had together."

"Did you get a nap in at all?"

"No. I wasn't as tired as I thought I would be when I got off, but I did get my assignment done."

"Do you want me to bring Sherice home or do you want to come get her? I don't have a problem bringing her to you even though you said you would come get her."

"No, I'll come get her. I need to go out to pick up a few things for her. Sometimes shopping with her can be challenging when she sees everything she wants and I'm constantly telling her no."

Brian laughed. His daughter has his persistent spirit.

"Okay, well we'll be here at the condo. I'm about to give her dinner and we're going to read."

"Thanks Brian, I'll see you in a few. I hear you ran into Lance today."

"Yeah, he approached me when I came in the door. I take it you've talked to him? What have you decided to do?"

"Well, he called me and I told him we needed to talk. He wanted to do it tonight, but I told him I was tired. I plan to talk to him tomorrow to try and explain that he and I can't see each other anymore."

"Are you sure you don't want me there with you? The guy creeped me out today and I don't want him flaking out on you."

"Lance is harmless. He'll be upset, but I'm sure it'll be fine."

"If you're sure then I'll leave it alone, but I get a vibe from him that's unsettling."

"Don't worry okay? I'll handle this and it will be fine."

"Okay, I'll drop it. Say, is there a problem if I want you and Sherice to spend the night with me? I know she has daycare in the morning and you have work. I promise to have you up early so you're not late and I can drop Sherice off. I want to hold you in my arms all night."

The bright smile that she knew was on her face said everything.

"No, that's not a problem and I want that, too. I need to get some clothes together and I'll be over in a bit. Is there anything there to eat because I haven't had dinner or I can bring something with me?"

"I have plenty here for us to eat. I'm about to feed Sherice and I'll make us something when you get here.

How is that?" he asked.

"Sounds wonderful. I'll see you in a little bit."

"Okay, be safe and I'll see you in a few."

After hanging up, he still couldn't shake the feeling that though Sherry was confident that the conversation with Lance would go well, he felt otherwise. Lance was on his way to a great relationship with Sherry until he showed up and now that he's back in her life, she was backing away and he had a feeling Lance wasn't going to like it. It was never his plan to come between him and Sherry, but he wasn't going to apologize for still loving the woman who was always meant to be his. Turning his attention back to his daughter, he finished pulling her meal together while they waited for Sherry.

CHAPTER 19

Lance fumed at the scene that unfolded before his eyes. He was planning to surprise Sherry after church by coming by and taking her and Sherice out to eat to one of their favorite places. He was beginning to feel like a stalker because something told him that there was something going on again between Brian and Sherry, but he wasn't sure until he followed her to a downtown condo the other day after Brian picked up Sherice.

He had gone by Sherry's house hoping to talk to her when she emerged carrying what looked to him like an overnight bag. He watched her drive into the private underground garage, meant for those living in the building. He couldn't get in so he parked outside and waited to see what time she would leave, but she never did. He assumed it was where Brian was staying while in town.

A few days ago, he looked Brian up and found a connection to him and his rich brother, Duron, who owned a very sought after architectural firm in Atlanta, so it wasn't a surprise that Brian would be staying in an expensive condo.

He sat outside that condo looking and feeling like a fool

until around one in the morning, he realized Sherry wasn't coming back out. She was spending the night. He didn't bring the subject up with her later the next day when he called her at work to see if she was free for lunch. They needed to talk and he wanted to fight for their relationship.

For months, he had been moving toward a more loving relationship and was hoping to take things to the next level, but at every turn, Sherry told him she wasn't ready, yet she was ready enough to have sex with Brian again after all this time, even though she was in a relationship. If she needed to be satisfied sexually, he was more than ready for the job, but it was clear what they had was at risk of being over, something he wasn't ready for. It wasn't him she wanted anymore; it was Brian Knight.

Sherry's interest in him had waned since Brian showed up and he suspected there was more going on besides the two of them ironing out how to parent Sherice together. That was the story Sherry told him, but he didn't believe it. When he'd asked her to lunch, she told him she was busy, but that they needed to talk soon, face-to-face and to him that wasn't good. He figured she wouldn't want to have that conversation with Sherice around and he would be safe if the next time they got together, he could show her that the three of them were meant to be a family, which is why he decided to wait and show up after church.

His plan had already crashed and burned when just as he was about to get out of his car as service let out and he spotted Brian walking up to meet Sherry and Sherice on the steps of the church. It was obvious Sherry was expecting him and after she said goodbye to her parents, they walked toward his car. What burned him even hotter was the moment he saw Brian pick Sherice up in his arms and then joined his hand with Sherry's. They walked hand in hand like two lovers.

Lance grabbed his phone and called her to see if she would say what she was actually doing. He watched as she looked at her phone and to his surprise, she answered it where he thought she'd let it go to voicemail.

"Hello Lance."

He lightened his tone though he was hot as fire mad. He watched her look up at Brian, probably telling him who was on the phone.

"Hello, my love. How are you this sunny Sunday?"

"I'm great."

"I was hoping I could interest you and Sherice in a late lunch. I figured you may be out of church by now and that I would chance calling you."

"Oh, can I take a raincheck. I have some things to do and Sherice is going to be with her father for the rest of the afternoon. I've been calling you because I was hoping we could talk. Are you free tomorrow evening? Perhaps we can meet to talk."

"Do you want to come to my place? I can cook us dinner after work?" he said.

Perhaps if they were alone at his place, they could get back on track.

Lance watched the look on her face as she tried to come up with an excuse to not meet in private.

"I was hoping you could come by my house," she said.

Lance knew that meant she had something bad to say to him and she didn't want to be alone at his place. He needed more time.

"You know, I forgot I have this thing after work tomorrow. Why don't I call you Tuesday and perhaps when you pick Sherice up from daycare, we can grab a bite to eat. I miss you two and I'm starting to feel like a third wheel or should I say fourth," he said glumly.

"You're not a fourth wheel, Lance, but we do need to talk. Tuesday after work is fine. I'll see you then," she said.

"Okay. I miss you Sherry and I love you," he said and waited for her to respond.

"I'll see you Tuesday," she replied and hung up.

"That sounded brutal. What happened?"

"I think Lance has a feeling that things are over, but he doesn't want to talk about that. He told me he misses me and he loves me."

"He's in love with you? How do you feel about him?"

"Brian, I told you, things have been pretty casual, like a good friendship and I know deep down inside he has to know that it wasn't going to end with me and him falling madly in love. I wasn't leading him on and I've been pretty honest that I wasn't ready for a deeper relationship with him. We've never been intimate and I've never declared love for him. I am sorry that I haven't been honest with him lately and I know I should be. I haven't been able to focus on him and for that I'm sorry, but I need to talk to him sooner rather than later and let him know that things aren't going to work out."

"You know he's going to assume that you and I are back together and will probably guess that we've been sleeping together. Are you going to tell him if he asks?"

"I don't know that he needs to know that you and I have been intimate again. Are we back together again?" she asked.

Brian stopped walking and moved Sherice higher on his shoulder since she'd fallen asleep before they reached the car.

"I don't know what we are until you handle things with Lance. I wouldn't want to be the guy who thinks he's getting somewhere with a woman without knowing that she has possibly moved on to someone else. I love you as much as I always have and we have a lot to work through, but I want to do it together."

"I love you, too, Brian and I know it's not right having Lance just hanging around as if what he and I have is going to turn into something more. I'm going to tell him Tuesday that he and I are over and he can move on and find a woman who will love him back. I hope that doesn't sound too harsh because I'm not trying to be. I wasn't expecting for all of this to happen with you, but now that it has, I don't want to have him waiting around for something that's never going to happen."

"I agree and Lance needs to know. Why don't we go back to my place to let Sherice have her nap and then we'll get lunch before going to the zoo later," Brian said.

Before Sherry could respond, Brian pulled her close and when his head dipped toward her, she excitedly met him halfway as their lips touched.

**

Lance sat dumbfounded in his car as he listened to the exchange between Brian and Sherry before he watched them kiss and the blood in his body boiled like hot lava. Brian Knight was kissing his woman and not only that, but he'd heard Sherry tell Brian she loved him. He heard them talk about the fact that they'd had sex and they probably have done it more than once. Sherry must not have realized that she hadn't disconnected their call before dropping it in her purse because he'd heard every word. Here he was, for months pouring everything he had into a relationship with her only to have her spread eagle for her daughter's father the moment he drops back into her life after over two years of no contact. How dare he come in and steal his woman away? Sherry and Sherice were meant to be his family, not Brian's. He may not be Sherice's biological father, but he was planning on having the role of father to her and now Brian Knight has stepped in and ruined everything. This reminded him of his past relationship with Malina all over again and just like Malina regretted messing around on him, Sherry would regret it too and so would Brian. He didn't deserve coming in second place when for the past six months, he had been in first place, racing toward the finish line where he and Sherry would one day end up as husband and wife.

He watched them as they got in the car, smiling and laughing like a loving couple. He hated the family scene before him and pictured himself being where Brian was.

They were going back to Brian's place to have sex and he was left sitting here, longing to be in Brian's shoes. What kind of fool does she think she's dealing with? Well, Brian would regret the day he decided to come to Maryland under the guise of getting to know his daughter when his real plan was to steal Sherry away. He wasn't about to take that. He didn't take it with Malina and he wasn't going to take it with Sherry either.

**

Sherry entered the living room after putting Sherice in her crib and found him sitting on the floor instead of on the sofa.

"Why are you sitting on the floor?" she asked.

"Well, I started out picking up the few toys that had

fallen under the table here and I just stayed down here. This floor is quite comfortable. Come join me," he said.

"I'm going to grab a bottle of water first. Do you want one?"

"No, I'm good. You know we need to make plans for my family to come to town. Everyone is excited and just need to know the day they should arrive. I'm thinking of having something here at the condo, that way we won't overwhelm your parent's house with all of my family. This place is large enough for a celebration. It's past time that we officially welcome my baby girl into the Knight family."

Sherry came back in the room and sat next to him on the floor.

"I agree and I'm just as excited. This place is huge and I think that's a great idea. How is next weekend? Is that too soon? I know they all need to make arrangements."

"Don't worry about that. As soon as I give them the date, they'll be prepared to fly in immediately, trust me on that. They cannot wait to meet Sherice. I'm going to order some food and maybe you can work on a cake and some decorations or something."

"You mean like it's a birthday party?"

"Well, it is a party and I want to celebrate my daughter's introduction to her family and I want to do it big."

"Okay, I can do that and I'll let my parents know. My dad usually works on Saturday, but for this he'll make an exception."

"You know, I'm thankful that they've been nice to me after all this time knowing I've been absent for the past two years."

"That wasn't your fault, it was mine. You didn't know about Sherice and I know if you had, just like you came immediately when you found out about her, you would have done so earlier if you had known. I'm doing like you said and putting all that in the past and so have my parents."

"Well, I'm glad it's in the past and right now, I wouldn't want to be any place other than right here with you and Sherice."

"This is perfect, isn't it?"

Brian lifted Sherry and placed her in his lap and held her close.

"This is beyond perfect and I'm not sure what I'm going to do when I go back to Atlanta and you're here."

"You'll have Sherice with you, at least for a few weeks."

"I know, but right now I'm talking about you and me. There is no mistaking that Sherice is mine and she always will be. I have you in my arms again, something I never thought would happen and to think that there will be a day soon where you will be miles away from me and I'm sure it's going to feel more like a universe away."

Sherry turned and held onto him tightly, getting as close as she could.

"I'll be here whenever you come to town and whenever I can, I hope to visit you in Atlanta. I don't know what's next for us, but as long as I know there is an us, I can live with that. I feel like I'm getting another chance, I never dreamed would be possible, but here I am, in your arms, being loved. I will take whatever part of you I can get and I want you to know that I'm here, baby. I'm right here," she said and leaned into the waiting kiss she knew would greet her as she watched Brian's lips get closer and closer.

"I love you."

Sherry knew she would never, ever tire of hearing those

words escape his lips.

"I love you, too. Now kiss me before our daughter wakes up.

Brian smiled and placed a soft kiss on her lips before going in for more.

"I aim to please," he said.

CHAPTER 20

Brian reached feverishly around on the nightstand for his ringing cell phone before it woke Sherry and Sherice up. When he found it and looked at it, he should have known it could only be Duron who would be calling him at an ungodly hour of the morning. Slowly and quietly, he slipped his arm from under Sherry's naked body and after getting his fill of all of her lusciousness, he covered her back up before slipping out of the room to find a quiet spot to talk. Slipping on his jeans, he walked out into the main room of the condo.

"D, really? Do you know what time it is? This had better be an emergency," Brian said.

"Bro, I've been waiting for you to call me back from our conversation yesterday and to also let you know that the family and I are coming in this morning sometime before noon. Mom and Pop are traveling with me, Taija and the kids and Mike and Loren should be getting in a little after that. Jake and Kim and their kids arrived late last night and are already checked in at the Four Seasons Hotel in downtown Baltimore. We're all staying at the same place. I wanted to catch you before things got hectic here with getting everyone up, dressed and to the airport. Tyrone and Victoria aren't going to make it because they're still out of the country and not coming back for a few more days."

"That's good to hear and I did call you back last night; twice. You didn't pick up and I didn't leave a message."

"Oh, that was you calling? I was a little pre-occupied with my wife. The twins had finally fallen asleep and you know, sometimes we have to get it in when we can get it in! You'll find out soon enough, man," Duron jested.

"Trust me, Sherry and I are already finding ways to get it in the minute we put Sherice to bed."

"You guys have been pretty much living together lately?"

Brian walked into the kitchen to put on coffee. It was clear to him that his brother wanted to have a lengthy morning conversation.

"I wouldn't call it that, but we have been spending a lot of time together, day and night and I love waking up, not just to Sherice in the morning, but to Sherry."

"You are going to be a lost cause when you return to Atlanta and when is that exactly?"

The fact that he would soon have to return to Atlanta had been far in the back of his mind because he had been focused on the here and now and that's his time with Sherice and Sherry.

"I've been here a couple of weeks and I know it's time to return. Most likely it will be sometime in the next week or so after the celebration this weekend."

"Well, you know we're here for you when you get back with Sherice. Mom is already planning all kinds of things for Sherice and she's having an extra crib brought into her house in case she ends up with all of the grandkids at once. She's the only woman I know who can handle all of our kids. I'll let you go because I know it's early. We'll see you in a few hours."

Once the conversation was over, Brian, in the stillness of the early morning, had to deal with the reality that time was winding down for him and he would have to leave Sherry in Baltimore. He knew he would see her again soon when he brought Sherice home, but the thought of going back to Atlanta without knowing how the state of their relationship would be impacted was nerve-wracking. They needed to talk about their future and find a way to exist without miles between them. He went back to the bedroom to see if Sherry had woken up.

"Good morning."

Brian smiled when Sherry looked over at him with one eye opened and one closed, clearly not ready to wake fully yet.

"Is it morning already? I feel like I just fell asleep and my body feels like I ran a marathon last night. "

Brian chuckled.

"Do you really want me to respond?" he said laughing harder.

Sherry attempted a smile.

"You've got jokes I see."

"I'm just saying that last night was a marathon of sorts and a very enjoyable one too."

Brian crawled back in the bed and snuggled up to her, cradling her body close to his.

"Will I ever get used to your ravenous sexual appetite?" she asked.

"There is no such thing baby. As long as you are who you are, I will never get enough of you. We need to get up. Duron called early this morning to let me know everyone was flying into today. Jake and Kim and their kids are already here, probably still asleep like any sane person should be at this hour."

"Sherice isn't up?" Sherry asked.

"I was just about to go get her. Are you keeping her home today or is she going to daycare? I know you're off to help prepare for my family coming in today."

"I was thinking about that and I think I'll take her to daycare for a little while, otherwise, we won't get much done. There's food and decorations and so many other things to deal with."

"Do you want me to drop her off?"

"I'll do it. I need to stop at home and pick up my mother. She wants to run around with me and she wanted a chance to meet your parents today after they check-in. My dad will be by later, sometime after work."

"Are you sure? You may run into Lance. You never did tell me what happened when you talked to him."

Sherry moved to get up while they talked.

"Well, we talked on Tuesday when I picked Sherice up. He was getting pushy and making demands for my time and I got frustrated. He walked me to my car and we started talking. I had hoped we could be civil and sit down and that he would give me a chance to really explain that I don't mean to hurt him. Before I had a chance to say anything, he told me that he already knew I wanted to talk to him to break things off and wanted me to just say it, so I did. I wasn't mean about it and I took my time and explained that I hadn't planned on falling back in love with you or getting involved with you at all, but the time we had spent together brought back the love we once shared and that you and I realized we still had unfinished business. I told him about my reasoning for breaking things off with you before and how it was all a big misunderstanding. I told him he needed to find someone who would love him the way he needed to be loved and not wait around for a woman who was unsure of her own situation."

"How did he take it?"

"Surprisingly enough, he took it very well. He said he was prepared for it because he could tell we were drifting apart. He wished that I would have given him an honest chance to prove he could be just as right for me as I felt that you were, but he understood and knew that the right thing to do was to bring my family together, meaning you men and Sherice."

"Do you think it's wise to leave Sherice at that center? It seems like there's no bad blood, but I would feel better if you looked into a new center for her."

"I agree, but I think for today, she'll be fine and shortly she'll be leaving with you for a few weeks and in that time, I can think about my next move. For now, I'm not worried about running into him. I saw him Wednesday and Thursday and he was cordial and reminded me that he really did wish me well. I appreciated that."

"Well, if you feel that you're fine with it, then so am I. Why don't I go get Sherice ready while you get ready?"

"Sounds like a plan. We work well at this together."

Brian thought that that worked at parenting perfectly.

"Yes, we do."

He kissed her sweetly and went to get his feisty daughter who was already up and screaming for him to come get her out of her crib.

"Good morning!" he said to Sherice the moment he entered her room and found her standing in her crib.

"Dada, up!"

"I know you want out," he said reaching down to pick her up.

"Today is a big day for you. When mommy picks you up later, you're going to meet your other grandparents, some uncles, aunts and cousins who have been waiting to meet you. We're going to have a party just for you. You like that?"

"Cake."

Brian laughed. His daughter knew what she liked.

"Yes, cake, but first breakfast and then daycare."

**

Lance had been waiting for Sherry to bring Sherice in. A few days ago, they'd had a brief conversation where she pretty much told him that she didn't want to see him anymore and that she only wanted to be friends. Friends? After all the time he had invested in her, wining, dining and being the perfect patient man and that's it, it was over? He wasn't ready for it to be over. All he had to do was win her back over and he was planning to start that this morning.

He stopped and picked up a dozen yellow roses, her favorite color and purchased two tickets to a traveling play he knew she wanted to see that was currently at the Hippodrome theater in the city. She was going to love it and before long, he would have her forgetting all about Brian Knight. He had spent most of the night before searching vacation packages to some of the most exotic and romantic islands where they could finally seal their love. That was all they needed to do, he thought. She needed to be alone with him where no one else could enter her thoughts or their time finding each other again. He loved her and that should be enough for her.

Finally having a chance to get out of his office after speaking with a parent, he went straight to the receptionist area to wait. As soon as he got closer to the door, he saw Sherry rushing to get into her car. He had missed connecting with her.

"I missed speaking to Sherice's mother? I told you to let me know when she arrived," he said to the receptionist.

"I'm sorry Lance. After she walked Sherice in, she came out to let me know that Sherice wouldn't be here for a few weeks and that she knew she still had to pay for the first week Sherice was away because according to the contract, she has to give a two-week notice for extended time away from the center. She also said she may not be coming back and wanted to know about our cancellation policy. I discussed that with her because you were with a parent and then she turned to leave. I forgot all about it. Do you want me to call her back in? I think she was heading to work, but I'm not sure."

"No, don't worry about it," he said as he watched her drive away.

Lance needed to sit down. He felt light-headed and thought that if he didn't sit, he would fall down. Sherry was taking Sherice out of the daycare and not just for a day or two like she had done in the past, but it seems she was looking to do it permanently. That meant he would never see Sherry again because she would have no reason to come by the center anymore and he wouldn't be able to win her over. What was he going to do?

Turning, he walked back into his office and slammed the door.

"That Brian Knight ruined everything. I should be

happy and in love and I would be if it wasn't for him."

Brian didn't have anything that he didn't have. Any man can make a baby and he could give Sherry all the babies she wanted if she'd just give him another chance. Now that chance had walked out of the door. He rushed over to his computer and pulled up Sherry's record to see what the receptionist had logged in as Sherice's last day. Finding the file, he checked and after being picked up today, Sherice all of the days for the rest of the summer were zeroed out, which meant Sherry had officially given notice to remove Sherice. After today, she would be gone and he would have no reason to casually stop by her house since they were no longer, officially dating.

His head hurt. His heart hurt and any minute, he felt like he was going to be sick. She was lost to him. After today, the love of his life would be lost to him.

Lance began grinding his teeth and hitting himself on the side of the head. How could he have been so stupid? He had let her use him and toss him away like he was nothing just like she had done Brian. This was Malina all over again and this time, unlike how he let Malina off easily, Sherry wasn't going to be so lucky.

"If she thinks she's gotten rid of me, she had better think again. No one was going to take her away from him; no one.

CHAPTER 21

"Brian!" Sherry screamed into the phone the second he answered.

Before he could get a word out, Sherry screamed again and he couldn't make out what was wrong. His heart rate sped up thinking something was wrong with Sherice. He needed her to calm down enough for him to find out what was going on.

"Sherry, I don't understand you, baby. What's going on?"

"Something's wrong?"

"Wrong? What's going on?"

"I came to the daycare to pick up Sherice and they told me she wasn't here and that Lance had taken her out to the playground in the back and yet they are both gone. His car is gone and Sherice is gone. I've been calling his phone and it goes straight to voicemail as if he turned it off."

Brian grabbed his keys and sprinted out of the condo where he had been straightening up in preparation for the party the next day. All of his family had arrived and Tyrone and Victoria had flown in. After Duron told them why he was inviting them to Baltimore, they cut their honeymoon short and flew in. Thoughts of any festivities went out the window as he rushed to his car.

"What's his number?"

He listened as she ran it off to him.

"Have you called the police?"

Brian's heart rate was going crazy as he patiently waited for the elevator. Not able to keep still, he ran to the stairwell and not caring how many flights he had to go down, he skipped as many steps as he could to get to the bottom. His daughter was missing.

"No, I didn't know if it was that kind of situation. We've been looking around and can't find them anywhere."

"Call them, Sherry. Call your father and get him to get some guys on this. I know he's with the city department, but I'm sure he has connections. He has our daughter without your permission and that means he's taken her. Where would he go? Where does he live? Send it to my phone."

"Call the police and I'm on my way. Are you still at the daycare center?"

"Yes, and the center just called them and I had another teacher call my mom and she's on her way, too. My dad, is already on his way."

"Alright, stay right there and I'm on my way."

He hung up and immediately dialed Lance's number and like Sherry said it went straight to voicemail. His phone pinged and he read the address Sherry had sent him to where Lance lived. He tried Lance by phone again.

"Lance, this is Brian, Sherice's father. We need to know where you are with Sherice. You can call me on my cell phone or call Sherry. She's really concerned about Sherice just as I am."

He hung up and exhaled. It took everything out of him to remain calm when what he wanted to do was threaten him. He knew there was something strange about Lance, but he never thought that Lance would take his anger over the end of his relationship with Sherry out on Sherice. Before he dialed Lance again, he dialed Duron, who had landed earlier in the day and was probably relaxing at the hotel until later when they were planning on connecting.

"D, I have a problem," he said the minute he heard Duron's voice.

"What's up?"

"That guy I told you Sherry had been seeing, but broke it off with has Sherice."

"What do you mean has Sherice? Like kidnapped her?"

"I don't know, but it looks that way."

"Have you called the police?"

"It looks like he took her from the daycare center where she goes and where he works. The center called the police and I'm on my way there now. Her father, I'm sure is also all over this with men of his own."

Brian finally reached the garage level and ran as hard as he could to his car.

"I'm on my way. What's the address to the daycare? I'll get Jake and Mike and we're on our way the second I'm off the phone," Duron said.

Brian gave him the address.

"Don't worry bro, we'll find her. Do you know what he's driving?"

"I've seen him driving a silver Maxima. I don't know the tag number. Sherry may and hopefully she's giving that information to the police."

"We're on our way. Jake is in the room on one side of

me and Mike and Loren are on the opposite side. Try to keep calm and we're on our way. I won't tell mom what's happening yet. She hasn't met her granddaughter and already some fool is playing a game with her life."

Brian's anger boiled over and the threat he wanted to level at Lance came out as he vented to his brother.

"He's dead, D. If I get my hands on him, he's dead."

"Brian, pull it back. Don't do anything that will keep you away from your daughter. We'll find her and she'll be fine. I'm on my way," Duron said and hung up.

Once in the care, Brian dialed Lance again and to his surprise, this time after it rang, he answered.

"You're not getting her back," Lance said to him in a sinister voice.

In the background, Brian could hear his daughter crying and he almost lost control of his car as he exited the garage, barely avoiding running down a few people who were crossing the street. His mind raced in all directions with fear.

"Lance, what are you doing? Bring Sherice back."

"I don't think I'm going to do that. You took something from me and now I'm going to take something from you."

To him, Lance's voice sounded like some sinister horror movie character. He definitely wasn't operating on all cylinders.

"What did I take from you? Sherry? She wasn't yours for me to steal from and my daughter has nothing to do with this."

"You love her and I love Sherry and now you know what it feels like to have someone you love snatched away from you."

Brian weaved in and out of traffic hoping he wasn't

pulled over by the police. He would end up wasting precious time in finding his daughter. He continued to rush, but slowed down.

"Sherice is a baby, Lance. You want to deal with someone, then you deal with me. Come deal with me and give Sherice back to Sherry. They don't deserve this. It's me you want, so come get me. It's me you want to take your anger out on, not an innocent baby. You said you love Sherry, yet you take her baby away."

"You think I don't know you've been screwing my woman? I've known it for a while, even before she broke up with me. I waited for her to come home one night and around midnight, I realized she wasn't coming home and the next day you show up to pick Sherice up at school. I put it all together. She was mine and you swooped in and snatched that away from me."

"Lance, I understand you're upset, but what happened has nothing to do with my daughter. Bring her back and talk to Sherry about what happened. Don't hurt Sherice," he begged.

"Hurt Sherice? You think I would hurt her? I love Sherice just like I love her mother. They're supposed to be my family and now instead of that, the three of you are living happily ever after. Sherry didn't care that she ripped my world apart. She made me wait and wait for us to get closer and here you show up and she climbs right into bed with you just like old times, huh? You should have stayed in Atlanta."

Brian could hear Sherice crying.

"Lance, don't you hear Sherice crying? Listen to her screaming. You say you love her and yet you don't care that she's afraid right now. Listen to her!" he shouted.

"Well, you know what, she'll be fine with me. You and Sherry wanted each other and didn't care about my feelings, I don't care anything about yours. See how it feels when something is taken away from you that you love. If Sherry wants Sherice back, she can have her as long as she comes to me and makes things right. We were meant to be together or none of us will be happy ever again."

Before he could plead with Lance again, the line disconnected.

Brian's phone rang as he sped through traffic and answered when he saw Sherry's number.

"What's going on baby? Any word yet from the police on where he could be? I just talked to Lance and he sounds crazy. I could hear Sherice crying and he didn't care. It sounded like he was driving. Do you have any idea where he could be?" he shouted with fear.

"No. I want my baby back Brian," she cried.

"I know and I'm going to bring her back. I'll be there in a few minutes. I'm not far away. I had to take another way around because traffic was bad. I doubt he would go home, but where else would he go?"

"I don't know," Sherry said crying, barely able to speak.

Brian drove erratically through traffic on I-95 when he saw a Maxima that matched Lance's fly by on the other side of the highway. He caught a quick glance and would bet his life that he'd just past Lance. Seeing an emergency break in the road, he sped up to it, made a U-turn and sped toward the car.

"I think I see him. Call your father and tell him that Lance is driving on I-95 toward Washington. I just turned around and I'm following him."

"Okay," Sherry said before hanging up.

Nervously, she dialed her father's phone when she looked up and heard sirens coming toward her. Her father leaped out before the car had even stopped. She ran toward him.

"Dad!" she screamed. As she ran into his arms, she saw more cars pulling up and spotted Duron as he jumped out of a truck.

"Sherry? Where is Brian?" Duron asked.

"I was just about to tell my father that Brian called and said he's tailing Lance on I-95 going toward Washington. Duron grabbed his phone and jumped back in the truck, no doubt to find Brian. She also saw Brian's brother Jake and another guy in the back of the truck Duron was driving.

She heard her father balk out orders over his police radio and a few of the cars that showed up with him took off in the same direction that Duron had taken off in.

"Sherry stay here. Your mother will be here in a minute. I'll call and keep you posted, but don't worry because I'm going to find Sherice and that jackass Lance will regret the day he made the decision to take my granddaughter."

Sherry couldn't talk because all she could do was cry.

**

Brian tried calling Lance again the moment he got close enough to the car to see that it was him. He was able to see inside in the back and noticed that Sherice wasn't in a car seat and Lance probably had not put a seat belt around her either which meant she was vulnerable if he crashed. He had to get Lance to pull over. He was about to call him again when Lance looked over and saw him right before he sped up a little faster.

"Damn!" Brian screamed and continued to dial Lance's number hoping he would pick up again. After a few tries, he did.

"Lance, look, Sherice isn't secured in the back of the car. You have to slow down and let me take her out. If you want to run, you do that, but give me my daughter. If you crash or if someone hits you, you could kill her. If you love her as much as you say, then you won't want that to happen!" he shouted, trying to keep his cool.

"Back off, Brian! I mean it, back off or you'll regret it. I'll call Sherry and she and I are going to take Sherice and move away and live someplace where we can be happy. They were doing fine with me before you showed up."

"Look man, I'm sorry about how things turned out, but don't hurt my daughter," Brian said in a much calmer voice. He was hoping to bring the tension down a few levels in hopes it would calm Lance down also.

"Sherry and Sherice belong to me!" Lance shouted before looking into the mirror when he heard police sirens coming up behind him.

Brian looked behind him and saw several police cars, city and county, following him.

He watched in horror as Lance crossed over several lanes of traffic toward the expressway exit. He was about to speak into the phone again and his heart stopped. His next words lodged in his throat as he looked in horror as Lance tried to exit the expressway and missed the turn. The car turned on its side and slid off of an embankment. Though it didn't roll over and over, the fact that it turned on its side and he knew that Sherice wasn't secured in the back terrified him. Not caring that the car was still in drive, the minute he reached where they were, he leaped out of the car and ran over to them where he could hear Sherice screaming at the top of her lungs.

The wheels of the car continued to spin as he climbed up on the side and reached for the back door. As soon as he opened it, police cars surrounded them as he reached inside to reach for Sherice. She didn't look to be injured, but he wasn't sure as he reached down for her cautiously. He tuned out the fact that Lance was crying and screaming how sorry he was from the front seat, but Brian didn't care. His only concern was getting to his daughter.

"Sherice, baby, it's Dada. I'm here," he said going down into the car carefully. He pulled her slowly into his arms and saw blood on her bright yellow top. He couldn't see where it was coming from until he turned her over and saw that the side of her head had several cuts.

"Brian, I'm here. Is she alright?"

He looked up at the door and saw Jake's face. Thankful that his brother was a doctor, he knew giving Sherice to him was the best choice.

"I don't know, Jake. There's a lot of blood," Brian said, unable to hold back the tears. He didn't want to frighten Sherice further by crying, but he couldn't help feeling helpless. The minute she saw how upset he was, she screamed even louder.

"Hand her up to me and let me check her out. An ambulance is on the way, but I want to check for any breaks and to see where the blood is coming from. We have to get her out of the car, but in case she has injuries we can't see, hand her too me carefully," Jake said.

Brian reached her up to Jake and Duron, who he could also see through the window. He also saw Sherry's father and other men who had gathered around. While he handed her to Jake, he climbed out behind her as men worked to free Lance from the front seat. Getting him out appeared to be harder since it seemed he was stuck behind the steering wheel.

Exiting the car, Brian ran to where Jake and Duron were taking a screaming Sherice toward an oncoming ambulance.

"She's okay, Brian. I think she's okay," Duron said as he walked with Sherry's father toward the ambulance that had now stopped.

He quickly looked back at the car as Lance was finally being pulled out. He walked over to tend to his daughter as a paramedic checked her out.

"How is she?" he asked, impatiently reaching for Sherice who was crying out and reaching for him.

"Brian, let me check her out. The fact that she's crying I'm sure is a good sign," Jake said.

"I need my baby. Please, let her be okay."

"I got her, Brian. You know I got this."

"Brian, she's in the best hands possible," Duron said, trying to comfort him.

"I'm a doctor," Jake said as the paramedics jumped out.

Brian stood to the side pacing as Jake barked out orders for what he needed in order to check Sherice out. While he worked, Brian called Sherry to let her know he had Sherice.

"Is she okay?" Sherice screamed.

"My brother Jake is checking her out, but she seems okay. The car had an accident and I think she may have a cut or something, but she's not unconscious and as you can hear, she's having no problem screaming."

"Is that Sherry?" Jake asked.

"Yeah."

"Tell her we have Sherice and I'm checking her over. I think she's going to be fine, but we're getting her to the hospital so that she can be checked out thoroughly."

"Okay," he replied.

"I want her taken to Hopkins. I have privileges there and I'm calling ahead to let them know you're on your way," Jake said.

Knowing that for the moment, Sherice was fine, Brian dropped his phone to the ground and walked back toward the car with long, strong and powerful strides with a murderous spirit just as the men had taken Lance out. Before he could think about his next move, his fist made contact with Lance's face over and over. Though several men tried to pull him back, Brian used the strength he didn't know he had and went at Lance again, this time knocking him to the ground where he let loose all of the rage he'd felt since hearing that Lance had taken Sherice. His rage was fueled by the fact that Lance could have killed his daughter and all he saw was fire as he pounded away until Lance lay limp on the ground and men were finally able to pull him off.

"Brian! Stop! Sherice needs you. Stop!" he heard Duron saying behind him.

"This bastard could have killed my daughter!" he shouted and struggled against the men who held him.

"I know, but he didn't and the police are here now, so let them deal with him. You need to get in the ambulance with Sherice. She's calling for you and you're probably the only one who can calm her down. She's scared and she needs you!" Duron said, trying to sound calmer.

Brian shook off his rage as thoughts turned back to his daughter and hearing her cries, he shook loose of the hands holding him and ran back to the ambulance, climbing inside.

"We're going to meet you at Hopkins. A unit is already on the way to take Sherry and my wife there. A few of these patrol cars are going to escort your brothers through traffic while you ride in the back with Sherice."

Brian, with a tear-stained face looked into Mr. Braxton's eyes and he turned his focus squarely on his daughter. He shook his head and sat down as the doors of the ambulance closed and they took off. Alone in the back with Sherice and one of the paramedics, Brian held his head down and cried a silent thanks that his daughter was going to be alright.

CHAPTER 22

Brian and Sherry saw a nurse rushing toward them and they turned to meet her halfway. Brian knew that she could only be coming to them with an issue with Sherice and the look on her face was one of worry.

"What is it?" Brian said breathlessly and with a voice laced with worry.

He watched as the nurse took a moment to catch her own breath.

"Your daughter is doing fine, but we are having a hard time getting her to calm down. You have one strong little girl and she has a will that is just as strong."

"We can hear her screaming. What's happening back there?" he asked.

"She's fine, but we're ready for you to come back now. I don't want to give her anything to calm her down and I'm hoping you can help with that."

Before the nurse could get another word out, Brian moved around her with powerful strides to get to his daughter's side as quickly as possible. He knew he never should have let them convince him and Sherry to give them a few minutes before they could come back to the room. He hadn't been a father to Sherice long, but he knew she had that Knight stubbornness and she also had the same feistiness as his sister Loren. He could hear her screaming all the way down the hall and knew that unless she saw a familiar face, she wasn't going to let up.

He walked without thinking about stopping and could hear Sherry rushing to keep up with his long strides as her heels clicked on the white tiled floor. As soon as they reached the room that was to be assigned to Sherice, they rushed over to the bed where another nurse was trying to console Sherice while another tried to get Sherice to lay on the bed, something she clearly wasn't going to do, at least not quietly.

He watched as Sherry got close and tried to console her.

"Baby girl, it's okay. Mommy is right here. You have to stop crying and let this nice nurse finish checking you over. You are scaring everyone here because you won't stop crying."

Brian watched as his daughter flailed her arms about and kicked her legs to keep anyone from touching her. All he saw was terror when he looked in her eyes. As soon as Sherice laid eyes on him, she screamed louder.

"Dada, dada, dada!" she hollered for him.

Not caring what anyone said or thought, he rushed to her and picked her little body up in his arms. As soon as he did, he felt her wrap her tiny arms around his neck as tight as she could, making sure everyone knew that nothing was going to pry her from his arms. She was still crying to the point that her whole body shook and racked from the magnitude of how hard she was crying.

"Shhhh...Everything is alright, baby. Dada is here and I

got you. I need you to stop crying, okay?" he asked, soothing her by rubbing her back, hoping to encourage her to stop crying.

Sherry walked over and joined him in caressing Sherice so that she felt comforted enough to calm down.

"Sherice, Dada has you," Brian crooned softly into her ear while cradling her and rocking from side to side.

Though her cries quieted as she laid her head on his shoulder and gripped his neck even tighter, her body still shook and he continued trying to calm her down.

"Mr. Knight?"

Brian turned toward one of the nurses who called his name.

"Yes?"

"Do you think she will let you lay her in the bed? I just need to check her vitals and then the doctor will come in and talk to you about her examination. Sherice is going to be fine and that bump on her head from hitting it on the side of the door will go down. We'd like to keep her overnight and put a monitor on in order to keep an eye on her breathing for the night. I think with you here, she may calm down enough to let us get everything on her."

Brian shook his head and walked to the top of the bed where he tried to lay her down.

"Dada is going to be right here, but I need to lay you on the bed and let this nice lady make you all better."

When he tried to extract her death-grip hold on him, she started crying and hollering again and there was no way he would be able to survive watching his daughter go through this.

"How about if I lay on the bed with her? I don't think she's going to just lay here and not be frightened."

"That's fine, you can do that. We can work around you holding her. This will only take a minute."

Brian sat down on the side of the bed and slowly laid back, taking Sherice with him as she continued to lay snug in his arms with her head on his shoulder. He was happy that they were able to exam Sherice in this position. He and Sherry waited patiently until they were done until she stepped out a few times to update their families on what was happening. She came back in following behind the doctor.

"Well, Sherice is going to be fine. She's got a bit of a concussion which we want to watch tonight and the cuts on the side of her head aren't deep. She'll be fine," the doctor said.

"When can we take her home?" Sherry asked.

"She can go home in the morning. I want to monitor her sleeping tonight. I don't think there are any issues, but since she's here, let's have the nurses keep an eye on her and if she's back to her lively self in the morning, we can discharge her. Now, one of you can stay here in the room with her tonight if you like. I assume it will be you?" the doctor said looking at her.

Sherry looked to Brian and knew what he was thinking, so she spoke up first.

"Are you sure we both can't stay?"

"I'm sorry, we don't allow more than one parent in the room overnight. It's really not set up for two additional people.

"I'm not leaving," Brian interjected.

"Okay, so it will be you, sir?" he asked.

"It will be both of us," Brian said sternly.

Brian gave the doctor a warning look to not test him.

There was no way he was letting Sherice or Sherry out of his sight even though Lance was in jail with little to no chance of getting out.

Sherry's father had informed them that a deeper look into Lance's background had produced a prior case of domestic abuse against a former girlfriend who refused to press charges against him, so the case had been missed. It hadn't come up in any background check because Lance's sister owned the daycare and a background check on him didn't produce the information that would have kept him from being able to go into business with her in the first place. For now, a judge wasn't going to release him and Brian hoped he'd get the help he needed. For tonight, he didn't want to worry about Lance or anything else other than Sherry and Sherice. If he couldn't stay in the room with Sherice, he would be more than happy being uncomfortable in the family lounge across from her room. He'd never get any rest and he knew Sherry wasn't leaving.

"I can only have on bed brought in. The room isn't big enough for two beds in this private room," the doctor said.

"That's not a problem. I'll be fine in that chair over there. I don't need to sleep, but I do need to be here with my daughter."

Sherry waited to see how the doctor would push back, but the look on Brian's face told him this was an unwinnable fight for the doctor.

"Okay, okay. I understand. I have two small children at home as well and I've known your brother, Dr. Jake Knight for a lot of years and he would hunt me down if I didn't allow you both to stay. I'll have a cot brought in with some bedding and we'll get some fluids for Sherice. No food for her tonight. Does she drink from a sippy cup or a regular cup?" he asked.

"Definitely a sippy cup," Sherry said.

"Okay. There will be staff in throughout the night to check on her, but if at any time, something seems off about her behavior or her sleep isn't calm, push the call button and someone will be right in. I'll be here all night and they know to call me with any emergency; otherwise, I'll see you all in the morning."

"Thank you," Brian said. He looked down at Sherice who had finally calmed down and was falling asleep.

"Should we let her sleep now or keep her awake?" Sherry asked.

"After experiencing the lungs on your daughter, I say let her sleep, but watch her breathing."

Brian listened as the doctor gave them a few more things to look out for before leaving out. He told them the family could come in one at a time, but by nine, they all had to leave, which was actually an hour past visiting hours, but for Jake, he would make an exception."

Family came in one at a time to see that Sherice was okay and by the time, his mother and father had shown up to see her, she had fallen asleep on Brian's chest. A few times, he tried to move to lay her on the bed and the minute Sherice felt him moving away, she would fuss and grab onto him tighter. He remained where he was until he knew she was good and sleep. He had to curve his legs off of the side of the bed that wasn't meant for anyone over six feet tall like he was.

Now that everyone, including Sherry's parents, his brothers, Mike and Tyrone had come and gone, Brian and Sherry were left to the quietness of the room as they watched Sherice sleep, not sure either of them would find the kind of slumber that their daughter was now enjoying.

"I can't believe I brought him into our lives. How could I not see that Lance was out of his mind? How could I have missed the signs that he was getting out of control? You tried to warn me that something was off about him," Sherry said, sitting down. She wasn't ready to lay down on the cot that had been brought into the room for her. She needed to talk.

"There was no way for you to know that he would lose control and take Sherice."

"Brian, he could have killed our baby. He could have killed her!" she screamed and caught herself, remembering they were in the hospital.

"I know, but he didn't and she's right here with us and as the doctor said, she's going to be alright. Come here baby, touch and feel her. She's right here and she's going to be okay."

"I brought that maniac in our lives. As I think back on the conversation I had with him earlier this week, there were signs that something was off. He started telling me that he knew it was coming because he knew I'd been intimate with you, spending the night with you and avoiding him. He talked about what our life was supposed to be and how it still could be if I would remember why I left you in the first place. I told him it was all a misunderstanding and that though you and I had talked through all of that, it wasn't the reason behind why I was breaking up with him. I told him I needed to focus on me and Sherice and that I wasn't in a place to give him the kind of relationship he wanted. I apologized profusely for any hurt feelings and I hoped he would be able to move on. I thought by the end of the talk, that he understood. He said he did and even gave me a hug before leaving. He told me he understood and that we could remain friends and that I would still see him at the daycare because Sherice went there. He didn't seem upset or angry and in fact, he seemed quite calm."

"How did you end the conversation?" Brian asked adjusting Sherice when she began to whimper.

"Is she okay?" Sherry asked.

"She's fine. I think she was just getting comfortable. I'm going to try and lay her in the bed in a few minutes. I think she's really sleep now. So how did the conversation end with Lance?" he asked.

"Oh, right. Well, he wished me well and said he hoped we could still be cordial when I came to drop off and pick Sherice up. I looked on line at a few places that I was going to check into while she was with you later this summer and when she came back, I was going to transfer her. I didn't want things to be strained with Lance and I knew that if you were here visiting and either dropped off or picked her up, it could be an uncomfortable situation. The way he looked was strange and I picked up on it right away, but dismissed it. Then a few days later, this happened. I saw him Wednesday and Thursday and he was fine. I dropped her off this morning and didn't see him at all. I spoke with the receptionist for about ten minutes about the time Sherice would be away and then that I was probably going to transfer her out, but I never saw Lance. I didn't think he was there. I don't know what actually made him take Sherice out and the receptionist said Lance must have done it when the class was outside for recess which was right around the time that I showed up early to get her since I knew your family was coming in today. I wanted to get her home, get her changed so that we could meet you at the condo. When I got there, they couldn't find her. One of parents who was leaving when I got there heard us talking and said she had seen Lance walking to his car with Sherice. She knew that Lance and I had been seeing each other, but still thought it odd that he would be leaving with her. She knew that staff were never to leave the grounds with any of the children. That's when we knew something was wrong."

"Sherry, don't beat yourself up about this. Sherice is fine now and Lance is right where he should be. They're lucky they pulled me off of him because I could have killed him. I have never, ever been that mad before. I kept hitting him and couldn't stop."

"Duron told me about that when I got to the hospital. I hear you beat him up pretty badly before you were pulled off of him."

"Yeah and I think the cops didn't try as hard as they could to pull me off. He kidnapped the granddaughter the police commissioner and I think to them, he had it coming and I needed that contact between my fist and his face because now I can move on and focus on you and Sherice. I poured all my anger out in each punch that landed on his face. He'll think twice before he ever attempts to come near me or my family ever again."

Sherry began to cry.

"I'm sorry, Brian. I keep messing up."

Brian moved to lay Sherice on the bed and after raising the bars on the bed, he moved to comfort Sherry. He didn't want her carrying around anymore guilt. He'd had enough of that and now that Sherice was fine and Lance was in jail, they could move on with their lives.

"Don't cry, baby," he said pulling her into his embrace where she cried harder, but silently.

"I'm so sorry," she continued crying.

"I know and it's okay. We will get through this and put it behind us and we'll do whatever we have to do to make sure Sherice doesn't have any long-lasting effects because we're still talking about and dealing with this. I love you and I told you there is no responsibility around all of this anymore. Let's look ahead to raising our daughter and seeing what direction our lives go in. Now, why don't you go ahead and lay down. I know you need some sleep because I know how exhausting this day has been. I'm going to stay up and keep an eye on Sherice," he said kissing her forehead.

"Are you sure?"

"Yes, I'm sure. Go ahead and lay down. I'm going to pull this chair closer to the bed and sit here."

"She's going to be okay, right?" she asked.

"Yes, she is because she has you and she has me. We'll give all the love she will need."

Sherry laid down and got as comfortable as a person could get on a cot.

I love you," she said and closed her eyes.

"I know, baby. I love you, too."

Brian covered both of his girls up, said a silent prayer of thanks and sat in the chair beside the bed and settled in for a long night.

**

Duron walked into his hotel room, closing the door behind him and when he turned around, Taija was standing in front of him.

"How is Sherice?" she asked.

"She's fine. She has a concussion and they're keeping her overnight in order to monitor and Brian and Sherry are staying at the hospital with her."

"What the hell happened? All of this is just insane!" Taija said.

"Yes, it is. Where are the twins?"

"I just put them to bed. Your parents came by to see them and after they left, I gave them baths and put them down."

"Give me a minute and I'll tell you all about it. Right now, I want to go kiss my children," he said and leaned down and kissed her sweetly.

Taija knew Duron was thinking about Brian and what could have happened to Sherice that didn't. Going through something like that would make any parent want to embrace their own kids.

"Okay, I'll be in the other bedroom. I need to call Loren back. She said Chase was a little fussy after the long flight from California and she wanted to get him to sleep."

Taija went into the bedroom and called Loren's room.

"Hey, Loren. How is Chase?"

"He's finally asleep. I think it was the long flight, but he's good now. Is Duron back? Mike just walked in."

"Yes. I think they came back together."

"Mike said Sherice is going to be fine and that the hospital just wanted to monitor her overnight."

"Duron said the same thing. I asked him to tell me what exactly happened, but he wanted to see the kids first. After what Brian is going through, I don't blame him."

"Yeah, Mike did the same thing. I told him I had just gotten Chase down and he wanted to pick him up. He didn't care and said if he woke up, he'd get him back to sleep. When I left out of the bedroom, he had picked Chase up and sat with him in the chair next to the bed. I decided to give him some alone time with him."

"I can't imagine what Brian and Sherry are going through and I wish there was something we could do to help. I feel helpless just waiting around," Taija said.

"Well, Mike said that the hospital would be releasing Sherice in the morning and that Brian told him he was planning to bring Sherice and Sherry back to the condo with him to stay for a few days. Do you think it would be out of line if we had dinner prepared for them when they got home? I can call Brian and make sure it's okay. I know we all want to lay our eyes on Sherice tomorrow and without being too intrusive, I think they would appreciate having family around when she came home. I can call and tell Sherry's parents to meet us at the condo and you and I can make sure everything is all set up for them. What do you think?" Loren asked.

"I think it's a great idea. We'll need to get in the condo. I'll ask Duron to get Brian's keys in the morning."

"Okay, call me early and let's figure out what we can plan together," Loren said.

Taija turned as Duron entered the bedroom looking exhausted.

"I'll do that. I'll call you early," Taija said and hung up.

"Was that Loren?" Duron asked.

"Yes. We were talking about helping out in some way and thought though the party was probably off for tomorrow since Sherry and Brian have Sherice to worry about, we thought we would still have some food delivered and have all of the family there when they brought her home from the hospital. Mike said Brian would be bringing

Sherice to the condo when they released her. Is it too much to have everyone there when they arrived?" she asked.

"I don't think so. I think it's a great idea."

"Can you check with Brian and see about getting his key? We want to get in and set everything up?"

"Can I check with him in the morning? Tonight, I want to make love to my wife because I need her. I need to feel you," he said coming over and pulling her into his arms.

Before she could respond, Duron was already untying the satin robe that covered her naked body.

"Yes, baby and you do know that the twins and I are alright. I know that something like this can make you remember how important family is."

"That lunatic could have killed my niece today," Duron said.

Taija reached up to caress his face as she began removing his clothes after letting her robe slip from her body to the floor.

"I know, but he didn't and she's going to be alright and so will Brian and Sherry. Everyone is alive and this family is intact."

"I know and tonight, I don't want to focus on anything, but loving you."

Naked and more than ready for her, Duron lifted Taija up in his arms and after laying her in the center of the bed, he joined her, moving into her widespread, inviting legs and joined his body with hers, thankful that he had her to love.

CHAPTER 23

After a week that Brian would like to forget, he was alone with Sherice and Sherry at the condo. Sherice had been released from the hospital a week ago, and life for her was back to normal. The doctor had told them to watch for any signs of trauma, but they didn't see any. She had bounced back into the happy little girl she was before the accident. His family had stayed an extra day until Monday and they had spent the weekend together as a family having fun and trying to put the drama with Lance behind them. He was happy that Sherry's father had taken a few days off and he and his wife spent the weekend getting to know his family. It looked like they were finally going to be able to put the drama with Lance behind them and get back to being a family.

He was happy to hear that the judge agreed with the state's attorney's recommendation that Lance be held until he could be evaluated which included a sixty day stay at a facility where they all hoped he would get the help he needed. For now, getting their lives back on track was the priority and that meant that he would soon need to return to Atlanta and wasn't sure Sherry would be up to letting Sherice go without her after what happened. Her job had given her a few weeks off to deal with her home life. For the rest of the week, they had done a lot of fun things with Sherice which included another trip to the zoo, the Baltimore Aquarium and lots of trips to the playground, Sherice's favorite place.

In the midst of all that fun, the time was coming for him to leave and he and Sherry would need to talk about what will happen when he leaves. His heart hurt knowing that now that he had her back in his life, where she should have been all along, he was about to separate from her. He knew people had long distance relationships all the time, but he wasn't sure how it would work for them. He walked out of Sherice's bedroom after finally getting her to sleep. The highlight of his day was reading to his daughter at night and hearing her call him Dada, something he would never get tired of hearing. Now, he was about to have one of the toughest conversations of his life.

"Is she finally sleep?" Sherry asked as she cleaned up the tons of toys Sherice had scattered all over the room.

"It took three stories and some serious coaxing before she got to the point where she couldn't keep her eyes open any longer."

"Would you say she's back to normal?"

"I think the only people who aren't back to normal are you and me. Sherice is definitely back to her delightful self where her daddy is the most important person in her life. I'm sorry, but I think you have officially been bumped down to the number two position," he bantered and moved out of the line of fire when Sherry threw a stuffed animal at him.

"You go jokes!"

"Hey, don't be mad at me because my daughter thinks

I'm her superman."

Sherry walked over to him.

"You know, you're my superman, too and I love you."

Brian moved in close and nuzzled her neck.

"I love you, too. These have been the best weeks of my life except for last week of course, but other than that, I cherish this time we've had."

Sherry stiffened in his arms.

"What's wrong?" he asked pulling back to look in her face.

"We're going to have to talk, aren't we?"

Brian shook his head, yes.

"I have loved being here, but I need to get back home and we still need to talk about whether Sherice goes with me for a visit or if you aren't ready for that after what she's been through. I know it's tough and whatever you decide, I'll be okay with. If you want her here with you, then I'll figure out a way to get back here for a visit as soon as I can. Maybe we can cam-chat every evening and I can still read her stories at night. It won't be the same, but it's something."

He tried to sound convincing hoping she would believe he was okay with whatever decision she made, but deep down, he was struggling with the idea that he not only had to go back home without her, but he'd have to go home without Sherice.

Sherry knew it wasn't what she wanted; not for her or for Sherice. She wanted Sherice to have time with Brian and his family and if anyone would keep her safe, he would.

"Brian, if you still want to take Sherice with you, you can. Is two weeks enough? I'm not sure I would be able to survive with her being gone longer than that. I also don't think I could send her back to that daycare or any other daycare right now. I have one more week off and then I have to go back to work. I don't trust Sherice with anyone other than you and your family and my parents. My mom is thinking of retiring to be home with Sherice until she's older. That mess with Lance terrified her to the point that she's ready to leave her job in order to watch Sherice and allow me work and finish school. I need some time to think about it, so why don't you go ahead and take Sherice with you while I work on things here at home. By the end of the two weeks, I'm hoping you and I can work out other visitation arrangements, but right now, I need to know about us. You going back to Atlanta and me staying here isn't really the typical relationship and I don't know what that means. I'm scared to think that I could lose you again and I'm not sure I can survive that; I know I can't."

Brian knew he should be happy about her willingness to still let him take Sherice with him, but he still felt sad. Like her, he knew that they would now be states away from each other just when they had found their way back. Like her, he didn't know how to handle it and right now, he didn't want to.

"I would say let's sit down and talk about it, but tonight, all I want to do is take you to bed and think about this situation tomorrow. I'll be here for another couple of days and we can talk more about this in the morning. Right now, I just want to love you. I don't know how long it will be before I'll get to go to bed and wake up with you beside me, so I want to take advantage of the time we have left. Is that okay?" he asked.

"Yes," Sherry said softly. She could look in Brian's eyes

and see that he needed her like he never has before. His world had fallen apart and he took the weight of keeping them safe. He feigned being the strong one for all of them, but right now he wanted to be vulnerable with her and let his guard down. She could see that he didn't want to think, plan or figure anything out. Now that their daughter was safely sleeping in her bed behind a locked door with them, he wanted to let go and just feel. Now was the time for her to take care of him and let him know that with her, he will always find a place of peace. He would always get the love and support he needed unconditionally. For her, he only needed to be. Seeing his need, she reached her hand out to him and when he placed his hand in hers, she walked toward the bedroom where they could shut the world out and focus only on them.

"Where is Sherice's monitor?" he asked.

"I have it. She had a busy day and will sleep all night. Let's focus on you," she said as they entered the bedroom.

Brian's gaze followed Sherry as she walked around the room, dimming the lights, setting the scene for love. Being able to slow his life done even if it was just for one night was all he needed besides the woman who was the focus of his attention tonight. When she turned around and looked at him his world stopped and he could finally stop with it, at least for the night. His heart swelled with so much love for her, he hurt and all that matter was losing himself in her love tonight. At the same time, they walked toward each other and his eyes followed the path of her hands as she reached up and loosened the pink silk tie that held her robe together. When she opened it and the sides fell away and slid slowly to the floor, he lost the ability to move and speak. Underneath was a soft pink, lace two-piece lingerie set. The bottom hugged her generous hips, revealing a flat stomach that led up to a sheer, lace bra where her breasts strained against the confines of the cups, practically begging to be set free.

Walking over to her, he pulled her into his arms, lifted her up and walked over to the bed, placing her in the middle.

He stripped off his remaining clothes and then joined her where he welcomed into her open arms.

Brian came to her in a time of need and the only thing he needed from her was her love, something she had plenty of for him.

"Make love to me," she whispered and pulled him down on top of her, joining their lips. The kiss was slow as she passed her hands down and around his chiseled arms. She toyed with his lips before doing the same with his tongue. Against all odds, they were here and here is where she always wanted them to be. If they had to be apart, she needed him to know that he would always find his heart's desire in her arms.

"You are all I need, Sherry. Just you. I've always needed just you, like this, loving me and letting me love you."

Brian kissed his way down her body, kissing her skin through the thin material of her bra. As he slid lower, he found her pebbled nipple and teased it to an even harder peak. Reaching up, he slid the cup to the side and drew the tip into his mouth, using a sucking motion that he knew she'd feel the pull further down her body, in the apex where her thighs met, creating a moisture that readied her for his entry. When he drew back, Sherry took that moment to run the tip of her finger across his lips and keeping his eyes locked on hers, he sucked the finger into his mouth, kissing it, sucking it, loving it. When she moaned out her pleasure he knew that she was already getting close. Moving further down her body, he smiled as her hips wiggled showing her frustration with how slow he was going joining their bodies. Tonight, he wanted to go slow, enjoying every bit of her and erasing the drama of the past few weeks, concentrating on love.

"Brian," she sighed.

"I'm here baby, needing you, loving you. When I give to you, I give even more to myself."

Brian moved even further down her body until his face was planted in the area between her legs. Sliding his hands down, he lifted her hips and pulled her panties down her legs, tossing them to the floor. He parted her legs even more and when his face came in contact with her mound, he inhaled, letting the scent of her engage all of his senses and he was tuned into what her body needed and what it needed, he needed it for himself.

Opening her legs as wide as he could, he lowered his head and pressed his tongue to her center and her hips jerked up in his direction. Keeping his tongue nestled against her, he swirled it around matching the swirling motion Sherry used to guide her hips to get what she needed. When he used a sucking motion on her hard nub, she flew apart, muffling her screams as her body shook like an earthquake riding out the torrent of waves that flowed through her body to him.

While still in throes of ecstasy, Brian slid up her body and captured her lips, diving into her mouth the way he was about to dive into her body.

"You're mine. All mine, now and forever," he said as he used his hips to slide in between her legs and as soon as his hardness came in direct contact with her moist center, he easily slid in.

"Yes, love me!" Sherry mewed as Brian began moving his hips with powerful strokes, going deep penetrating more than just her body; he was going deep into her very being. Before long, she had to hold on to his shoulder as his strokes grew harder, once again guiding her toward a powerful climax. He rode her, she rode him and together they escaped to a place where only love and passion existed.

"I love you Sherry. I love you, I love you, I love you!"

Unable to hold back anymore, Sherry let loose and let her orgasm overtake her. She knew Brian wasn't far behind her as his moans turned to growls as his body erupted, he quivered getting everything he needed from her.

"Yes, baby," she said making sure he knew she was right here with him.

Brian didn't know how long his body quaked, but he couldn't seem to stop his hips from moving as his orgasm went on and on. Something amazing started happening the moment he thought his body was calming from the powerful explosion he'd just experienced.

Sherry started moving her hips again, holding him captive in her body, milking him, getting more and giving him even more. His body and mind rose to the occasion again and for the first time, right after he'd just experienced an orgasm that took his breath away, another quake slammed into him and he climaxed again and this time, he saw stars and rockets as he squeezed his eyes together tight thinking he was about to have a heart attack. With the love of his life is the only way this feeling could happen, he thought. Only with the love of his life. He continued to shutter even as he felt Sherry's hands caressing his back as her legs gripped his hips even tighter holding him in place.

Love was all he felt and love from her was all he needed. When the waves finally began to subside, he moved to take his weight off of her body, but she held him in place.

"Don't move. I need you just like this," she whispered in his ear.

"I need you so much, baby," he uttered.

As Sherry continued to caress him and whisper her love for him, Brian leaned his head into the space between her head and her shoulder and closed his eyes. I love you was the last thing he heard before falling into a deep slumber.

**

Brian was startled awake by a dream where he couldn't find Sherry and Sherice. He had been running through a dark tunnel screaming for them and everywhere he looked, they were nowhere to be found. The terror of it shocked his mind awake as he sat up straight and looked to be sure Sherry was still in bed with him. The room was dark so it wasn't yet morning. He waited a few moments for his heart to stop racing before he finally got up and went to check on Sherice. Grabbing a pair of boxers, he picked up the monitor to listen for her cries and left the bedroom.

Breathing a sigh of relief at seeing Sherice sleeping peacefully in her crib, he didn't go back to bed, afraid he'd wake up Sherry. Instead he went out to the living room and sat down on the sofa and looked out over the darkened sky. Brian couldn't sleep. His dreamed reminded him of how much his woman and his little girl meant to him and he knew he would be nothing without the two of them. What bothered him most was leaving and trying to get back to some semblance of the life he had in Atlanta. He already knew that there would be no life with them all together, but he didn't know how to make that work. He'd been fixing things for weeks, but this he couldn't find a remedy for that would allow them to live the lives they were currently living.

He wanted Sherry with him and Sherice in Atlanta, but he knew he couldn't ask her to give up her life for him. He also didn't know what he would do when he would have to bring Sherice back and leave her while he traveled back home alone. His little girl was everything to him and so was Sherry. After being away from her for over two years, he couldn't imagine going back to a life without her in it every day. He had been thinking about making some changes that could involve him giving up his life in Atlanta and moving to Maryland permanently. There were tons of teaching opportunities and of course, he could continue to work for Duron remotely from anywhere. It would be easier for him to change his life than it would be to ask Sherry to change hers. He didn't know what to do, but he knew that thoughts of indecisiveness kept him from sleeping, so he may as well stay up.

**

Sherry rolled over hoping to snuggle up to Brian and she found his side of the bed empty. She looked around the room, listened and didn't hear anything. Perhaps Sherice had woken up and she didn't hear her. She got out of bed, put on her robe and went in search of him.

She walked out into living room after checking Sherice's room and found Brian sitting in the dark, not watching television or listening to music, two things he loved doing.

"Brian? Are you okay?"

269

He didn't look at her and she went around and stood in front of him. The moon provided a lot of light in the room, so she could see that he wasn't smiling, but looked like he was deep in thought.

"What woke you up?" he said looking up at her.

"You weren't there and the bed felt cold. I thought perhaps Sherice had woken up and you'd gone to her. Is something wrong?"

"Yes," he responded immediately. "Come here, baby."

Sherry went to him and moved to sit on the chair next to him when he pulled her into his lap where he pulled her close.

"What's wrong?"

"I'm leaving in a few days."

"I know and you're taking Sherice with you. What's wrong?"

"I'm leaving *you* in a few days."

Sherry wrapped her arm around his neck and leaned into his chest.

"I know. I've thought about that, too. Neither of us expected to be back together again, but we are and that's something we'll have to deal with. I've never had a long-distance relationship before and I don't know how well they work, but the love I have for you is boundless. It's infinite and never ending and I don't care how many miles are between us, I will still love you endlessly. We'll see each other when you bring Sherice back and we'll figure out something after that. I don't have the answer right now, but I love you and you love me. We have our love at last, the way it was always meant to be. That can help us overcome anything."

"You still have the rest of the week off, right?"

"Yes."

"Come with us for a few days to Atlanta. You can do your class on-line from anywhere and you don't have to be at work until next Monday. That's almost a week away and you can help me get Sherice settled in. Before all this, when we first talked about Sherice coming with me for a few weeks, I had Loren have her team in Atlanta turn one of the bedrooms at the house into a room for Sherice along with adding a playground in the backyard. You can come help me get her room together, shop for whatever her favorite things are and see how things are going to be for her for the second week. I want you to feel comfortable with what I'm preparing for her and I would feel better if you saw it first-hand. I know it's asking a lot, but I need you; I want you. I'm not sure I can deal with you being here and Sherice and I being in Atlanta without you. I need a little more time."

Sherry knew she wanted that, too.

"Are you sure? I know this was about Sherice and I don't want to impede on you and your family's alone time with her. She's just as much a part of your family as your brothers and sister's children. She is going to have so much fun in Atlanta."

"You are a part of my family, too because Sherice is and I want you there. It would give us both some relief from worrying about this and we could revisit it in a few days before you leave to come back to Baltimore."

"I would feel better going to Atlanta with you. Sherice has never been on a plane before.

"Then let's make that happen. I'll make some travel arrangements and as soon as you can get your things packed and ready to go, we're out of here."

Sherry lit up like a Christmas tree. Brian was right. She had time off from work and she would feel better if she accompanied Sherice for the first few days and she would get more time with Brian.

"I'll have us packed before the end of the day. How's that?"

"That's perfect and so are you."

"Well, why don't we go back to bed and you can show me how perfect you think I really am."

**

While Sherry took Sherice and went home to work on packing what they would need for the trip to Atlanta, Brian called his family, starting first with his mother.

"Mom, I was hoping you would be home."

"Where else would I be this early in the morning. Is everything okay? How is Sherice? I miss my grandbaby. I didn't get enough time with her."

"Well, I'm about to remedy that. We're coming to Atlanta tomorrow. I was planning to stay here a few more days and bring her back for about two weeks for a visit, but since Sherry is coming with us, we're going to leave tomorrow. I just got off the phone making flight arrangements and we're flying in early tomorrow morning. Sherry is home packing and I'm packing up the condo. I have a lot of things to ship home and the carrier is coming in about an hour to pick up everything except my overnight bag. I was calling to let you know we'd be there tomorrow and you won't have to miss Sherice, at least not for the next two weeks or so."

"Oh, that makes me so happy and I know your father will be, too. We sat up talking last night and he was overwhelmed by how fast our family has grown and he especially misses Sherice since we didn't get a lot of time with her besides those few days we were in Baltimore."

"Yeah, I'm calling everyone to let them know and I already know I want to have a cookout at my house this weekend. The playground in the backyard that I'm having constructed should be up by then and Loren is having her team turn one of my bedrooms into a bedroom for Sherice and another into a playroom."

"Wow, you have a lot going on. Do you need someone to pick you up at the airport?"

"No, my car should still be there where I left it when I flew here. I just wanted to update you on the latest. I'll call you tomorrow when we land."

"Okay. Have a safe flight and kiss Sherice for me."

After hanging up from his mother, he called Duron.

"Hey, D."

"Hey, Bro. What's good?" Duron asked.

"Besides the fact that I'm coming back home to Atlanta tomorrow and bringing my daughter with me? What could be better than that?" he asked.

"Really? That's good to hear man. What can I do to help? You need the jet to fly in and pick you up?"

"No, I'm good. I have flight arrangements and I'm excited because this will be Sherice's first plane ride."

"What about Sherry? How is she handling being away from Sherice?"

"She's coming with us at least for the rest of the week. We'll deal with the aftermath later in the week. I'm getting everyone together at my house on Saturday to finally have the big party for Sherice that we had in mini-version of after she came home from the hospital."

"Okay, you know Taija and the kids and I are there. How

is Sherice after all that excitement?" Duron asked.

"She's showing no signs of any trauma afterwards. She's back to her happy little self where I'm still the light of her life!" he jested.

"Right!" Duron laughed. "What's the latest on Lance? Any word?"

"The latest is Lance is getting the help he needs and after his stay in treatment, he'll still face some charges. I don't think he'll be foolish enough to come after Sherry or Sherice again."

"Yeah, not after that ass-whooping you gave him. I thought you were going to kill him with how hard you were hitting him."

"Man, I unleased someone I didn't know lived inside of me."

"When it comes to your children, trust me when I tell you that you would do anything to protect them. If I were in your shoes, I would have done the exact same thing. I'm glad things are looking up for you in your personal life. I know it's been pretty rough, but you have your daughter and you have your love back."

"True that and I've never been happier. I'll see you tomorrow."

CHAPTER 24

The party was in full swing, the grill was smoking, family had come out and there was laughter and fun in the backyard around the pool. Brian smiled at the happy occasion celebrating his daughter after returning to Atlanta. Sherice had settled in easily around the family and like the rest of the grandchildren, Brian noticed that the first person Sherice had developed an instant love for was his mother. She wasn't the only person who had settled in nicely.

Sherry had been back in Atlanta and they had established a routine as if it was the most natural thing in the world for them to be sharing their lives together again. In the few days since they had arrived, she had even gone to visit a few of her friends from college who stayed in the area after graduation, who were shocked and excited to know that she'd had a baby. Right now, that baby was being pushed by her grandma on the new built swing set he'd had installed, knowing how happy it would make her. The minute she saw it, he had to chase after her because she bolted right for it, tripping a few times on the grass, but she didn't care and neither did he. He was too happy that she was loving her new surroundings to worry about anything else.

"Brian, you outdid yourself with those ribs. You're almost as good as me when it comes to grilling," Duron said walking up, handing him a beer as he continued cleaning the grill as the festivities began wrapping up. His nieces and nephews were winding down and he could tell they needed naps.

"Hey, a man is always a master at his own grill," Brian said.

"I'm glad you thought of this because everyone is having a great time and my niece is beautiful. She actually gave me a hug and a kiss on the cheek today. She smacked my cheek afterward, but at least I got that kiss, especially after the first few days of her running to the hills every time she saw me."

"Yeah, she does that with everyone for a while after she meets them, except or me of course. The minute she saw me, she loved me. I have that effect on women," he grinned.

"You definitely have an effect on women. Sherry looks happy."

"She is, at least for now. She's flying back home tomorrow without Sherice. I'm going to take her back in another week. It's going to be hard and I know how I would be if it were me. You and I can't begin to understand how that would be for a mother. Any thoughts of asking her to say for good?"

Brian had thought of nothing else. He needed it to be her idea and not his. He wanted Sherry to want a life with him in Atlanta and not be asked and then agree for any reason other than she couldn't imagine living apart from him. He knew how he felt and had prayed all week that the subject would come up and he would welcome her with open arms.

"I've been thinking about it. I've been unable to think of much else except for the fact that she's going to be leaving tomorrow, heading back to her life in Baltimore."

"Are you worried about Lance getting out one day and coming for her again?"

"Not at all. I'm worried that we'll drift apart."

"Then don't let it happen. Do something about it and do it fast. I see her walking around here smiling and laughing with everyone, but I also get the feeling she's hiding sadness for the sake of all of us. She's a good one, Brian. Don't let her slip away a second time," Duron said and walked back over to his family.

Brian cut his eyes to Sherry who was standing off to the side watching all of the fun and when the locked eyes, he winked and blew a kiss her way. When she mouthed she loved him, he put his hand over his heart letting her know he loved her, too.

As people continued to come over and thank him for the fun afternoon, the crowd dwindled down until the only people left were him, Sherice, Sherry and his parents. He walked over to join everyone just as his parents were saying goodbye to Sherry.

"We're glad you came to Atlanta with Sherice and I know she's going to miss you this week, but we'll keep her happy and smiling for you," his mother said.

"Thank you and thank you for welcoming not only Sherice, but me as well. I appreciate it," Sherry said.

"Dear, you are and always will be a part of this family. I know my son loves you and aside from that, we love you, too. Always remember that. Now, it looks like this little sweetie here is getting tired. I'll hand her to you, clean up a few more things and then my husband and I are heading home. You have a safe flight tomorrow and I hope you'll come back for another visit soon."

Brian watched the exchange and he saw what looked like Sherry on the brink of crying.

"Why don't you take Sherice inside and get her a bath and changed into pajamas," he said to Sherry, giving her an escape.

**

Sherry was on the brink of tears and she didn't want to break down in front of Brian's parents. She took Sherice by the hand and walked into the house, hurrying up the steps to the bedroom. The happiness that everyone else felt all day was not what he was feeling. She was sad and feeling a touch of anxiety knowing that in less than a day, the scene she saw in the room with everyone enjoying each other's company would not include her as she returned home to Baltimore.

Picking Sherice up in her arms, she hastened her steps to get to a place where no one would see her tears. She was hurting ad it wasn't because she was leaving Sherice in less than a day, though she was going to miss her baby, she was also going to miss Brian and the more she thought about being away from him, the more it pained her. What was she going to do knowing how miserable she was going to be to once again be separated from him. It wasn't enough that they were back together, but they would soon be living apart and she wanted him; she wanted him day and night. She took Sherice into the bathroom to give her a bath and get her ready for an early night.

**

"Mom, can you and dad let yourselves out? I'm going to go check on Sherry."

"I'm glad son. I noticed a change in her right before she turned and left the room. Do you think something is wrong?"

"I don't know, but I'm going upstairs to find out and put Sherice down for a nap."

"Okay, son. I'll talk to you tomorrow. I know Sherry is about to return home and I bet that's what's wrong. We'll give you the space you need to deal with this. Let her know we all love her."

"I will and thanks for embracing her, mom."

"Nonsense. We're family and that includes not just Sherice, but her, too."

Brian turned toward the steps and when he reached the top of the stairs and walked toward his bedroom, the door wasn't quite closed all the way and he thought he could hear Sherry sniffling as if she'd been crying. He pushed the door and entered the room just as she turned to look at him and then quickly looked away. Clearly, she'd been crying and her eyes were swollen and red.

"Mommy sad," Sherice said. Brian looked at her and saw that Sherry being upset was about to upset Sherice.

"No, mommy is fine."

Sherry smiled at her so that she could see nothing was wrong. She was afraid to say anything not sure if she'd break out in tears. She pleaded with Brian with her eyes, hoping he'd see that she was barely holding on and she didn't want Sherice upset.

"Sherice, how would you like to go with granny and grandpop for a little while and Dada will pick you up later?"

Sherice perked up and smiled while clapping her little hands with extra excitement as he lifted her in his arms.

He turned and left the room, grabbing his cell phone from his pocket while he walked back down the steps with Sherice in his arms.

"Mom, how far did you and dad get? Can you come take Sherice with you for a while? Maybe let her spend the night and I'll pick her up in the morning before church?"

"Sure. Is everything alright with Sherry?" she asked.

"I'm not sure, but I don't think I'll get to the root of whatever is wrong with Sherice here. Looks like she and I need to talk."

"We're pulling back around to the house. We just pulled out of your driveway, so we're still right here. I'll come in and get a few things for Sherice and we'll keep her as long as you like. What time is Sherry flying out tomorrow?"

"Her flight leaves at five in the evening."

"Okay, come pick up Sherice in the morning, so that she can see her mother before she goes back home."

"Thanks a million, mom."

**

With Sherice gone, Brian finished cleaning up and went in search of Sherry.

He took the steps to the bedroom two at a time and saw Sherry packing for her returned trip home. As he entered the room, she didn't look his way or utter a single word. He walked over and leaned against the dresser, crossing his legs at the ankles as he crossed his arms across his chest. Something was wrong and he wasn't going anywhere until he got her to open up. They'd spent years apart because the last time something weighed heavy on her, she left without talking to him. He wasn't having that again.

"Sherry, what's wrong? Whatever it is, let's talk about it. Sherice is with my parents for the night and I don't care if we're up all night long, I never want to see you crying again for any reason."

He didn't get a response, but what he heard was more sniffles.

"Are you going to tell me why you're crying? Talk to me please. If you need me to just stand here for support, I'll do that, too."

He waited until she was ready to talk. When she was, he watched as she turned to him.

"I love you. Since you've been back in our lives, I don't think I've said that enough, but I do; I love you. My tears aren't a result of anything anyone has done and certainly not about my unhappiness with you, because I am the happiest I have ever been."

"Baby, you know I love you and I don't want you to doubt that. You and Sherice are my world. That doesn't explain what has you so melancholy. The fact that you love me is a great thing, not something that should make you cry. I'm going to go out on a limb here and assume this has something to do with you leaving tomorrow."

Sherry looked up at him and she was once again on the edge of crying. How could she leave him and her daughter and go back to her life in Baltimore with hopes that they can figure out a long-distance relationship.

"What happens to us when I go back to Baltimore? I know Sherice will be here with you, but I'm wondering if what we've been sharing is because we were together, but now that I'm going back home, I don't know what to expect. I don't want to ask too much of you after what we've been through, but the way I love you, it saddens me when I think that when I feel like we're getting to a really good place, I'm going home and you'll be here. I know we talked about you coming to Baltimore to see Sherice and having her spend time here in Atlanta with you, but I can't help, but wonder what's next for you and me and if there will be a you and me once I go back home. All day I've felt like I did when I walked away from you the first time."

He should have known her struggle was about them. He'd felt her slipping away from him for the last few days and now he knew what it was all about. He wasn't doing enough to reassure her that she was his life and there was no other woman for him, but her, and if the only way he was going to be able to have her was long distance, then he was willing to deal with that. He needed to know what she wanted.

He walked away from the dresser and sat down on the foot of the bed.

"Come here, baby," he said taking her hand and pulling her into his lap. He saw the trickle of a few tears stain her face as they ran from her eyes and reached up and swiped them away.

"I'm sorry if it sounds like I'm putting any kind of pressure on you to figure this out alone. Tell me what you want? What do I need to do to put a smile on your face?" he asked. He knew he would do anything for her including move to Baltimore if that meant they would be happy and not apart.

"I don't mean to make you worry," she said.

"I'm always going to worry about you. That's what being in love is; it's the good, the bad and the worry. What if I move to Baltimore? I don't want us apart either and I can work anywhere. You and Sherice deserve to have the life you have been living. We can plan or future together, there."

"I can't ask you to give up your life here in Atlanta. Your work is here and your family is here."

"You and Sherice are my family and I have no problem making my life wherever you are. I want to do whatever I can to keep you and my daughter happy."

"Brian, that's not what I want and you haven't put any pressure on me," she admitted.

"Baby, you have to talk to me about what's in your heart and on your mind. We've been down this road of you keeping things from me and I never want to do that again, so talk to me."

Brian lifted her chin, bringing them eye to eye.

This is it, Sherry thought. Now was the time to be open about everything. She exhaled and let it out.

"I don't want to go back to Baltimore. I want to stay here with you. I want Sherice to have you in her life every day and not just holidays and summers. She loves you so much and loves saying Dada all day, every day. She lights up every time you enter a room and she doesn't like to be away from you for too long. I feel anxious every time I think of getting on that plane and leaving you both here. I don't think I can have a life without you again."

Brian knew that was all he needed to hear. He needed her to be the one to set the tone and path for what would happen for them next. It was the only way that he knew she would truly be invested one hundred percent. It had to come from her. Now that she had admitted what was in her heart, it was time for him to take the lead.

"Let me make something very clear, so that there is no

doubt. You never, ever have to leave here. I love you and I would like nothing more than to have you and Sherice here with me in Atlanta every day. I had been contemplating moving to Baltimore because now that I have you both, I don't have a life if it doesn't involve you every day. If you never want to leave, then unpack because this is just as much your home as it is mine."

"Are you sure? Having Sherice is one thing, but now you're taking me on all day every day and I can be a handful," she joked.

"Mmmm, I love how you fit in my hands perfectly. Every single, soft, sexy curve of you. What about your job? I know you can do school from anywhere, but what about work? What about your parents? You have family, too."

"My parents would understand that I have to make my own life and you and Sherice are my family, too. It's more important that I build my life with the man I love and get back to the love I never should have walked away from. I have a second chance with you and I don't want to blow it by being far away. I've waited what feels like a lifetime to finally have a love like this. I'm getting this kind of love at last and I have no plans of ever letting it slip through my fingers again. I think deep down, I knew I was meant to always be with you. I could never give myself to another man the way I have with you, which is why I never have. I don't want to be away from you again and my life and Sherice's life is wherever you are. It's a lot easier for me to move than for you to pack up your life and move away. Besides, your family deserves more time with Sherice and I don't want to take that time away from them. My parents would love to visit Atlanta often to see Sherice and we'll visit them in Baltimore. I just want you. As for work, there are labs everywhere and Atlanta has the Centers for Disease Control and I would love to work there."

"Then, it's settled and let me be the first to welcome you home."

Picking his love up, he locked their lips in a love-filled kiss and he laid down on the bed with her embraced in his love and love was the only thing on the menu tonight.

CHAPTER 25

"Good morning, Mom. How is Sherice?"

It was mid-afternoon and he and Sherry had finally ventured out of the bedroom. Now that she wasn't returning to Baltimore for good, they still had to make plans to pack up and move all of her and Sherice's belongings and have them shipped to Atlanta. Sherry had ventured to his downstairs office to call her mother and make plans. He took the extra time before leaving to pick up Sherice to call and check on her.

"She's in her world laughing and giggling with your father. We've discovered she loves riding on his knee as he pretends she's in an airplane."

"That's funny because she loved the plane ride here. I think I'm raising a natural born traveler."

"I was wondering what time I would hear from you. We were hoping to take her to the Atlanta zoo before you came to get her. We saw a commercial for it last night and she ran over to the television like it was an aquarium full of fish. The excitement in her eyes told me she has a thing for animals."

Brian chuckled silently.

"I know. I already decided I was going to buy a large tank for the house and let her pick out some fish. I think she'd love it. Go ahead and take her, there's plenty of time before I pick her up later."

"Are you sure? Doesn't Sherry want to see her before she flies back home?"

"Yeah, mom, I'm sure. If fact, she can stay as long as she wants with you guys today because Sherry isn't going back to Baltimore. She's going to move here to Atlanta."

"Oh, my prayers have been answered. I didn't want to say anything, but I wondered if that was what she was struggling with and whether or not that option was on the table."

"We talked about it and it's the best thing for us all."

"Well, in that case, as your mother, I hope you plan on doing something a little more permanent than just shacking up. I'm not prying, but I wouldn't be your mother if I didn't express my opinion."

"I hear you and you don't have to worry about that. Call when you get back and Sherry and I will come and pick her up."

Hanging up the phone, he took the steps two at a time and heard Sherry moving around in the kitchen.

"Hungry?" she asked.

The look Brian gave her told her that he was hungry for more than just food.

"Really, Brian?" she laughed out loud.

"Always when you're around, but right now I could use some sustenance. You know how to drain a brother of all of his energy."

"Speaking of that, with me here permanently, I need to get some kind of birth control before we hear the pitter-patter of little feet running around behind Sherice."

Brian walked over and pulled her snug against him and leaned down to place small kisses along the column of her neck.

"Would that be so bad? Don't answer that. You have school to finish and I know you want to work and Sherice is a handful, so yeah, before I put my foot in my mouth, we should talk about that. I can continue with condoms for now, though we have been hit or miss with remembering to use them."

"We need to stop spinning that wheel. I could check in with my doctor when I go back home to pack for the move, but I will still need to connect with a doctor here."

"Well, why don't you call Taija and ask her for a recommendation. If she's not pregnant again already, I'm sure she's using something."

"Right, because you Knight men barely let a girl come up for air!"

"You love every single minute of it. How about we cook breakfast together. I'm thinking a big meaty omelet."

"What about Sherice? Should we go pick her up?"

"She's getting ready to go to the zoo with mom and dad. I think if she had to choose, we would lose."

"Then breakfast it is."

Brian turned her around and teased her lips before she wrapped her arms around his neck and pulled him toward her, taking full control, diving in over and over, smiling when he moaned in her mouth."

"Goodness woman. I hope I survive you being here every day."

"Haha, you'll survive lover boy. Go ahead and get breakfast started and I'll call Taija. I think I need that appointment sooner rather than later."

"Yeah, you do," Brian slurred out and blinked wickedly.

**

"Hi, Taija, it's Sherry. Did I catch you at a bad time?"

"No not at all. I was just putting the twins down for a nap after getting in from church. How are things going? Are you sad about leaving us yet?"

"Things are actually going better than expected and there is no sadness going on over here. I've decided to stay in Atlanta and move here permanently."

"I'm happy to hear that because it also means things are going well for you and Brian."

"Things with Brian are incredible. I love him so much and can't believe I ever walked away from him."

"That was right before I met Duron, but I heard about it and I'm glad you found your way back to each other."

"Us being together is the reason I'm calling you. Brian and I have been intimate and playing roulette with the possibility of me getting pregnant."

"Girl, I know what that's like. Those Knight men have insatiable appetites."

"That appetite is crazy, but I love every single minute of it. I'm calling you because he and I talked about birth control and because I don't know any doctors in Atlanta, he suggested I ask you if you could recommend one that I could make an appointment with as soon as possible so that I can get on the pill."

"Your timing is great. I have a checkup coming up with my doctor tomorrow. I'll call her to see if she can squeeze you right before or right after me. I'm sure it won't be a problem."

"That would be great."

**

"You're in great health Sherry. When was your last gynecology appointment?"

Happy that Taija's doctor was able to get her in for an appointment, Sherry thought back to the last time she'd seen her doctor back at home. She and Taija decided to make a day out of it by getting in some shopping. Now that she was moving to Atlanta, Brian told her to redecorate any way she wanted and she wanted to start on the bedroom. His room was definitely a space made for a man and though she wouldn't change much, she liked being able to add a little bit of herself. The biggest priority was taking care of birth control. They loved Sherice, but she wasn't sure Brian would be ready for a new baby just yet.

"About six months ago. I wasn't scheduled for another yearly exam for quite a few months. If you need a more exact date, I can check the calendar on my phone."

"No, that won't be necessary. A ballpark timeframe is good enough. Are you planning to live in Atlanta full time? If so, if you want me to be your doctor, I'll need to get a copy of your medical files from your current doctor."

"Yes, I just decided to move here, but I can do that right away. You come highly recommended by Taija."

"I love Mrs. Knight and her twins are the cutest. I've been her doctor since she had them."

"So, what kind of birth control do you recommend?" Sherry asked as she finished strapping her shoes on her feet.

"Birth control? I know that's why you came in today, but you won't be needing that anytime soon and as soon as you finish putting those cute heels on, you can take them back off again because I need to have an obstetrician come in to examine you for a more precise date."

Sherry wasn't sure she heard the doctor correctly. Did she just say obstetrician?

"What? What kind of more precise date? A date for what?" she stumbled out.

"You're pregnant. I had a full gamut of tests run on your blood and urine and some preliminary results are in and one is that you're pregnant. I'd like an obstetrician to come in and tell you how along pregnant you are. I'm thinking you may not know that since you didn't know you were pregnant."

Sherry stood so fast, she almost fell over.

"I can't be pregnant. I came in for birth control to keep from getting pregnant!" she shouted and then apologized for how loud she had spoken.

Sherry felt like she was going to faint as Dr. Oslow smiled at her.

"Why don't you have a seat? You look like you're about to pass out. I think the idea of birth control at this point is out the window and it's not a GYN you need, you need an OB."

Sherry's pulse quickened as her heart felt like it was beating outside of her chest. She was pregnant. She and Brian were going to have a baby; another one. To say she was shocked would be an understatement.

"Do you need some water? Perhaps you should lay down? You don't look to well."

"No, what I need is a drink, but that's not going to happen, you know, with the baby in me and everything."

"I'll give you a few minutes to let this sink in. Have a seat and I'll be back in."

Sherry fell back in the chair and lowered her head

between her legs. As soon as she heard the word pregnant, she began to feel like she was going to be sick. Baby? They were going to have another baby? She couldn't be too far along because they've only been intimate a little over a month. What was she going to tell Brian? Mulling all of those questions in her head, she looked up when there was a knock on the exam room door.

"Come in."

Taija poked her head in and Sherry was relieved that she had someone to talk, too. Her mind was crazy along with the rapid beat of her heart.

Taija entered the room and knew something was wrong.

"What's wrong Sherry? The doctor came out and asked me to come in with you while she got another doctor? What doctor and what's wrong? Should I call Brian? Did you call Brian? You don't look so well. What's going on?" Taija was rattling questions off too fast for her to answer.

Seeing unshed tears in Sherry's eyes, alarms started going off in her head as she fumbled around in her purse for her cell phone.

"I'm calling Brian."

Sherry perked up enough to stop her.

"No, don't. It's okay. Everything is okay, at least I hope so."

"Okay, you had me nervous. You wouldn't say anything or answer any of my questions."

That made her smile.

"You didn't really give me a chance to answer any of them because you were shooting questions at me so fast."

"Well, I walked in and you looked like death. I was worried and I ramble when I'm worried. So, what's going on?"

No beating around the bush, Sherry blurted it out.

"I'm pregnant."

"You're pregnant? But we came for birth control," Taija said and then they both laughed.

"Apparently, I'm a little late for that."

"I'd say you're a little late for a lot of things. How are along are you?"

"I'm not sure, but it can't be more than a month or so. Sitting here I was thinking that it didn't occur to me that I missed my cycle. In everything that's happened, I haven't thought about it."

"That's understandable."

"It may be, but I'm not sure how Brian is going to react. I don't think we're ready for another one so soon."

"Ready? There is no such thing as being ready. You and Brian have rediscovered your love and a baby could only enhance that, not hurt it. Have you seen how much he loves Sherice? Oh, my goodness, I thought Duron was bad with the twins, but Brian has him and Jake beat in the daddy being wrapped around his daughter's finger game. Sherice is definitely in control and you will have your hands full when she gets older and pits you against each other," Taija laughed.

Still stunned, she tried to laugh along with Taija, but reality kept smacking her in the face. She was going to have another baby.

"We are just getting back on track. I don't know how Brian is going to take this."

"I know it's shocking, but you know he is going to be ecstatic, you'll see."

"I sure hope so because ready or not, another baby is on the say," she said just as the doctor knocked and entered with what she assumed was the Obstetrician.

**

Sherry paced nervously back and forth across the bedroom floor while Brian put Sherice to bed. Thankfully it gave her a little extra time to get her thoughts and words together. She'd held in the news that she was pregnant all day.

After leaving the doctor's office where it was confirmed that she was a month along, she and Taija went out for comfort food and girl talk since she couldn't have a drink. By the time she arrived home, she felt better about the pregnancy, knowing that Brian wouldn't see it as a bad thing. She had a feeling he would be happier about it than what she initially felt. As he entered their bedroom and they were alone, it was time to tell him he was going to be a father again.

"I'm going to take a shower and I was thinking that you should join me. I haven't been able to think of anything else, but you in that sexy ass dress you've had on all day. Did you go to your doctor appointment in that? You look good, my love. I'm also playing by your rules, though they are only your rules."

Brian reached into the nightstand and pulled out a box of condoms and smiled when he turned back around to show her what was in his hand.

"Condoms?" she asked, laughing.

"Hey, you're the one who wanted to talk about birth control and even though I know you went to the doctor today to get on the pill, I'm sure there's still a risk until they actually kick in."

"Condoms, huh?" Sherry asked again. Now was as good a time as any to tell him, she thought.

"Thank you for taking responsibility for birth control

until I get the pill, but we won't need them," she said calmly.

Brian walked around the room removing his clothes and tossing them in the basket.

"We won't?" he asked, clueless.

"No, we won't. We can toss the condoms at any time."

"The pill works that quick huh?"

"No, it takes a few weeks when you're on the pill."

"What? I don't understand. We don't have to use condoms, but the doctor didn't put you on any type of birth control?"

"Yeah, she said there was no need since we're already pregnant, one month pregnant to be exact and she said at this point, birth control would be useless. Like I said, you won't be needing that box and that sure is a mighty large box!"

Sherry was trying to serious and funny at the same time and she started laughing when what she said finally sunk in for him.

"Wait? You're pregnant?"

She nodded yes and in an instant, Brian screamed, ran over and picked her up into his arms, completely covering her face with kisses.

"I'm going to be a father again?" he shouted.

"Yes, and why don't you wake Sherice with all of that hollering. You'll be the one up trying to get her to go back to sleep."

"That's nothing. I'll stay up with her and the new baby and all of the rest of the babies we're going to have."

"Whoa, slow down cowboy; one Knight baby at a time."

"I love you so much! I know we weren't planning for any more kids right now, but I hope you're as happy as I am."

"I am. I wasn't sure how you'd react. I know how much you love Sherice, but I wasn't sure enough about us to know that you would be this happy."

Brian frowned. Did he just hear her say there was an issue in the air about their relationship?

"You were questioning our relationship?" he asked.

"No, I was questioning myself. Being pregnant again took me back to my first pregnancy and that was without you. I was being melancholy about the past."

"That was then and I'm here now and I'm more than ready. You've got me baby, forever," he stated, making sure to confirm for her that everything about this pregnancy is a good thing. There is something I haven't told you about our life back then. I was planning on asking you to marry me that summer, but things fell apart and it didn't happen. I kept the ring and I have no idea why until today. I love you and I never want you to question where we are in our relationship We are exactly where we need to be and that's together. There is only one thing missing in adding some permanency to our situation, sealing our family."

She didn't know what was happening when he stood up, went over to his closet and came back with a small black box in the palm of his hand. Her eyes pooled with happy tears the moment he got down on his knees.

"Brian?"

"Let me finish. This isn't because of the new baby, but because I finally have my love at last. You are my love and my life and I want to marry you. Now, before you answer, you need to know that this isn't some spur of the moment thing. If you call your father, he'll tell you that I spoke to him last night and asked him for your hand in marriage. He gave his approval immediately, so this was in the works even before you told me about the baby."

"I don't need to check with him because I don't care when or how, all I know is I love you and I would be your wife, today, tomorrow and forever!"

Brian reached up and held her face in the palm of his hands as he leaned over, capturing her lips with his. He suckled them, satisfying their need to be close and sealing their love for a lifetime. He pulled back and looked her in the eyes.

"I have my love at last and it feels so good!!"

EPILOGUE

Loren's excitement over being back in Atlanta, even if it was for just one week to attend her sorority's fundraiser, couldn't be contained. She looked over at her husband Michael as he snored lightly with their son sprawled across his chest, also fast asleep. It wasn't too long after their flight aboard the company jet had taken off from California that she noticed it would be a quiet flight.

Heading to Atlanta for the first time in months, her excitement kicked up to a new level because she was also heading home in time for the birth of her brother Brian and his wife Sherry's second child, a girl they were going to name Zoe. The past eight months had flown by with a lot of excitement. Besides the announcement that Sherry was pregnant with their second child, the family had loaned their support in helping them move all of her belongings to Atlanta after deciding to stay with Brian on a more permanent basis, which included their fairytale wedding a month later and a trip to Hawaii for their honeymoon. They were now settling in to their new life as husband and wife and she couldn't be happier for them.

She was startled when her husband suddenly woke up

with a jolt when the captain came over the speaker system telling them they would be landing soon and that they should be buckled in. Michael jumped the minute he heard the captains name.

"It's about time you woke up. I had to resort to entertaining myself for this entire flight. Both of you abandoned me, preferring to sleep," she said, smiling.

Michael stood with Chase still in his arms as he walked over and kissed her sweetly on the lips.

"Our kid tires me out more than running a multi-million-dollar company with Tyrone and your brother and you know how demanding your brother can be," he joked.

"Well, get ready for more of that since you insisted on coming with us to Atlanta."

"What? I wasn't going to have you both gone for over a week without me and besides, it was time for me to make a trip back to the Atlanta. I haven't been here since the wedding either. Have you talked to anyone today?"

"I talked to my mom this morning and she said Sherry was on bed rest for the next two days and then the doctors are going to induce if she doesn't go into labor. They wanted her at the hospital to be sure she didn't get out of the bed, but she promised she wouldn't if they would let her stay home until the delivery date. Of course, Brian is making sure she doesn't have to lift a finger. Her parents are flying in from Baltimore tomorrow and mom has been at the house everyday helping with Sherice and looking after Sherry while Brian acclimates to working at the firm. How's he working out?"

After a few years of begging Brian to join his architectural firm, he finally agreed and after they returned from their honeymoon, Brian took over the finance division and their newly formed mentorship program where they gave college seniors a paid internship. She loved the idea that his company respected other companies that offered non-paying internships, but Duron, Mike and Tyrone knew that with as hard as times are, everyone needs a little extra in the pocket, especially a college student. They even partnered with several other businesses who were adopting the same mentoring program including Xavier McIntyre and his Baltimore law firm, whom Duron had signed on as a client a few months back. She knew that Brian also appreciate being able to set his own hours which allowed him more time to look after his very pregnant wife.

"I don't know why we didn't bring him on earlier than this. He has been a huge asset bringing on a new perspective in diversifying our financial portfolio. I'm looking forward to the all staff meeting since we'll have everybody in Atlanta. What do you have planned besides checking in on your Atlanta office?"

"After we get settled in at the condo, I'm going to meet Taija at Brian's house to give my mom a break today. She has been a trooper helping out around their house with Sherry bedridden."

"Do you want me to keep Chase with me?" Mike asked as he placed his son in his car seat and strapped him in, careful not to wake him.

"No, I'll take him with me. I'm sure Duron will have you running in circles doing everything while you're here. He'll have fun with his cousins.

**

Brian walked into his bedroom where he encountered a very bored Sherry sitting up in bed acting like she was reading another magazine. He knew she wasn't and only wanted him to think she was okay with being on complete bedrest.

"You know you're not reading that magazine so you can stop faking on my account," he said smiling.

As he got close, he leaned down and kissed her and what started out as a very innocent kiss, quickly turned heated as he took the kiss deeper and deeper. He tried pulling back and then he heard the sound of her moaning and knowing that meant she wanted more, he gave her more, finally pulling away knowing the kiss could only lead to more kissing and nothing else.

"Aww. That's all I get? I really miss you," she said.

"I know baby. I miss you too, but you know what your doctor said."

"I know, but I am starving for you and I know you're going through something," she said as her eyes traveled down his body, resting on that area she loved so much. If she was abstaining, per doctor's orders, then so was he.

Brian laid down across the bed and placed his head on her stomach, caressing his child.

"Not making love to you has been extremely hard, but I am a man who can control his libido especially when his very beautiful and very pregnant wife is this close to having our baby. I'm fine and trust me, the hand action from last night you gave me, hit a brother off just right," Brian kidded.

Sherry playfully punched him on the shoulder.

"You are so nasty, but you know I love it when you get like that."

"I know you do and don't worry too much about anything, especially sex right now. The only thing on my mind is you having a healthy baby."

She was about to respond when the sound of high heels clicking on their steps were heard.

"I hear there's a pregnant lady in here someone!" Loren shouted.

Sherry perked right up.

"Is that your sister I hear?" she asked him.

Brian, with a guilty look on his face, was in on the plan to surprise Sherry with an afternoon of girl talk with Loren, Taija and Victoria, Tyrone's wife.

"It sure is!" Loren said coming through the bedroom door followed by Taija and Victoria.

"Oh, my goodness! I'm am so happy to see all of you. Is the whole family in town for this baby's birth?"

"Of course, we are," Taija exclaimed.

"I know I wouldn't miss this," Victoria added.

"So, two more days of being in this bed, huh?" Taija asked Sherry as Brian brought in more chairs for them to sit in at her bedside.

"I don't need a chair. We're about to climb up on this big ol' bed with Sherry and dive into some girl talk," Loren said.

"Where are the kids?" Brian asked.

"They're all with mom. I tried to bring Chase with me, but mom fussed because she doesn't get to see him as much as she gets to sees Duron's kids, so she almost demanded I leave him at the house with her. I don't think she was going to let me leave with Chase even if I wanted too," Loren said.

"The twins are there, too. When I stopped by to pick up Loren, your mother insisted I leave the twins with her today. I thought we were giving her a break by spending the day with Sherry, but she didn't want a break. She wanted a day with her grandkids."

"She just left a message on my cell phone right before I came up to check on Sherry and I bet it's her asking me to drop Sherice off after pre-school. I'll leave you to your girl talk while I go pick up my baby girl. I'm going to stop at my mom's, but I'm reachable by cell if anyone needs me for anything."

Sherry wave him out of the room.

"Go, leave, Brian. I'm going to be fine," she said shaking her head and her fingers at him, pointing him toward the door.

"So, Loren, Tyrone said you're in town for your sorority's event this weekend, too?" Victoria said.

"Yeah, that and the birth of my niece will be the highlight of my week."

"What's the event?" Sherry asked curiously.

"Well, we're having another bachelor auction. The last one we had where Duron met Taija was such a huge success, they want to do it again."

"That was the best night of my life," Taija added and snapped her finger added emphasis to her excitement.

"Who are the men this time? Are any of them returning from before? I know Duron isn't since he's taken," Sherry asked.

"They have a whole new group of guys this time. Can you believe just about all of the guys who participated in that auction a few years ago have all found love through that auction, either directly with someone who was there that night or through someone who bid on them for someone else?"

"Really? How many guys? All of them?" Taija asked.

"No, not all of them. I know the stories of twelve other

guys besides Duron who got lucky in love because of the auction."

"Oh, you have to tell us these stories," Sherry said.

"Some are pretty steamy," Loren said.

"How did you get the stories?" Taija asked.

"Well, I was a part of the committee from the last one and I was asked to take part in this event and reach out to some prospective men since my team did a great job the last time. I started by reaching out to some of the guys from before and let me tell you, when they told me their stories, I had to stop periodically and go in search of my husband after hearing it because they left me that hot!"

"Whew!" Sherry said, fanning herself. "I could use a little hotness right now. I'll take anything to help pass the time by. This baby has two more days and then I'm kicking her out. I miss my husband and all of his hotness. Let's hear about these stories."

"Are you sure?" Loren asked, looking from Taija to Sherry and then to Victoria and each lady smiled, ready to listen.

"I don't have any place to be. Duron is picking the kids up from Ms. Barbara later this evening, so I have hours to hear about all twelve stories. I can have Estelle bring us some food up when we get hungry."

Estelle was the woman who took care of Taija and Duron's house, cooking, cleaning and helping with the kids.

"Thanks for loaning Estelle to us to help out around the house while I'm laid up. She is the best and I notice that Sherice isn't as picky with her food as she is when I cook."

"She is amazing. Okay, Loren, let's hear the stories. I haven't read a romance book in a minute. Give us all the juicy details and don't leave anything out."

"Alright, don't say I didn't warn you," she giggled.

"I'm warned, not spill it," Sherry added.

"Let me grab my IPad to give you a little background on each guy to set the scene for you."

Loren searched around in her bag, grabbed her IPad and pulled up the old biography information on all the guys.

"I remember how hot looking they all were, though none compared to my baby Duron. Still, the hotness factor in the room that night was off the scale."

"It sure was and I remember each of them. Well, let me see if I can pull up the names. The stories were so hot, I should know them by heart. The twelve bachelors I spoke with are Kyle, Diego, Tristan, Maxwell, Jordan, Terrence, Julian, Jensen, Nicholas, Gideon, Harlan and Gabriel. I'm going to start with Gabriel Santos's story."

"Oh, his name sounds exotic," Sherry said.

"It is and he was. Take a look at his picture," Loren said passing it around.

"Oh, yeah, he's hot, though he has nothing on my man!" Victoria said.

"His full name is Gabriel Santos and at the time he was thirty and owned a men's customer clothier store in Atlanta. Men from all over the country visit his stores for their custom-made shirts, so you know he was looking good that night. From what he told me, he almost missed the event because he was running late and they almost didn't let him in because he wasn't dressed. He told me the hottest story about him and one of my sorority sisters, Taylor, who served as a hostess for the event. Thankfully, she found him a place to change and was able to get him in before the actual auction had taken place, but what it took for him to get there, is the stuff that the hottest romance you could ever read could never make up. After I talked to him, I talked to her because they are a couple, living together and planning to get married. That night, they told me a story of their adventure in a changing room that will blow our socks off. You asked for it so here it goes. It started when he showed up to the event after leaving the gym with his clothes in a carryon bag and somehow, he'd left his wallet with his identification in the office. He knew if he took the time to run back to get it, he would miss the auction all together. He took a chance on showing up and of course, they wouldn't let him in until Taylor ran into him and offered to help. Now, I know why she seemed to have disappeared for a while that night."

Loren looked at Sherry and Taija noticing their full attention as she continued.

"I may need a drink for this conversation," Taija said and they all laughed.

"You just might. Anyway, earlier in the day, before the auction, Gabriel had gone to the gym to get his usual workout in and decided to take his clothes for the black-tie event with him. Losing track of time, by the time he went to shower and change, he was about thirty minutes away from the start of the event. Rushing to get there, he grabbed his tuxedo and raced to the civic center. When he got there, he tried to use his charm to get in without any identification, but even with his sexy, exotic looks, his charm wasn't getting him anywhere with the gatekeepers until Taylor, who was running late herself, entered and heard the conversation. Explaining to the who she was, they let him in. He wasn't dress and so she escorted him to a room where he could change into his tuxedo. Wait until you hear what happened when they found themselves stuck behind a door that locked once they were inside.

Read more about Gabriel's story in, "Twelve Bachelors for Sale", available July, 2017.

Enjoy this teaser chapter, a look *into "Behind Closed Doors"*, a new sexy romance novel from Cheryl Barton, available in April 2017.

"So, do you know for a fact that Kennard is working today or was all of this scheming a waste of time?" Yasmine asked.

"Stop your worrying. You'll get to see your man today. I told you, the record company receptionist and I are tight and she would never tell anyone about you. Kennard's assistant will be leaving out and will be gone for about an hour and that means you have one hour. Kennard has to respect the level of risk you are willing to take to prove to him that you're interested in him. I planned this out perfectly if I must say so myself. I haven't worked for these slippery slope lawyers for the past year and not learn how to scheme and be conniving. Trust, I've helped sneak in enough side chicks for the married guys that I should go into business for this stuff," Aria laughed.

"Well, just make sure you keep dumb and dumber from finding out that I'm not in here with you."

"You know what, let me take care of that right now."

Yasmine watched Aria as she straightened her clothes and stood taller in her five-inch stilettos and pranced to her office door.

"Girl, I swear I'm correct. Let me ask your guys here who's right," Aria said loudly, putting on a show for the two bodyguards sitting in the waiting area. Yasmine knew it was all for show and a part of their plan to get her back out of the office unseen. She decided to play along to add more drama to the scene.

"I say I'm right, but feel free to ask someone else their

308

opinion," she hollered.

"I'm telling you I'm right. Let me ask Lars and Roman." she said.

"Say guys, Princess Yasmine and I were having a discussion about penis sizes. I was telling her that I like them really long and very thick and that men know how important size is to a woman and we wanted to know what you thought? Are men as preoccupied with how big they are if they know women are all about the size?"

Yasmine had a look of horror on her face before she placed her hand over her mouth to stifle her laugh. Leave it to Aria, miss bold and beautiful, to not hold punches on a topic that she made men squirm. She was glad they were friends because she could live vicariously through her boisterous friend. Being a Princess had its limitations, especially with the opposite sex. The fact that Aria could make such a statement with a straight face didn't surprise her. Nothing surprised her when it came to her best friend.

Yasmine watched as Lars and Roman turned as white as ghosts and looked to each other, not believing what they were just asked. They shouldn't be surprised since she relentlessly flirted with both of them every chance she got.

"What?" Lars said in response.

"Well, it's part of our lunch discussion and that's the tamest of the subjects. I figured, since we have the two of you sitting right out here, you can be our male perspective on everything. Trust me, the topics I have planned are going to blow you away. So, what do you say?"

Both men stood straight up out of their seats.

"Uh, we're going to take you up on that offer and hang out in the employee lounge. You said it was down the hall this way right?" Lars said, looking in any direction that wasn't at her.

"Are you sure? Well, if you really want to do that, yeah, it's at the end of the hall and cut a right. There's actually a nice lunch buffet in there today if you want to indulge. I know you feel like you can't let the Princess out of your sight, but I don't know how many questions I may need to ask you to break our tie in the discussions. I guess we'll have to figure it out for ourselves if you're going to the lounge."

"Yeah, why don't we do that because I'm starving. What about you Roman?"

"Yeah, me too. Tell Yasmine, if she needs us, we're a few steps away and she has her panic button."

Aria faked a smile.

"Uh, huh. I'll let her know," she said and shut her office door back.

"You are out of your mind!" Yasmine shouted and jumped up and down with excitement. There was always such a rush being around Aria.

"I'm telling you, that performance was Oscar worthy. If nothing else, you know I can make a guy run away!" she shouted. "Now, let's get you upstairs to see your man. Did you bring condoms? If not, I keep a supply in my office drawer."

Yasmine snapped her head around so fast, she thought it would break off.

"Stop assuming I'll need a condom for anything. I simply wanted to see him and let him see that I'm not some stuck-up Princess, which is what he called me the last time I saw him. I like this guy and you know that and why do you keep a supply of condoms in your office? Just what do you do in here besides work? It's a law firm!"

"Oh, it's not for me. These attorneys may look like they're all work, but after hours and sometimes during the day, they get busy with all kinds of women and they can't be caught buying condoms since all but one of them is married. I get an extra added bonus by keeping them supplied with things like pens, paper, condoms and the morning after pill."

"What? You have the morning after pill in that drawer?" Yasmine asked, shocked.

"You don't want to know. Now, take a few of these condoms and get your pretty ass upstairs. You're wasting time with me when you could be getting busy with the sexiest man in LA."

Yasmine huffed at her.

"I told you, it's not about that."

"Well, it should be. It's been months since you've gotten laid and you're overdue, unless you've hooked up with someone since Vegas and that was six months ago, you're due. I can't have you walking around in heat all the time. Even a Princess needs to get her some and when I tell you there isn't a better specimen walking around then Kennard Jackson, I mean it. You've set your eyes on a beast of a man!"

Yasmine tried to look away to not give away the secret that she hadn't had sex in six-months which occurred on their girl's trip to Las Vegas.

"It doesn't matter because like I said, I just want to see him."

"Yasmine, no one just *sees* Kennard Jackson; they get a taste, a sample or a whole damn meal. If I were his type, I would have tried getting in those jeans a long time ago, but he likes his women, slim with big asses and large breasts and you fit that bill to a tee. Ugh, you frustrate me so. I have to teach you how to be a little more like me."

"Whatever."

"Okay, let's get you upstairs. There is an exit to the fifteenth floor through the office over here. I'm going to call Cindy, the receptionist up there, to let her know to let you in. Those doors only open from that side. She'll get you to Kennard's office unnoticed and take as long as you need. I'm going to laugh ever so often just in case dumb or dumber comes by to check on us. Now, get going. When you're ready to come back down, she'll call me," Aria said pushing her towards the hallway that led to another door.

Yasmine bit her bottom lip, still unsure about what she was about to do. Throwing caution to the wind, she pushed the door open and rushed up the stairs.

Just as she reached the landing to the fifteenth floor, the door opened and a blond woman escorted her in.

"Hi, how are you? I'm Cindy and when you're ready to leave, have Kennard buzz me. I don't know how long his assistant will be, but if she comes back, I'll need to distract her to allow you time to get out unnoticed. Kennard's in his office which is the large set of doors at the end of the hallway. No one else is back there and I'll make sure no one comes back that way. He doesn't have a meeting for a few hours meaning you should be good to go," she said smiling.

Yasmine didn't respond, but shook her head signaling she understood as she walked quickly to the large set of dark redwood doors at the end of the hall. As she reached them, she looked back at Cindy who was still making sure no one saw her. She leaned toward the door and could hear Kennard talking on the phone. Taking in a deep breath, she knocked softly and waited for him to acknowledge that he heard it.

"Come in," he said.

"Here goes nothing," Yasmine said softly and opened the door.

She stood in the opened doorway until he looked up and saw her standing there. Whoever he had been talking to had completely lost his interest. For what seemed an eternity, they looked at each other as if they were strangers wondering what they were doing. To break the obvious trance, she smiled and waved a few fingers at him. When Kennard didn't move or respond, she didn't know what to do next.

Kennard had to blink several times to be sure the woman he saw standing in front of him was actually there.

"Yasmine?"

From the look of things, she was alone which surprised him since he never saw her without her security detail.

"I'm sorry if I'm disturbing you," she stuttered out.

"Disturbing me? Are you kidding? You're joking right? You standing in my office looking like a dream? There is no such thing as you disturbing me.

"It looks like you're busy on a phone call," she said.

Kennard looked at the phone in his hand, forgetting he was having a conversation before she showed up.

"What this? Hey, Ben, I have to go. Let's continue this conversation a little later. I'll have my assistant ring you back later when I'm free because right now, anybody other than this gorgeous woman who is standing in front of me is obsolete."

Before his caller could respond, Kennard hung up and then reached for his phone again, tapping the intercom.

"Leslie, hold my calls and visitors, please."

Yasmine pointed to the outer office.

"Oh, she's not out there."

"She isn't? Then how did you get in here?" he asked inquisitively.

"Cindy."

"Remind me to make sure Cindy gets a raise. Now to what do I owe this surprised, but extremely welcomed visit?" Kennard asked.

The last thing he expected was to see Princess Yasmine standing in his office and to say she was gorgeous was again an understatement. She was even more beautiful than the last few times he'd seen her.

"Well, the last time we talked you called me a stuck-up princess and I wanted you to see that I'm not like that at all. I am a Princess, but I'm not stuck-up."

He eyed her from head to toe and his body hardened instantly.

Damn! He said inwardly. How could this woman do this to him every time. All he needs to do is look at her and his body reacts like some teenager.

Kennard stood from behind his black and gray marble-top desk, pushing his chair back as he walked around it to get closer to her. He smirked at his erection knowing that this was his state every time he set eyes on her. He purposely adjusted himself so that she could see him do it. He wanted her to know without a shadow of a doubt, that he wanted her, as much as he could read from her body language, that she wanted him.

He tried to reign in his desire for her and his boys reminded him that he was way out of his league with her, but he couldn't help himself. His eyes loved gazing upon her and his hands throbbed like his manhood at the thought of touching her. His lips wanted to devour hers with a powerful kiss and his tongue wanted to taste her until she screamed his name and only his name. He knew he should care more that she was engaged to marry another man, a man she herself had only met once in person, but he didn't care. The fact that she was here, in his office was enough for him to know that she didn't care about her impending marriage either. Right now, all he knew was that he was looking at her and she was real.

Finding words seemed impossible as silence ensued and neither said a word. Yasmine began to look uncomfortable and he liked that. He didn't want her comfortable; he wanted her aroused.

"Umm, maybe I should leave. I don't want to cause any trouble, especially for Aria, with my being gone."

"Aria is your friend right? She works for the law firm a few floors down from here. What does she have to do with this?" he asked, curiously.

"She planned all this out for me to slip away from my detail in order to sneak up here to see you. We are supposed to be having lunch in her office and I have about an hour before Lars and Roman, my detail, will probably go in and check on me."

"Oh, then you have an hour, so don't rush off. You came to see me and I'm glad you did."

Kennard walked even closer to her as Yasmine backed up toward the door. Forgetting that she had closed it, she stopped when she encountered the door at her back.

"Ooops," she said, knocking into it.

"The door is closed," he said.

"So, did you come all the way up here just to see me or was there something else you wanted."

"I.I.I..don't know," Yasmine stammered.

"You don't?" he asked, sauntering up to her until he was only a breath away.

Yasmine wanted to look away from his piercing stare, but couldn't. Kennard was so damn sexy there was no way any woman would be able to take her eyes off of him. The way he was looking at her made her skin feel hot and moist and her thighs throbbed.

"Why are you so damn fine?" she asked, abruptly. She even caught herself by surprise by what she blurted out.

Kennard laughed and threw his head back.

"You know I get that a lot, but until this very moment, I never cared to pay much attention, but hearing it from you, I'm honored you notice and I'm thankful you said it. I never thought you'd be that bold. How bold can you be? I mean, I know how to make some pretty indecent overtures, but I don't want to scare you away."

"Am I sweating? I swear it's really hot in here?"

"Yes, you are and it's only hot right here in this space right around you and me."

Kennard reached out and placed his hand on the door right at the side of her head. When she turned to look at where he placed his hand, he leaned in and quickly kissed the side of her neck.

Now, he's done it, she thought. Not only were her thighs really throbbing, but now her sex was, too. His lips were soft and wet against her neck. Should she dare ask for more? Did she come for more? Was Aria right? Did she want Kennard to take her, like this in his office, behind closed doors? Hell, yes! Turning her head back to him, she held his stare and dared him to make another move.

"Like that?" he whispered close to her ear.

"Yes," Yasmine said softly.

Without thinking, she linked her finger in one of the hooks on his jeans and pulled him up against her and the moment she felt his erection, she knew what she came for. She should have taken Aria up on her office with the condoms.

"Oh, damn. I see you aren't stuck-up. You're a woman who knows what she wants. Well, you know what, I'm a man who knows what a woman wants and definitely what she needs and your need is written all over your beautiful face.

"I only have about forty-five more minutes?" she said, seductively.

Completely out of character, she wasn't holding back knowing she may never get an opportunity like this again.

"Sweetness, there is a lot that can be done in the forty-five minutes you have left, or should I say forty minutes because I want to be sure you have at least five minutes to make your escape back downstairs."

Yasmine looked at Kennard and to her he was a tiger that has set his eyes on his prey. His eyes seemed to darken as she began to feel his aura all around her.

With one hand on the door, Kennard used the other to use a finger and trace the small area where he'd placed a kiss. From there he used that same finger to travel down her neck until his finger rested in the middle of her large cleavage. He loved a woman with large breasts and Yasmine's were perfect. He watched her as she watched his finger and noticed her breathing had become erratic. That's exactly what he wanted. He wanted her to want him as bad as he wanted her.

"Forty minutes, huh?" she asked.

"Shall I show you what I can do in forty minutes behind closed doors?"

"Yes," she said without a hint of hesitation.

Kennard leaned into her neck and moved his mouth up to her ear.

"Turn around, place the palm of your hands against the door and hold on. It's going to be a bumpy, yet very enjoyable ride."

Read more in April 2017 when "Behind Closed Doors" is released.

Princess Yasmine had an image to uphold as the daughter of the King of a country. She was pledged in marriage by her father in order to build her family's wealth, but a few last flings wouldn't hurt anybody, or so she thought.

Kennard Jackson is a music mogul and playboy and is known for satisfying the ladies. For the first time in his life, he found a woman who was beyond his reach until she made the first move and then all bets were off.

Get books 1 – 3 of the Bachelor Series

Book 1 - Bachelor Not For Sale – Now available

Even self-proclaimed "bachelors for life" meet that one woman that makes them want to slow down and second guess bachelorhood. After suffering through the heartache of what he thought was true love, Duron Knight meets and becomes enchanted with bombshell Taija Charles.

Taija has heard a lot about Duron and all of her body

senses are on overdrive when she meets the handsome bachelor face to face. As the sparks fly, Taija plans to show Duron how she can help him mend his broken heart with real love and the right amount of lust.

Book 2 – A Designed Affair – Now available

In the follow-up to "Bachelor Not For Sale", Loren Knight has been engaging in a secret love affair with her brother Duron's best friend and business partner, Michael Bailey. He is everything she could want and more in a man, but she believes the risk is too great for any type of relationship with him beyond the bedroom door.

Michael Bailey has been fighting his attraction to Loren for years. He has stayed away from her out of respect for his best friend and business partner. Now that he and Loren have finally given into passion that they both have been craving, can Michael convince Loren that what they share is worth the risk?

Book 2 – A Perfect Combination – Now available

In the third installment following "Bachelor Not For Sale" and "A Designed Affair", Tyrone Davis is the king of one night stands; nicknamed, Mr. Love Them and Leave Them. He learned to perfect it from his two best friends, Duron Knight and Michael Bailey. He never imagined a one night stand would have such a lasting impact, but that's exactly what happened.

Victoria Alston couldn't forget the incredible night she

spent with Tyrone Davis, someone connected to one of her best friends. The next day, she disappeared, returning to reality and the fiancé she'd left in Boston while on business travel. They both soon discovered that it wasn't just a one night stand, but a perfect combination for love.

From Cheryl Barton – "Un-Break My Heart" – Now Available

Dr. Mackenzie Ellis suffered a loss so great, she never thought she'd fall in love again, especially with someone close to her.

Travis Blackwell, III never dreamed of crossing the line with Mackenzie until his heart would no longer allow him to deny the love he has for her and the passion he wants to share with her knowing that he is the key to mending her broken heart.

From Cheryl Barton – "Bossy" – Now Available

Cassidy 'Bossy' Bostic came from nothing, but knew she would be something. Pregnant and alone, she was forced to run from her past in order to have a future. Her rise to the top as the owner of a fashion dynasty is what dreams are made of, but her hard, icy persona could have her living a lonely existence.

Drake Montgomery, a rising attorney heading toward the political arena, has fallen in love with the 'Bossy' mogul only to discover it's 'Cassidy' he loves, but 'Bossy', not so much.

Can their hot, steamy romance melt even her cold, icy heart? Only time and love will tell.

From Cheryl Barton – "Heartthrob" – Now Available

Cade Weston, Hollywood's most eligible bachelor and named the world's sexiest man of the year, lives life at the top with a bevy of beauties at his beck and call, people providing his every desire and more money than any one person should have.

Callie Hurston struggles to make it as a stylist to the stars in a world where women are intimidated by her beauty and men are interested in her body and not her talent.

Cade thought he had it all until he has a chance meeting with Callie and decides to take a chance on her talent and ends up taking an even bigger chance with his heart.

Can the playboy turn in his player's card and give in to love?

From Cheryl Barton – "His Halloween Promise" – Now Available

Dylan Kennedy and Savannah Eaton-Kennedy may be divorced, but that doesn't stop them from indulging in some pretty hot and sexy encounters.

A divorce decree may mean that their life together is over, but Dylan has a promise to keep that could bring his wife back where she belongs; in his life permanently.

From Cheryl Barton – "Home for Thanksgiving" – Now Available

Firefighter Nicholas Sullivan is going home for the holiday after he was sidelined due to an injury on the job. Guilt over a life lost has kept him away from his family's ranch in Montana and now he's forced to face his past demons and deal with a self-imposed life of regret.

Veterinarian Parker Wingate's first encounter with the handsome firefighter was less than pleasurable. She sympathized with his hurt, understood his pain and before long, felt his love.

Knowing the holiday season is ending soon, can Nick go from living in love for the moment to allowing himself to finally live in love forever?

From Cheryl Barton – "A Better Man" – Now Available

Phoenix Graham is living her best life with the best man, her fiancé, Carson Stone, heir to the Stone Tower Hotel Empire. Her perfect life is shaken up when a handsome, rugged and extremely sexy mysterious man moves in across the hall and she begins to see that the rose colored glasses she had been seeing life through were blinders. She soon discovers that Carson was the best man for her until she takes notice of a better man and his name is Gavin Black.

What's a girl to do when the best doesn't get better and better is what she craves?

From Cheryl Barton
Book 5 of the "Amorous Occupations" series
"The Electrician" – Now Available

The party invitation said everyone had to wear a masquerade mask the entire night, a New Orleans tradition. Dara Marshall couldn't resist the opportunity to spend an uninhibited night of passion with National Football Association coach Nelson Riley, the guest of honor, knowing that her identity was hidden by her mask.

Dara's world turns upside down when she discovers the gorgeous coach is the newest client of her father's business and after she's sent on a job at his condo, she does everything in her power to not give away the secret of who she is.

Nelson could never forget the sexy temptress he'd spent an unforgettable night with, even when she tries to hide behind a mask and baggy overalls.

ABOUT THE AUTHOR

Cheryl Barton lives in Maryland and in her spare time she loves to read espionage novels, cook, watch Sci-fi movies, spend time with family and friends and enjoy Maryland steamed crabs.

Find more romance and inspirational novels by Cheryl Barton on her website at www.cherylbarton.net.

I am because you read and I thank you! - Cheryl

Connect with me

Visit my website at www.CherylBarton.net
Twitter – @Author Cheryl Barton
Instagram – AuthorCherylBarton
Facebook at Author Cheryl Barton
Email – Cheryl@CherylBarton.net
Blog - https://mswriterinmd.wordpress.com/